QUANTUM LEAP

INDEPENDENCE

A NOVEL BY

JOHN PEEL

**BASED ON THE UNIVERSAL TELEVISION
SERIES *QUANTUM LEAP*
CREATED BY DONALD P. BELLISARIO**

BOULEVARD BOOKS, NEW YORK

QUANTUM LEAP: INDEPENDENCE

A Boulevard Book / published by arrangement with
MCA Publishing Rights, a Division of MCA, Inc.

PRINTING HISTORY
Boulevard edition / August 1996

The Putnam Berkley World Wide Web site address is
http://www.berkley.com

ISBN: 1-57297-150-9

BOULEVARD
Boulevard Books are published by The Berkley Publishing Group,
200 Madison Avenue, New York, New York 10016.
BOULEVARD and its logo are trademarks
belonging to Berkley Publishing Corporation.

PRINTED IN THE UNITED STATES OF AMERICA

10 9 8 7 6 5 4 3 2 1

For all my friends in the Moriches Bay area

CHAPTER
ONE

The first few seconds of any Leap were always the worst
for Sam Beckett. To be catapulted into an unknown situation, looking at the world through God-knew-whose
eyes, and trying to make sense of things before disaster
struck was never very easy.

Having a knife held to his throat didn't make the proc-
ess any easier.

"Well?" growled the knife wielder, pressing slightly
harder with the blade. The knife wasn't well cared for,
but the slightly dulled blade was still sharp enough to
break the skin of his throat and start a drop of blood
trickling downward. "Are you with us, Sam Beckett, or
not?"

Still trying to determine where he was, being ad-
dressed by his given name threw Sam. Had he somehow
Leaped back along his own time line again? Had his
mysterious guiding Fate thrown him back, unprepared,
into an earlier version of himself?

No; that couldn't be the case. For one thing, to the
best of his Swiss-cheesed memory, he'd never been held

1

at knifepoint in his life. That didn't mean much, of course, because as a result of the Quantum Leap he had made, he seemed to have left a lot of the molecules of his memory back in the year he had started from—whenever that might be. Besides, second, he doubted if he'd ever forget the look of the man who was glaring at him in the gloomy light of the cabin.

Sam's eyes had finally adjusted to the low level of lighting. He could see that he was in an old-style wooden-walled room. The only lights were small, sputtering oil lamps: one on a bare wooden table in the center of the small room, and another being held by one of the group of men in the room. Without turning his head—not a wise move at this point—Sam could see eight men besides the one whose bad breath was in his face and the one whose knife was in his neck. Another man held Sam's hands behind his back, not tightly but with a steady grip that suggested business. The men all wore similar clothing: knee-length trousers with stockings below, rough-looking shoes, white shirts tied at the throat and wrist, and waistcoats in various dark colors. One of the simple chairs in the room held a pile of what looked like long coats.

This was clearly not the twentieth century.

"Answer me, Samuel Beckett," Bad Breath growled. "Or I swear I'll slit your throat with pleasure." He increased the pressure slightly, and Sam felt another trickle of blood.

The rest of his questions could wait for a moment. This had gone on far too long. Sam tensed his muscles, studying the hold the man behind him had on his wrists. It would take a second or two to break, by which time Bad Breath only had to press slightly.

Sam took half a pace backward, crowding the man

2

holding him and retreating just slightly from the blade. Before either man could react, he slammed his foot down hard on his captor's instep. The man gasped in pain, and his grip loosened enough for Sam to whip his right hand free and up in an arc. As he struck, Sam twisted his head slightly. His hand slammed into the knife wielder's hand, sending the blade upward. It barely missed taking Sam's ear with it, but he was now free of immediate threat.

Whirling about, Sam brought his fist down into the stomach of the man who still held his left hand. The man *whoof*ed and collapsed to the dirty floor, clutching his stomach and freeing Sam. Pivoting on his left foot, Sam kicked out with his right. Bad Breath took the full force in his stomach. He grunted, his eyes bulged, and he flopped to the floor, gasping for breath. His knife clattered into the darkness.

Ready for a further attack, Sam stood waiting, watching the other eight men, wondering who would be the next to try. To his surprise, none of them made a move toward him. This obviously wasn't a kidnapping or a robbery attempt, then, as he'd begun to suspect.

One of the men, a stout-looking fellow with thinning, graying hair, gave a short bark of amusement as he contemplated Bad Breath. "Well, John Kirk, maybe that'll teach you better manners, eh?" Kirk gasped for breath. The speaker chuckled again, then fixed Sam with a shrewd eye. "But that's not really an answer, is it, Samuel? Now, tell us: where do you stand?"

Ah, a disagreement between—well, "friends" was obviously too strong a word. Acquaintances, maybe? No . . . a clandestine meeting by night, with too few lights. *Conspirators*.

What had he Leaped into this time?

"I don't like being coerced," Sam finally replied, studying the faces arrayed in front of him, seeking a clue. "When I give my word, I mean it to be believed because I speak it, not because some fool holds a knife to threaten me." He was playing for time, hoping someone would say something to let him know what he was supposed to be committing to—or against.

"Well said, Samuel." The speaker was a lanky man with straw-colored hair that hung untidily and unevenly over his thin, worried-looking face. "This is disgraceful." He glared at the men with him, daring them to argue. "We're acting worse than the Tories do. Is this any way for free men to behave?"

Bingo! That was enough for Sam. "That's right," he said quickly. He realized he was going to have to be very careful about how he spoke. He'd Leaped back further into the past than ever before. It wouldn't do to use any anachronisms here. "Do any of you think you can win a man's loyalty at the point of a knife? Isn't this a fight for freedom we're waging here?" He gestured at John Kirk, still wheezing on the floor. "Is that how you aim to win men to our cause?"

"Isaiah and Samuel are right," a third man stated. "I've always said that John is too hasty in his ways—though none can doubt his dedication to the cause, of course. We need people who commit themselves freely to freedom."

"Thank you, Joshua," said the man who had berated Kirk. He glanced shrewdly at Sam. "I don't believe you've yet given us an answer, Samuel."

"My answer," Sam said carefully, "is yes—provided we leave all knives outside these meetings in the future." He wished he knew precisely what he was agreeing to join. If he was careful, he should be able to

4

discover this in the course of the conversation.

"Then I believe that this concludes our meeting," announced the portly man who seemed to be the leader, dashing Sam's hopes. "If there are no further objections, I propose we meet here again early tomorrow forenoon, as planned." He glanced around, and then down at Kirk lying on the floor. "I trust you are satisfied, John?"

Having regained his breath at last, Kirk managed to stagger to his feet. Swaying uncertainly, he glared at Sam. "I'll hold my peace, George," he replied, wincing as he spoke. "For the present, at least." Clearly, he had no intention of forgetting what had happened.

"Good." George nodded at the other men. "Until tomorrow, then, gentlemen. To freedom!"

"Freedom!" the others chorused, with Sam joining in.

"Death to Tories!" added the man who had earlier been holding Sam.

"Well, let's not go *quite* that far, James," said George with a chuckle. "A pox on them, shall we say?"

"A pox on the lot of 'em," agreed another man. "And especially on King George."

Sam knew that this was mostly bravado on the part of the speakers, but it wouldn't take much to tip words over into actions. "Until tomorrow," he said firmly, turning toward the door.

He felt a hand on his arm, and glanced around to see Isaiah smiling uncertainly at him. "Samuel," the tall man said, "wait, I'll travel back to the path with you."

"Thank you, Isaiah," Sam said sincerely. That was one less problem to worry about—where he was actually going when he left this shack. Until Al turned up—and there was never any predicting when that would be—

5

Sam would have to stumble along and hope he didn't make too many mistakes.

Isaiah smiled gratefully. "I'll get our coats," he offered, turning to the chair where they were piled. Another problem solved.

As another loomed. John Kirk, a decidedly unfriendly scowl on his face, glared at Sam. "It's not over between us, Samuel Beckett," he stated. "I'm still not convinced that you're one of us."

Sam sighed and shook his head. "It's not over only if you refuse to let it rest, John," he replied. "I can assure you, there isn't a person in this room—or even in these Colonies—that believes in the cause of America's freedom more than I."

"Well spoken!" exclaimed George before Kirk could reply. "Sentiments that I fervently believe we can all echo, eh?"

There was another round of muttered agreement as Isaiah proffered a long coat. Sam slipped it on, then realized there was a woolen cap in one pocket and, following Isaiah's example, pulled it on his head.

"We'll go first," Isaiah said to the others. It wasn't really necessary, since none of the others had made a move for their coats. Sam strongly suspected that he would be the topic of discussion as soon as he was out the door.

"Until tomorrow," he said, nodding at them, then followed Isaiah out of the shack.

It was night outside, and there was only one feeble light, set atop a fence, burning fitfully in the still summer air. In its gloomy light, Sam could just make out large shapes in the field. Isaiah came to his rescue again, obviously eager to please. "I'll get our steeds," he offered.

Horses. . . . Well, Sam had already deduced roughly

6

when he had to be, so that wasn't too surprising. The automobile wouldn't be invented for over a hundred years. "Fine," he agreed, accompanying Isaiah to the gate. He waited while his companion collected two of the animals and brought them back.

Sam studied his: it was a fit-looking beast, though obviously more suited to farm labor than riding. Transporting people was clearly its secondary purpose. The animal shied, whickering slightly, as Sam moved to take his reins.

"Easy, boy," Isaiah said, puzzled. "It's only Samuel. No need to worry."

Not strictly true. When Sam Leaped, people saw him as the person he had Leaped into—somehow the aura of that person's presence clung to Sam, clouding their perception of him as he really was. If he Leaped into a woman, to the observers he *was* a woman, down to the last anatomical detail. But in reality he was still Sam Beckett, whatever anyone saw.

Except for small children and animals. Their less sophisticated and more instinctive minds bypassed that weird aura business and jumped straight to the reality: they saw Sam nothing else. Now the other Sam Beckett's steed could tell that the man standing in front of him was not his master, and was balking at being mounted.

Sam had been born and raised in farm country in Indiana, and he knew horses well. Moving gently, he stroked the animal. "Easy, boy," he murmured. "Everything's fine. No need to be spooked, is there?" The combination of soft tones and stroking calmed the uncertain horse. Sam smiled at Isaiah. "I guess he just got worried waiting," he said.

Isaiah accepted the explanation, and with a nod he

clambered inelegantly into his saddle. He obviously was not very comfortable, Sam noticed, as he mounted his own steed with ease. A slight jerk of the reins started his animal ambling down the path beside Isaiah's.

The stars burned crisply and clearly in the night sky. There were no lights to dim them. A sliver of moon hugged the horizon but cast sufficient light for Sam to see at least the outline of the path ahead. Obviously they would be making this trip at a slow pace. It was unusual for riders to be out this late—another indication of the clandestine nature of the meeting they had just quit.

Some of this was becoming clear to Sam, but he badly needed Al to make his entrance and help out with information. On the other hand, there was an excellent source of data right beside him, one who, Sam suspected, wanted to talk. "Well, Isaiah," he said in a friendly tone, "how did that meeting strike you?"

That was all the invitation his companion needed. As they threaded their way through dark masses of trees, following the thin path, Isaiah turned to Sam and shook his head. "To be truthful, Samuel, I was not at all happy with its tone."

"Nor was I," admitted Sam, touching his throat. "It became a little rougher than I'd expected."

"That's just John Kirk's way," Isaiah answered. "He's never liked you much, has he? I think in a group, he feels stronger. I think he expected George Townsend to back him more than he did."

Sam smiled. "I suspect George was waiting to see who was going to win between us."

"Aye. George tends to be like that, waiting to see which direction the wind blows in." Isaiah bit at his lip nervously. "Samuel, now that we've declared for inde-

8

pendence, I think the best and the worst is being brought out in us."

"That's always the case," Sam replied. "Some men rise to the occasion, while others seek only to profit from it. What is it that troubles you the most?"

"George and John seem to have taken over the Committee of Safety, Samuel. If you hadn't made your stand as you did, then I think the rest of them would have gone along with their suggestion to hang all Tories and sympathizers. As it is, you've deflected their aim, but I don't believe you've altered their purposes."

Ah! So that was it. The *real* Samuel Beckett—and it was confusing to think like that!—had provoked Kirk's wrath and suspicion by disagreeing with him publicly. That explained the knife at his throat. And *maybe* why Sam had Leaped in. The original Sam Beckett wouldn't have known the fighting techniques that he did, and it could have been a problem. On the other hand, that Sam himself was here should have been proof that the other Samuel Beckett hadn't been in grave danger. Or was it? The one thing Sam had discovered from Leaping was that nothing was certain. The past could be, and had been, changed a number of times. Mostly, it was up to Sam to change it back, but sometimes he'd altered it for the better. He'd saved Jackie Kennedy from being assassinated along with her husband, for example. Had he already changed the past by getting out of that fix with Kirk?

Again, there was no way to know until Al turned up. So where *was* Al? Sam already knew that he was way earlier in time than his own lifetime. This meant that he'd Leaped along his own bloodline again, into one of his own ancestors—this time another Sam Beckett. Sam wasn't too strong on his family history. There was only one Sam Beckett he recalled, and that man had been involved peripherally in the War of Independence. That was obviously the person he had taken over from.

But as to where and when he was, he had very little clue. It had to be after July 1776, since those men at the Committee of Safety meeting had referred to the Declaration of Independence—but not too long after. And what was this Committee of Safety business?

"Maybe not," he said in reply to Isaiah's comment. "But I've stopped them from going too far for now. What more can we hope for?"

"It'll be up to us to keep them in check, I suspect," Isaiah said. "Samuel, I'm not as brave as you are. Every time I want to act, I see Anne and our children's faces. Then I freeze. I don't want to do anything to endanger them. But in this uncertain time, *anything* I do could harm them." He sighed loudly and shook his head. "Samuel, I tell you, I do not know what to do for the best."

Feeling sympathy for his ancestor's friend, Sam managed a reassuring smile. "Isaiah, we *all* have families and children to think about."

"I know," Isaiah agreed. "You have your Hannah and Daniel. I'm not making light of that. And I know you must be worried for their safety as much as I worry for Anne and my two. But I can't simply forget them and act when I need to."

"Don't forget them. Not ever. They are the reason we're fighting King George. We want them to grow up free and responsible for their own lives and actions, not answerable to men appointed by a monarch, an ocean away, who cares very little for us beyond his coffers. But you have to decide what it is you believe in, and then stand up for it, Isaiah. Would Anne respect you if

10

you failed to do what you know is right? Would your children?''

"No," Isaiah said softly. "And they'd be right to fail to respect me. I *know* what I should do, Samuel, but it's hard for me to be as brave as you are. I guess I'm just a coward at heart."

Sam reached out and touched Isaiah gently on the shoulder. "You're a good man, Isaiah," he said confidently. "Bravery isn't easy for any of us. But when the time comes, you'll know what you should do. And I believe that you have the strength within you to do as you must."

Cheered by this encouragement, Isaiah sat straighter in his saddle. "Thank you, Samuel. Your words and your belief in me mean a lot. You've been a good friend to me ever since we moved here to Smithtown. I only wish there was some way I could repay you for your kindnesses."

"There is," Sam told him. "Stay strong in your beliefs. Be good to your family, and brave for our country. And don't mention your doubts to anyone else. If Kirk and Townsend hear that you're not a hundred percent behind them, they're not likely to be as sympathetic to you as I am."

Isaiah snorted. "That's for certain. Don't worry, Samuel, I'll keep my fears and doubts private." He reined in his horse. "Well, now we must part. I'll see you tomorrow, after noon, I trust. Stay well, and give my greetings to Hannah."

Sam was a little unsettled by this sudden leave-taking. "Uh, right," he said. He waved as Isaiah set off down a side trail, vanishing into the darkness in seconds.

Staying where he was, Sam studied what he could see about him. Trees, mostly, dark and tall shapes all about

11

him. There was the thin side path down which Isaiah had disappeared, and the slightly larger one they had been taking. Sam assumed that this led to wherever he was heading—but how far did he have to take it? Where was the turnoff to his home?

Staring around in the darkness, Sam knew that he was far worse than lost. Without help of some kind, he didn't have a clue to where he was supposed to be going.

Now what?

CHAPTER
TWO

"We have a real problem this time, people."

Admiral Al Calovicci winced at this observation, glaring at Dr. Verbeena Beeks. "Worse than normal?" he growled.

"Much." Dr. Beeks took her seat at the small table and poured herself a cup of coffee. She glanced around at the others, as if she were a teacher performing a head count.

Al sighed again. Dr. Beeks was a good-looking woman—almost any female was attractive to him for one reason or another—but sometimes her attitude really bugged him. Considering she was a psychiatrist, she often seemed oblivious to the effect she had on others. "We're all here," Al growled. "And awake. Now, are you going to tell us what's screwed up so badly, or not?"

Dr. Beeks scowled at him, but the others fought to suppress smiles. They knew Beeks sometimes rubbed the Admiral the wrong way. Dr. Donna Elesee didn't

13

bother to hide her smile; Gooshie almost had a choking fit fighting his; Tina smirked.

"Do you have any idea who's in the Waiting Room?" Dr. Beeks finally demanded.

"Not until you tell us," Donna answered, leaning forward slightly. "You're the only one who's been in there." She narrowed her eyes. "And you've issued orders that nobody else was allowed inside. We need to know why."

Dr. Beeks studied them all for a moment. "It's Samuel Beckett in there," she finally announced.

"Ouch," mumbled Gooshie. "You mean Sam's jumped back into himself again? That could be a problem, if we have to keep him from finding out about his own future."

"No." Beeks was obviously concerned. "Not himself. *Another* Samuel Beckett."

Tina frowned. "Another Sam Beckett? What are the odds against that? Unless. . . . You mean the *Waiting for Godot* guy?"

"No," She shook her head. "This happened once before."

That made Al wince. "He's way back in time again? Before the twentieth century?"

"Way before," Dr. Beeks answered. "This Samuel Beckett we have was born in the year 1752."

"Terrific," sighed Donna. "None of the computer files we've loaded into Ziggy go anywhere near that far back. We never thought they'd be needed."

"You're sure of this?" asked Al carefully, waving his cigar in the psychiatrist's direction. "I mean, maybe this character in there is cuckoo, or lying, or something."

Dr. Beeks straightened slightly. She was tired, and annoyed. "I *am* quite competent," she snapped, "whatever you may sometimes think. I've had a very interesting chat with Samuel Beckett, and I'm convinced he's genuine. When I first saw him, he took me for a servant and asked to see my master."

"I'll bet that went over well with you," Al growled.

"I made allowances for it," she retorted. "It served to point me in the right direction as to when he was from. He meant no insult, and when I replied that I was not a servant, he apologized, and suggested that I'd earned or bought my freedom. Further questioning elicited the response that he was Samuel Beckett, of Smithtown, Nassau Island, and believed that today's date is sometime in 1776."

"This is going to cause some serious problems," Donna broke in. "Aside from the fact that Sam's never Leaped this far back, and Ziggy's still having trouble physically locating him, there's the problem of Samuel to face."

"As I pointed out," agreed Dr. Beeks. "We none of us know precisely how much the Visitors recall when they return to their own time lines. It is probable—but *only* probable—that they undergo something of the same memory loss that Dr. Beckett experiences. In the case of people from fairly close to our time, I'm not too concerned that they might take back any memories or information to their own period. But in the case of Samuel Beckett, I feel very strongly that we can't afford to have him contaminated in any way, shape, or form. That is why I've placed him strictly off-limits to everyone but myself."

"Well, that's very thoughtful of you," Al snapped, "but I can't agree with it. I'm going to have to have access to this Sam Beckett to do my job with the other Sam. He's going to have to provide us with the information we need to help Sam on this Leap.''

''Also,'' Donna added, ''think of the historical data we could gather from Samuel! A man from the eighteenth century! If we could interview him and record it. . . .''

''Out of the question!'' Dr. Beeks said firmly. ''Even talking to him and asking questions might cause him to guess what is happening. We dare not risk it.''

''I've gotta have access to him,'' Al insisted. ''It's absolutely vital.''

''Not in this case,'' Dr. Beeks replied. ''I'm absolutely convinced that I'm doing the right thing here. We have to keep Samuel isolated. I'm as fascinated with him as any of you, but I aim to stay away from him as much as possible. We could cause serious damage to the fabric of history if Samuel Beckett returns with *any* idea of what is happening here.''

Gooshie leaned forward. ''I can see your point,'' he conceded, ''but you have to understand ours, too. I mean, I'd love to talk to this guy myself, but that's not important. Allowing the Observer access to the Visitor is.''

''I agree,'' Donna added. ''In the guidelines we've developed, we already decided that Al should be able to talk to the Visitors to gain whatever information is necessary to complete the Leap. Okay, this time the situation's a little more ticklish, but the principle is still the same. Al *needs* contact.''

Dr. Beeks glanced around the table. She was obviously realizing that if this came to a vote, she'd lose. ''All right,'' she suggested, ''how about a compromise? Admiral Calavicci can enter the Visitor's Room and converse with Samuel on a limited basis—only with me there to monitor the situation and with authority to pull the plug if I feel it is causing any serious problems.''

"I don't like it," Al snapped. "That means you can jerk me out of there anytime you want to, and for any reason you like."

"Credit me with a little judgment," Dr. Beeks demanded. "I would not do anything to jeopardize Dr. Beckett's mission or life. I simply want to be certain that we do not cause any inadvertent contamination of the time lines when Samuel returns to his own time."

"I think we could all agree on that," Donna said placatingly. "I'm comfortable with that compromise if everyone else is." She glanced about the table. Gooshie thought for a moment, then nodded.

Tina shrugged. "Sorry, Al, but I think Verbeena's right."

Faced with this decision, Al grimaced and studied his cigar thoughtfully. "I guess I have to go along with it. But don't provoke me." He sighed. "Now, is there anything else you can do to ruin our day?"

Dr. Beeks smiled. "Well," she admitted, "there is one other teeny complication."

"Why am I not surprised?" Al asked with resignation. "Okay, I'll buy it. Do tell."

"Samuel knows he is not in his own time, of course. That much is obvious to him. He has decided that he must have been killed, and this is Heaven. He seems to see me now as a black-skinned angel."

Al sighed again. "Boy, has he got the wrong woman for that role," he muttered.

CHAPTER THREE

"This would be a good time to show up, Al," Sam said. There was, of course, no answer from the dark trees. He shook his head. "It figures. He's waiting for a good time to either embarrass me or cause problems." Sam leaned forward in the saddle to stroke his horse's neck and ears. "I guess it's up to us, then, fella." His lip curled in amusement. "Well, actually, since I'm lost, I guess it's up to you. Go home, boy. Go home." He knew from experience that horses had a good sense of direction— generally. It would be just his luck to be astride a horse with the homing instincts of a frog instead of a pigeon. He gave the reins a gentle flick, and the horse started a slow amble ahead.

Well, that was a safe bet, at least. Since Isaiah had said good-bye and taken the turnoff, this was the logical route. But how far? Sam had absolutely no idea, so he had little option but to hope that the horse did.

Despite his uncertainty, this wasn't a bad ride. The horse went slowly, so Sam had plenty of time to enjoy the ride. There wasn't much to see, save for dark outlines of trees against the stars, but there was that marvelous expanse of lights across the sky. It was rare for him to be able to see the stars like this, and he relished the experience. He rarely had this much peace at any point in his Leaps.

There was the soft sound of wings in the night. An owl, most likely, after mice or moles. Maybe even a bat. Isaiah had mentioned living in Smithtown, and Sam recalled a place of that name on Long Island. According to what little of his family history he could recall, he thought that the original Samuel had been from Long Island. Sam's memory was always kind of fuzzy at best, but his last recollection of Long Island was a trip to Brookhaven National Laboratory a few years back. Well, about two hundred or so years in the future, technically speaking, but a few years back in his personal lifetime. Aside from the expressways and a few trees, most of Long Island seemed to be houses, shops, and factories. Where he was riding right now was probably a mini-mall in his own time. To experience it like this was a precious thing.

The experience soon paled, however. It was impossible for Sam to pretend that everything was fine and that he could simply relax and enjoy himself. If he had Leaped here, it was for a purpose. He didn't know what it was yet, but it was clearly tied into the Revolution. Samuel Beckett—his great-great-however-many-times grandfather was clearly involved in some aspect of the War of Independence. But what?

Sam's Swiss-cheesed memory was impairing his preparedness yet again. He wasn't sure, but he didn't think that he'd ever known much about the original Sam Beckett. He tried to concentrate, but very little emerged from the gloom. Born on Long Island—the first Beckett born in America, in fact—he had a son, Daniel, who continued the family line. That was all he recalled from his own memories.

However, Isaiah had mentioned a wife, Hannah. That made sense, even if Sam had no knowledge of her. And this horse and clothing suggested that Samuel Beckett was a farmer, as many of the colonists were. And farming was something of a traditional occupation for Becketts. What else could he deduce? The horse was a working animal, clearly, but also young and sturdy. That suggested the Becketts were reasonably well-off by the standards of their day. The clothing Sam wore was obviously handmade, but it was of good workmanship and fit him reasonably well. Aside from these facts, he had nothing to go on.

He needed Al to give him information. So where was Al?

The horse seemed to be happy enough ambling along. How much further did he have to go? There weren't any mail boxes at the end of paths to tell Sam where they were. Heck, there wasn't even a postal service yet. They had passed a couple of turnoffs that the horse had ignored. Sam eyed them suspiciously. "I hope you know what you're doing," he told the horse, "and you're not just as lost as I am." The horse snorted and kept walking.

The longer he traveled, the more frustrated and uncertain Sam became. Whatever he was supposed to be doing on this Leap, it wasn't getting done. Riding around in the night on a horse he wasn't even sure knew its way home couldn't be accomplishing much.

Where *was* Al?

Then the horse turned down a side path and ambled along it. Sam felt slightly better—at least they had to be getting close to where Samuel lived. Unless the horse was simply wandering where it liked.

"There's a nice bucket of oats for you," Sam told the horse, stroking its neck. "Once we get home, of course." He hoped he was telling the truth, and that the horse understood him. The animal whinnied and flicked its head, as if telling him to quiet down and let him do the work. Sam shrugged and waited, scanning the gloom ahead.

A moment or two later, he could make out a light through the branches, and then the path widened. The horse ambled on, toward dark shapes that resolved themselves into a small house and a barn. The light burned inside the house, dulled slightly by a curtain over the window. There was no light in the barn, of course— leaving a lamp burning there would have been criminally foolish. The horse halted by the closed door and snorted, shaking his head. Sam took the hint and clambered down. The barn wasn't large, but it was obviously the animal's home. Sam raised the bar on the door and swung it open on creaking hinges.

His horse wandered in ahead of him. Sam couldn't see anything in the darkness, but the horse seemed happy enough. Maybe there was a lantern by the door that he could light. Sam fumbled about, but succeeded only in slamming his shin on a log horse.

There was the sound of a door opening and closing, and he glanced around. Someone was heading across to him from the house, holding a light in her upraised hand. "Samuel?" he heard a pleasant feminine voice call anxiously.

"It's me," he replied. This had to be Hannah, his great-whatever-grandmother. "I'm just putting the horse away."

"Without a light?" There was a tone of affectionate humor in Hannah's voice as she arrived next to him. "Honestly, Samuel, I don't know what gets into you sometimes." She held out a small oil lamp.

Sam couldn't help staring at her. Initially it was simply curiosity as to what his ancestor looked like, but after a second it changed into something entirely different. Even in the flickering, uncertain light, it was obvious that Hannah Beckett was beautiful. Without a trace of makeup, or probably any other beauty aids, she had a clear complexion and long, full, dark hair. Her large, expressive eyes and her lips both showed evidence of humor about them. Her simple, full-length dress of dark material, couldn't disguise her figure.

"Samuel," she chided gently, "the poor horse is waiting for its feed. Aren't you going to stop staring at me like you've never seen me before, and satisfy him?"

Guiltily, Sam took the lamp from Hannah. Her touch was almost electric. Why was he acting like this? "I'm sorry," he replied. "I just can't help staring at you."

She laughed. "Trying to turn my head, Mr. Beckett?" She grinned at him. "I'm sure you're just as hungry as the horse. I doubt they fed you at that meeting of yours, did they?"

Sam didn't need to check that. His stomach was empty. "No, they didn't."

"Then I'll fix you some broth while you see to that poor animal." Hannah smiled again as she turned away. "Try not to be too long, Samuel. I've missed you."

"I'll be quick," Sam promised. He watched as she headed back to the house, and then reluctantly turned back to the horse, which was waiting impatiently just inside the barn. Sam had to force himself across the threshold into the building. He wanted to follow Hannah and just stare at her some more. "What's the matter with me?" he asked the horse.

The animal whinnied impatiently. It was obvious that all he was thinking about was food. Sam couldn't blame him. He glanced about the barn, thankful for the small lamp. There was a stall for the horse, and Sam opened the gate to it. The animal wanted to rush inside, but Sam stopped him. He placed the lamp on a convenient barrel, then stripped the saddle and bridle from the animal before allowing him into the stall. There was a trough with water there, and one with oats. Sam checked that they were reasonably full, as best he could around the head of the munching animal. Then he left the stall, fastening the gate behind him.

And jumped.

Al was standing there, head tilted to one side, watching him.

"You might have coughed or something," Sam complained.

"More fun this way," Al answered, taking the large cigar from his mouth and waving it about. "You look so . . . rustic here," he added. He wrinkled his nose. "I'm glad holograms can't smell anything. I'll bet it stinks in here."

Sam hadn't even noticed the odors. Now that Al had mentioned it, he realized that there were the usual farm smells he'd grown up with. "It's just nature," he pointed out.

"Yeah. Nature stinks." Al waved his cigar around again. "You like this stuff?"

"What I'd like most," Sam said, "are some answers. First off, where have you been? I Leaped here over an hour ago."

Al grimaced. "There's no need to get grouchy. There

have been complications. For one thing, it took Ziggy a while to figure out where you were.'' He grinned. ''Guess who you are.''

''I know who I am,'' Sam replied. ''I'm Samuel Beckett, my own great-great-however-many-times grandfather. And this is Long Island, sometime around July 1776.''

Al looked impressed. ''Sometimes I wonder why you need me at all.''

''Sometimes, so do I,'' Sam said. ''Can you help me out a bit here?''

Nodding, Al gave his handlink a good whack on the side. It chirped angrily at him, but seemed to settle down to offer information. ''You even look like you,'' he said. ''I mean, the original Samuel and you look almost like twins, except he's got a lousy haircut.'' He scowled. ''I'd have been here a lot faster if that ancestor of yours was a little more like you.''

''What happened?''

''When he appeared in the Imaging Chamber, he thought he'd died and gone to Heaven. Apparently, right before you switched places, someone had stuck a knife to his throat. Samuel thought he'd had his veins opened and died. He wanted to know if Dr. Beeks was an angel.'' Al wrinkled his nose in disgust. ''With her, I'd have suspected it was more likely the other place.''

Sam regarded the hologram of his friend. Al was dressed in a silver-and-purple, swirl-patterned shirt, bright yellow pants, red shoes, and an electric blue tie. His natty fedora was Day-Glo orange. ''You don't like Dr. Beeks much, do you?''

''Sure I do. It's just her opinions I have trouble with. She's got too many of them, and most of them disagree strongly with most of mine.''

24

"Anyway," Sam said, "I assume you finally got Samuel Beckett talking?"

Al grimaced. "Nope. Dr. Beeks is afraid we'll contaminate him with twentieth-century thinking or something, and has declared him out of bounds, except for emergencies. This, apparently, doesn't count as an emergency yet. She's promised to talk gently with him and try to get some useful information. And, before you ask, Ziggy doesn't have a clue as to why you're here."

"Why am I not surprised?" asked Sam with a sigh. "Okay, what *do* you have?"

Al smacked the handlink again, then tapped a few brief commands into it. "It's the eleventh of August, 1776," he replied. "You're on a small farm just outside of Smithtown, Long Island. Only back now it's known as Nassau Island. That's what the Dutch named it, you see, and nobody got around to giving it the right name yet. Everyone's getting geared up for one of the first battles of the Revolutionary War that's going to be fought right here in a couple of weeks. The British are going to win this one."

"Terrific." Sam frowned. "I'm on the edge of a war zone, I've joined something called the Committee of Safety, and you don't have a clue why I'm here." He thought for a moment. "Okay, see what you can dig up about this Committee of Safety and its leader, George Townsend. And see if Samuel knows anything at all about the upcoming battle. Maybe that's why I'm here."

"Will do," Al agreed. "Gooshie and the others are hunting up historical files to feed into Ziggy right now. We never expected to need anything this far back, so it may take a while. Well, if I've done all I can here, I'd better go find Tina." He grinned. "We've got a long night ahead of us, if you catch my drift."

"Yeah," Sam said wearily. "I catch your drift. Good night, Al."

With a final, leering wink, the hologram tapped the handlink. A rectangle of light opened behind him. He stepped back through it, and then the light zipped down to a small line of almost unbearable intensity before vanishing, leaving Sam alone in the barn.

His horse had apparently taken the meeting in its stride. It was cheerfully munching away on its oats. That served to remind Sam that he was very hungry, and that Hannah had promised to feed him.

Hannah. . . . His insides churned at the thought of her name, and it had nothing to do with hunger. At least, not *that* kind of hunger. "Steady," Sam advised himself. "You're acting like a giddy schoolboy going on a first date." The problem was that he *felt* like a giddy schoolboy going on his first date. There was something about Hannah that struck past all his mental barriers, all of his senses, and went directly to his heart.

It wasn't exactly love at first sight, but it wasn't far removed from it.

Knowing he was treading dangerous ground, Sam walked back to his ancestor's house.

CHAPTER FOUR

Hannah was waiting for him as he entered the small house. It was tiny within, and as simple as it had appeared from the outside. There was one large, L-shaped room at the front that did duty as living room, dining room, and kitchen. At the back of the house and to the right was a smaller room, clearly the bedroom. The door was slightly open, and Sam could see the edge of a large, wooden bed and a small cradle. That had to be where Daniel was sleeping.

"I was beginning to wonder if you were coming in at all this night, Samuel," Hannah said lightly, glancing up from the pot she was tending on the large, wood-fired stove. "Perhaps you aren't too hungry after all."

"I'm ravenous," Sam answered apologetically. "It just took me longer than I thought to deal with things in the barn."

Hannah chuckled. "Old Flighty playing you up again? I think you indulge that horse of yours too much. Rather like you indulge *me* too much." Her eyes crinkled as she smiled.

"You're worth indulging," Sam assured her. "And our horse is too valuable to us for me to get on his bad side."

"You'd best sit down. Soup is coming right up."

Sam did as he was told, taking a chair at the table. There was a loaf of coarse bread on a pewter platter, and a small tub of thick butter. Using a half-blunt knife, Sam hacked off two lumps of bread for them as Hannah ladled out two bowls of soup. Sam's stomach started growling as she brought the steaming bowls to the table.

It smelled delicious, and Sam was again aware that he had no idea how long it had been since he'd eaten. He was about to start when he realized that Hannah was giving him a quizzical look. "Something wrong?" he asked.

"Have you forgotten grace? I hope these men's meetings of yours haven't made you forget *all* of your manners, Samuel Beckett."

"They haven't," Sam assured her, flushing slightly. "But your soup smelled so good, I couldn't wait to eat."

Hannah laughed. "Ah! I might have known it was my fault." She placed her hands together and bowed her head, waiting.

Fortunately, this had been a family routine while Sam was growing up. Following her lead, Sam said, "For this food and this fellowship, we bless you, Lord. Amen."

"Amen." Hannah glanced up, her eyes sparkling. "*Now* you may eat."

"Good." Using a battered spoon, Sam did precisely that. The soup was a thick vegetable broth, heavy on the corn, with a light sprinkling of herbs. Sam was hungry to begin with, but there was no question that the food was excellent. He ate swiftly, then used the bread to mop

28

out his bowl. Hannah was still finishing hers when he sighed happily. "Have I told you lately how wonderful a cook you are?" he asked her.

"Not since our last meal. You're such a flatterer. You'll turn my head."

"It's such a pretty head." Sam was amazed how at home he felt with her. There were no modern conveniences, and he was almost two hundred years back before he had been born, but there was something very warm and comforting about this room. The *something* quite clearly was Hannah. She seemed to warm the room just by being there. Her eyes and mouth were filled with smiles and promises, and she seemed to be good-hearted and affectionate. Sam could see why his ancestor had married her. He felt rather envious of Samuel.

"So, then," Hannah said, finishing at last, "what was the meeting all about? You've been so mysterious about it that I know it must have something to do with the Patriot cause."

Uh-oh. If the real Samuel hadn't told her much, there was probably a good reason for it. Sam doubted it was simply chauvinism; everything he'd experienced so far suggested that Samuel and Hannah were partners as much as a married couple. "I'm not sure it's safe to talk too much about it," he temporized.

"Well, that makes a change," Hannah said, collecting the dishes. "Usually I can't get you to shut up, especially about the cause."

Oops. "You've probably heard more than enough about it, then." Sam helped her to clear the table. "I wouldn't want to tax your patience with further talk."

"Honestly, Samuel, sometimes you are quite impossible, do you know that?"

"So I've been told."

"Yes, and more often than not by me." Hannah pouted, but her eyes showed that it wasn't serious. "If you don't want to tell me, then don't."

"I won't," Sam said gently. "It's better if you don't know too much."

Hannah snorted. "In case the British come and torture me for information?" she teased. "Honestly, Samuel, I think you're enjoying all this pretended spy game a little too much. You act like a child sometimes."

"I *am* a child sometimes," Sam told her, with considerably more honesty than she'd ever know. "But I am also serious sometimes. And I am serious when I say it's for your protection."

Hannah smiled. "I know that. But it doesn't mean that. . . ."

She broke off as there came a loud banging on the front door. "Who could that be at this time of the night?" she wondered, looking a little worried.

"Let's hope it's not the British," Sam said, only half joking.

"They'd knock the door down, not rap." But Hannah looked disturbed as Sam went to open the door.

Uncertain of what he would find when he did so, Sam tensed, ready for action. As the door swung open, he saw a man in a cloak and tricornered hat standing in the doorway. There was a horse tethered to the fence behind him. As the door opened, the man looked up, a reassuring smile on his craggy face. "Samuel Beckett?" he asked.

Much relieved, Sam nodded. Not only was the man obviously friendly, but he was also clearly a stranger to the real Samuel. "Yes. And you are . . . ?"

"Benjamin Bradshaw," the stranger answered. "I've

come from Colonel Smith. May I?'' He gestured at the room behind Sam.

''Oh, yes.'' Standing aside, Sam let the man into the house. ''This is my wife, Hannah.''

Bradshaw removed his hat and gave a very low, polite bow. ''Your servant, ma'am,'' he said, then turned back to Sam. ''Forgive my intrusion this late at night, Mr. Beckett, but these are times when civility often must take the back seat to necessity.''

''Of course,'' Sam answered. ''But why are you here?''

''As I said,'' Bradshaw replied brusquely, ''I am here on behalf of Colonel Josiah Smith. I believe you know the colonel, do you not?''

Sam didn't, of course, but presumably Samuel did. Before Sam could frame a convincing reply, Hannah broke in.

''Of course we do,'' she said cheerily. ''He's my great-uncle. Is everything well with him?''

''Well and better,'' answered Bradshaw. ''He has just met with General Nathaniel Woodhull.'' That was a name Sam knew at least vaguely. An old detail from a school lesson popped into his memory. Woodhull had been one of the soldiers who had tried to defend New York City against the British. ''General Woodhull,'' Bradshaw continued, ''has appointed Colonel Smith to raise a militia regiment from Suffolk County. We are to march to join the defense of Nassau Island in a few days. Colonel Smith has sent me to see if he can count on the support of the men of this district, and he specifically charged me to ask you first.''

Talk about being placed on the spot! Sam had absolutely no idea whether his ancestor had joined the rebel forces in the upcoming battle or not. But he was clearly

31

expected to do so. Bradshaw was regarding him quizzically, waiting for a reply of some kind. Sam didn't know what to say. How could he possibly refuse? But if he accepted, what then? Was this why he was here? To change Samuel's response?

But from what and to what? What would Samuel have said? Recalling what Hannah had joked about earlier, presumably Samuel would have leaped—no pun intended!—at the opportunity to fight for his country in the upcoming battle. But Samuel couldn't have known what Sam did—that the patriots would lose the battle, and suffer grave losses with their defeat.

Would those losses have included Samuel Beckett?

But how could he possibly get out of this without looking like a coward or a traitor to the cause? Sam didn't know what to say or do. He looked to Hannah, hoping for a lead from her.

She saw the worry on his face, that was clear. With a faint frown, she said, "Is it me and the baby that worry you, Samuel? Lord knows, you'd be jumping in with your 'aye' fast enough otherwise."

"How can I *not* think of you both?" Sam asked her. "As strongly as I feel about independence, I have a responsibility to you and Daniel first."

Hannah scowled slightly, though he could see she was trying to be brave. "And what kind of a country will Daniel grow up in if you do not help free it?" she asked. "One that pays crippling taxes forever to a foreign crown? One with a king who cares not a whit about his subjects?" Then she smiled, somewhat sadly. "But here am I, preaching to the converted."

"You have a responsibility to the future," said Bradshaw gently.

Sam nodded, knowing that this simple sentiment

meant more than Bradshaw could possibly understand or mean. But to *what* future? The presence or absence of Samuel Beckett at the Battle of Brooklyn could hardly alter the outcome. The Patriots would lose, and lose badly. But his absence might mean that Samuel lived, and his participation might kill him.

On the other hand, how could Sam override Samuel's beliefs without good reason? To refuse to join the militia would be inconsistent and probably dangerous. Samuel might be seen as a Tory sympathizer—and in this day and age, that could be dangerous. Especially if the Committee of Safety were to hear of it. John Kirk already seemed to think that Samuel had dangerously pro-British leanings. To refuse to join the militia might increase the man's suspicions.

Maybe *that* was why Sam was here. Did Samuel refuse to join the militia and then incur the wrath of the Committee? Sam had already seen that they had almost been prepared to slit his throat on a mere suspicion. If they had what they considered proof, what would they do?

And if Samuel Beckett somehow died as a result of Sam's bad decisions, what would happen to Hannah and Daniel? And, as a result, what would happen to Sam himself? He was descended from Samuel through Daniel, who was sleeping peacefully in the bedroom, a helpless infant. If Daniel never grew up because Sam botched his Leap, what would become of Sam? His entire family would be effectively wiped out.

There was so much riding on a simple question, and Sam had very little to base his decision upon. To join or not . . . that was indeed the question.

Sam took a deep breath. The only thing he could do was stay true to his own and his ancestor's convictions.

The War of Independence was vitally important, not simply to Sam but to everyone, both currently alive and in Sam's own time. "I will serve," Sam promised. "In this time of crisis, how could I do anything else?"

Bradshaw clapped his arm. "Good man!" he said enthusiastically. "The colonel knew that he could count on you."

"But I'll need a few days to set things in order here," Sam added, looking with concern at Hannah. She smiled bravely, but it couldn't mask her fears.

"Of course," agreed Bradshaw. "I quite understand. I'll make certain another messenger calls in a few days to tell you where the gathering will be. Colonel Smith aims to raise his force here, and then march out toward Brooklyn. There will be plenty of time for you to join us."

"Fine." Sam nodded to the man. "I'll be there."

"Can we offer you some refreshment?" Hannah asked their visitor. "The soup is hot."

"And delicious," Sam added.

Bradshaw smiled and shook his head. "Thank you, but no. I have far to go this night before I can rest. Much as the smell is very tempting, Mistress Beckett," he added politely. "I had better be about my task."

"Then go in safety," Sam said, opening the door. It was getting simpler for him to think in eighteenth-century terms. He knew that some of the personality of the person he Leaped into always seeped across, and he seemed to be absorbing a little of Samuel's mind-set. It at least would help him in conversations.

"Thank you." Bradshaw bowed again to Hannah, then replaced his hat. "I'll be seeing you soon," he promised Sam, and swept from the room.

Closing the door, Sam turned back to Hannah with a

heavy heart. "I hope I've made the right decision," he said.

Hannah moved to join him, and placed her arms about him. Sam felt a chill sweep through him at her affectionate touch. He had to remind himself that it was meant for Samuel, not for him. "You have answered the only honorable way, Samuel," she said softly. "And I am proud of you."

"And what if I'm injured in the battle?" he asked, still uncertain. "Or. . . ." He couldn't bring himself to say it.

"Or killed? Samuel, God forbid that you should be harmed! I do not know what I would do without you. But I *do* know that if you stayed at home out of fear for Daniel and myself, then you'd become miserable and unsure of yourself. You'd have to turn your back on your most cherished beliefs, and that I could not accept."

"My most cherished beliefs are you and Daniel," Sam answered. "If I fight, it's for your sakes, not just my own. I do have a debt to the future."

"And you'll acquit yourself well. Of that I am certain, Samuel. I am very proud of you, and very frightened for you. But you are doing the only thing that you can." Before Sam could react, she kissed him.

It was like a fire inside of him. Sam had known many women in his Leaps, and most likely in his own, half-forgotten past. Yet this was somehow very different. It wasn't merely that Hannah was a very attractive, intelligent woman, supportive and understanding. There was something deeper inside of him, tugging him to her. He was drawn to her as he couldn't recall ever being drawn to any other woman.

Perhaps it was some overlap of his own personality

35

and that of Samuel. Sometimes that kind of thing happened on his Leaps. Part of the person he replaced stayed with him and helped to motivate his actions and conversations. And since he and Samuel were already quite alike, and even related, maybe the overlap was stronger than normal. Maybe it was Samuel's love for Hannah that stirred Sam so strongly.

Or maybe it was something else. Sam had never really believed in the old myth of love at first sight. Attraction, yes; interest, certainly. But *love*?

And yet, here he was, being shaken by strong emotions as his supposed wife kissed him. He couldn't help responding, but even as he did, there were alarm bells going off in the back of his mind.

If he didn't put a stop to this, Sam had a very good idea how this evening was going to end. There was, after all, only one bed in this small house, and he was theoretically married to Hannah. . . .

But—and it was an immense but—she was his ancestor. She was, in fact, his great-great-great-great-great-great grandmother. It was one thing to think of her academically as his distant relative, but quite another thing to be held and kissed by her.

He *couldn't* do anything about it. It would be incest. Well . . . Sam wasn't absolutely sure that this was the correct term for what it would be. Incest covered close family members, and he and Hannah were two hundred years apart. They weren't *that* close, really.

But some part of him owed its existence to her. Maybe only a percent or two, but it was there. Was that why he felt so drawn to her? Some attraction on a primal level? Still, whatever his feelings were, it hardly mattered. The facts were unchanged. Appealing though the thought was, Sam couldn't bring himself to respond physically to Hannah.

And she, being a sensitive person, could tell this. She pulled back from the kiss and looked at him, worried. "Samuel," she said, puzzled and a little hurt, "what is wrong with you? You've never needed more encouragement than this in the past. If you had, we'd hardly have Daniel now." She tried to smile, but Sam could see the concern in her beautiful eyes.

"I'm sorry," he mumbled, striving to find some excuse for his behavior that might make halfway decent sense to her.

"Is it Daniel?" she asked, anxiously. "Have I become unattractive to you since his birth? Is that it?"

"No," he replied honestly, "that isn't it. You've never looked more lovely or appealing to me than you do now." That, at least, was quite true.

"Then why do you not respond?" Hannah demanded. "If the fault is not in me, then. . . ." Her eyes opened wide. "Poor Samuel," she breathed. "Is it concern about this war of ours? Is that what distracts you so much?"

"Yes," Sam lied. "It's hard for me to push it from my mind. It's going to be a very rough time, Hannah." He considered how much he should tell her. He couldn't let on that he knew with certainty that the British were going to win this battle. But he could use the facts as an aid in making his excuses. "Hannah, I'm worried about the upcoming battle. Colonel Smith is going to be leading us into a fight. Now, we're good men, and willing to fight hard for our country, but the British have trained troops. It won't be an easy fight to win, and I'm very much afraid it would be an easy one to lose. The British know that if they lose control of New York, the

37

tide will turn against them. They're going to do everything they can to win this battle.''

Hannah took his hands in her own. "And you're afraid that we'll all lose out? That you may be killed, and Daniel and I will be left under the heels of a tyrant force? Is that it?''

"That's it exactly," Sam answered, relieved that he'd discovered a logical excuse for his reluctance. "And if you were expecting another child, then it would be even harder for you if I were killed in action.''

"Oh, Samuel," Hannah sighed, clutching him to her. "You're being so thoughtful and noble and so, so silly. If I were with another child, and you were killed, then at least I'd have something more to remind me of you. And what if something were to happen to Daniel? God forbid, but many children do die in infancy. If we had more, then at least there'd be a good chance of your name being passed down.''

"Trust me," Sam said, feeling very hemmed in by her replies, "my name isn't in danger of being lost just yet. Daniel is a strong and healthy child. He's going to grow up and be a father in turn.''

"I admire your certainty." Hannah snuggled close again. "But you needn't fear leaving me expectant, my love. I will survive it, if God so wills it. Come to bed.'' She looked up at him, her dark eyes expressive and filled with love and longing.

It was almost too much for Sam to refuse. He could feel his own body responding, and his resolve weakening. It was so damnably hard to refuse this woman anything she wanted. Especially when what she wanted was what he wanted.

Except in that small, rebellious, logical part of his mind.

Just as Sam was certain that he could take no more of this temptation, there was a wail from the bedroom. He jerked from Hannah's embrace, flushing guiltily. "Uh, Daniel's awake," he mumbled. "I guess I'd better go and see to him."

With a snort, Hannah pushed him aside. "Unless you've grown teats," she said, "there's very little that you can do for him right now." She made a mock pout. "Well, I suppose that resolves our ... discussion for now, Mr. Beckett. But it's far from over. I don't like to lose, as you well know." She started to unthread the ribbons that fastened the top of her dress.

Wanting to stay, Sam forced himself to turn from her and cross to the door. "I'm going to get a little fresh air," he called back. "I won't be long." Before she could reply, he hurried outside and closed the door. He leaned against it for a moment, breathing deeply and trying to get his emotions under control.

What was he going to do? It was bad enough being faced with the decision of whether to fight in the upcoming battle. Then, to add to that, he had his own great-whatever grandmother making advances to him.

Leaping was never easy, but it had seldom seemed to be so difficult before.

Keeping to the shadows, John Kirk slipped away from the Beckett house, his face set in grim resolve. He'd heard quite enough for now, and it was best to retreat before Samuel saw him lurking about. He'd spent a while pressed against the open window, listening to the conversations within. As he'd suspected earlier, Beckett was not the committed patriot that he pretended to be. He'd fobbed off Bradshaw for the moment with his promise to join the militia being raised, but he'd then privately admitted to his wife that he believed the British would win the forthcoming battle.

How could he be so certain? There was only one possible answer. Beckett was secretly a Tory and working *for* the British, not against them. He had cast his lot with the Loyalist cause, not the Rebels.

Therefore, he had joined the Committee of Safety not to help them but to hinder their work. To sabotage them, and to undermine the cause of liberty. Kirk was certain of this, though he knew that without proof, his certainty would not be accepted. He needed to have Beckett commit himself for the British cause, and that wouldn't be too difficult.

On the morrow, the Committee would be riding to Oyster Bay, to root out the traitors and Tories there. Unless he missed his guess, Beckett would do or say something there that would reveal his real allegiance.

And then Kirk would destroy him.

CHAPTER
FIVE

That night was hell for Sam. It was bad enough having to get ready for bed with Hannah, though the long night-shirts both donned over their clothes before undressing helped a little. It was all Sam could do to stop imagining Hannah's body as she removed her several layers of clothing. Then, lying next to her in bed simply refined the torture he was going through. Since it was August on Long Island, the night was warm and humid, so they had only a single blanket on the bed. Sam could feel Hannah against his back, and the soft rise and fall of her breasts as she breathed. Determined not to give in to his instincts, Sam spent several hours attempting to fight down his desires, without a great deal of success.

Surely he could control his urges! Hannah was just another woman. In his Leaping, he'd met many, and slept with quite a number of them, mostly platonically. Sex was not a necessary component of bed.

But Hannah was very different somehow, and Sam knew that logic had virtually nothing to do with what he was feeling.

Eventually he drifted off into a troubled sleep, to be wakened by the morning chorus of birds and Hannah poking him in the back.

"Lazybones," she chided him good-humoredly. "Time to get up and do the chores. Or did you think to sleep forever?"

"The chance would be a fine thing," Sam grumbled. But at least physical activity would take his mind off Hannah for a while—he hoped. He splashed water on his face to help him wake, then staggered outside to the privy. Afterward, he dressed discreetly under his nightshirt, avoiding watching Hannah as she did the same. Then he stumbled outside again to start the morning chores.

This, at least, was something he was used to. He might be back in the eighteenth century, but farm chores were farm chores, whatever the date. As the sun started to color the sky, and the black shapes of night resolved into structures and landscape, Sam could see that his ancestor's farm was quite large. It had to be more than twenty acres, which meant a lot of work for just Samuel and Hannah alone.

Behind the house were a chicken run and a pig wallow. There were a sow and six or seven piglets—in the mud and with their squealing eagerness to be fed, Sam couldn't keep an accurate count. He managed to dispense the swill to them without getting too filthy. As he did so, Hannah fed the chickens and collected eggs.

"Breakfast," she announced with a grin. "Ten minutes. Will you cut some wood and fetch the water?"

"Of course." Sam went to the stone-edged well and drew the leather bucket, using it to fill the pitcher that Hannah had set there. The water was sandy and brownish. Sam grimaced at the thought of drinking it as he carried it into the kitchen. Then he went back outside and split logs until Hannah called him in for breakfast.

Sam had managed to work up an appetite, and Hannah's cooking was just as good at breakfast as it had been at supper. She'd whipped them up corn cakes and eggs, with more of the rough bread. Sam eyed the brown liquid in his cup with suspicion, but forced himself to taste it. To his surprise, it was a chunk-filled cider, not the water. Certainly an improvement!

"This will set me up for the day," Sam said, finishing his plate.

"Hah!" Hannah snorted, "You and your appetite will be back at lunchtime, I'll warrant." She took his plate, then bent to kiss him. "And I thought *that* always set you up for the day."

"It certainly did," Sam answered, wanting more of the same but controlling the desire. "Will I get another with lunch?"

"As many as you wish," Hannah promised. "And more, if you discover your decision was wrong last night."

Didn't he wish! But he *had* to keep that door firmly closed. "We'll see," he temporized. "I'll have time to do some thinking in the fields."

Hannah grunted skeptically. "As long as you have the time to pick me more apples," she said. "Otherwise there'll be no pie for your supper tonight."

Sam made an expression of mock horror. "In that case, I'll pick apples before anything else." As he started for the door, he bent and gave Hannah a chaste kiss on the cheek. It sent a tingle through his every nerve. "Be good."

"And what else can I be with all this work?" Hannah grumbled good-naturedly. "Be off with you now."

It was both a relief and a shame to leave the house. Sam recalled seeing large baskets in the barn the previous night, obviously for the apples. The orchard portion of the farm was close beside the barn, so he headed there. In a few moments, he was happily gathering the best apples from the overloaded trees. It was clearly a good year for produce, and the work cleared his mind of less proper thoughts for the time being.

There was the flash of light that heralded the imminent appearance of Al, and then the hologram stepped into existence. He was dressed all in electric blue this time, clearly his notion of fashion sense. It hurt Sam's eyes to look at him too long.

"Well, if it isn't Farmer Brown," Al said cheerfully. "You look like you're enjoying yourself."

"It takes me back to my childhood," Sam replied. "It was a lot like this where I grew up."

"Yeah," agreed Al. "Except they had tractors instead of horses, and machines to do most of the work. And probably electricity and piped-in water. Jeez, how could people live like this?" He glanced with distaste at the mud, and then at Sam's dirt-specked clothes. "I'm glad I'm not really there. I wouldn't want to get my clothes all messed up."

Sam bit back his first response and settled for something more tactful. "Tell me you're here to help, Al."

"I'm here to help." Al eyed the half-full apple basket. "Thankfully, not with the chores. I'll just watch those, thank you." He tapped in a command on his handlink and then sat down, apparently in midair. Obviously he'd called up a chair in the Imaging Chamber, where his body was. "Okay, quick review time. The British are getting set to fight for New York City. The Patriots are

44

gearing up for a battle in a couple of weeks that they're going to get trounced in.''

"I know all of that," Sam objected. "In fact, I had a visitor last night after you left. A guy named Benjamin Bradshaw. He's an aide to Colonel Smith, the guy who's organizing the local militia for the battle. He wanted me to join the ranks for the upcoming fight.''

Al rolled his eyes. "Let me guess," he said, sighing. "You, noble soul and patriot, rushed to agree.''

"I didn't rush, Al," Sam objected. "I'm not stupid. I know that it might mean Samuel's death if he gets involved in the battle. But how could I refuse?''

"Just say no," Al advised. "Jeez, that bollixes up my projections.'' He smacked the handlink hard, and started to tap information in.

"What projections?'' Sam demanded. "You haven't told me anything useful yet.''

"Well, Ziggy's been computing all night, and Verbeena's been talking with Samuel. Boy, that guy really loves to talk. I'll bet he's got a donkey around here some place without hind legs. He's even got Dr. Beeks tuning out on him.''

"Get to the point,'' Sam begged.

"Okay, Ziggy predicts there's a fifty percent chance that you're here to prevent Samuel getting killed somehow. That business last night with the knife was just a warm-up, so to speak. Ziggy thinks Samuel's likely to be in big trouble over the next couple of weeks. It took me a while to access your family records. Somebody sealed them with a few strong defenses.''

"Me,'' Sam admitted, as a memory wafted back to him, "to stop people from peeking.''

"Yeah, and you did okay, too. It took Ziggy almost thirty seconds to break into the files. When I could stop her from making all kinds of comments about your childhood illnesses and how cute your baby pictures are, she told me there's not much there about Samuel.''

"I could have told you that and saved you the trouble,'' Sam grumbled.

"Yeah, well, you didn't. And even if you had, how would you know it for a fact? Your memory's not what it was, after all. Anyhow, Ziggy raided the Library of Congress next, and dug up some paydirt. It seems they keep the old militia records there, and she accessed Samuel's. He served for just a couple of months here on Long Island, then left for Westchester County. He fought there until 1782, then went back to private life. Ziggy tracked down census records that showed he lived until about 1800 or so—records aren't too good for that period—and had a couple of other kids.'' Al glanced up at Sam. "Provided, of course, he lives that long. Ziggy's half-sure that's why you're here.''

"And the other half?'' Sam asked.

Before Al could reply, there was a call from the house. Sam looked around and saw Hannah waving to him.

"Stop daydreaming, Samuel Beckett, and get those apples to me!'' she called. "Or it's no pie!''

Picking up the basket, Sam called, "Coming!'' and started back to the house. To Al, he added, "You wait for me here. I'll be back in a minute.''

But it was too late. Al was walking beside him. There had been shock on Al's face for a moment when he'd spotted Hannah, but that had been replaced by another look. Sam had seen the expression in Al's eyes all too often before. "You kidding?'' Al demanded. "This babe looks like a stunner. I owe it to myself to check her out.''

"You're a hologram, Al," Sam snapped. "You can't do anything."

"I can *look*," Al replied. "Boy, can I look. And she can't see me."

"And she's my relative," Sam added angrily. "Leave her alone."

"Whoa!" Al stared at his friend, scowling. "Do I detect a note of jealousy here, buddy boy?"

"Don't be stupid," Sam replied. "And be quiet." They were getting close to the house now, and he didn't want Hannah to see him apparently talking to himself. Besides, Al's ill-chosen words were irritating him. Al might be his best friend, but he could be pretty insensitive sometimes, especially where women were concerned.

"I *am* right," Al muttered, but subsided at Sam's angry glare.

Sam carried the basket of apples inside the house. Hannah was at the flour-dusted table, rolling out a corn-dough crust. "Leave them by the table, Samuel," she said, favoring him with another of her devastating smiles. Sam's heart leaped and fell at the sight. If only . . .

Al wasn't so reticent. "Hubba hubba hubba!" he exclaimed. "Now, is that a babe or is that a babe?" His eyes were almost bulging, and Sam was convinced he was overdoing his reaction to try and annoy him.

"I've got to get back to work," he said apologetically.

"I know," Hannah answered. She gave him a quick, corn-flour-laced peck on the cheek. "I'll see you at lunchtime. You've got a lot to get done if you want to make that meeting of yours this afternoon."

Sam had almost forgotten about the Committee of

Safety, so intent had he been on his work. "Right," he agreed. He lingered, reluctant to leave.

"Get along with you, now!"

Laughing, Sam did as he was told, heading toward the fields beyond the apple orchard. He glanced back, but there was no sign of Al. Sam had a very real suspicion that Al was checking Hannah out further, knowing he couldn't be seen. It irritated Sam, but there wasn't much he could do about it. Sooner or later, Al would reappear.

It was about fifteen minutes before the hologram did so. Sam was weeding the rows of corn that were almost ready for picking. Corn was a staple item in the diets of just about everyone in this period, he knew, and thus was one of the most valuable products of any farm. Not only would it be stored as ears and ground as meal for the family's use the following year, but a good deal of it would be sold or bartered for items that Samuel couldn't produce on the farm, such as salt and cloth. It was vital, therefore, that the corn be checked carefully and encouraged to grow.

Al arrived, walking through the tall ears of corn and shaking his head. "Boy, it beats me how you do it, but you really get some lookers. You know that?" He leered. "Must have been fun to come home last night, eh?"

"It was *not* fun," Sam snapped, ripping out weeds and wishing his hands were around Al's neck instead.

"No?" asked Al, innocence itself. "Hey, careful, you almost uprooted a perfectly good plant there. What's wrong? Mind on other things?" He leered again. "Can't say I blame you."

"We're not all obsessed with sex," Sam retorted, refusing to look up.

"No? Then you don't know what you're missing." A

48

pair of electric blue shoes ambled through the roots of the plant Sam was working beside. "Some days I don't know what's with you, Sam. If I'd made whoopee with a babe like that last night, I'd be in Heaven this morning. Not grouchy."

"I didn't make whoopee with her, and she's not a babe," Sam said angrily. "She's my great-whatever grandmother. So knock it off."

"Oh." Al removed the cigar from his mouth and studied the smoldering end of it thoughtfully. "So *that's* the trouble. You wanted some bingo-bango, but you had qualms. Boy, no wonder you're so grumpy today."

"I am *not* grumpy," Sam snapped. He finally looked up. "All right, maybe I *am* grumpy. But you're trivializing the issue, as usual."

"What's to trivialize?" Al asked innocently. "Boy meets girl, who thinks he's her husband. Boy and girl get it on, and everyone's happy. You should try it sometime. I only wish I could with her."

"Al," Sam said, with as much patience as he could pull together from the depths of his mind, "it's not that simple. She's my ancestor."

"Well, if this was 1995, maybe there'd be a problem. She'd be kinda thin and bony. But she's young and healthy—boy, is she *ever* healthy." He sketched a pair of breasts in the air. "Did you see the hooters on her?"

"Al," Sam tried again, "it's not simply a matter of sex. There's the moral factor, which you conveniently seem to have overlooked."

Al studied his cigar again. "You mean you're not really her hubby, and she only thinks you are?"

"No." It was obvious that this wasn't getting through to Al. "I mean the fact that she's my *ancestor*. Sleeping with her would be incest."

"How do you figure that?" asked Al. "You're probably closer related to Marilyn Monroe than to Mrs. Beckett back there."

"Al," Sam tried again, "she's my ancestor. If not for her, I wouldn't be alive. Part of my genetic makeup is from her. Sleeping with her would be like sleeping with my sister."

Al scowled and shook his head. "You're getting way too complicated here, Sam," he said. "So you share a couple of genes. Big deal. Sleeping with her would be like sleeping with a fifth or sixth cousin twenty times removed. There's nothing to worry about. Nada. Zip. Understand me?" He grinned. "Not that the thought might not add a little spice to the fun. Go for it."

Sam sighed. "It's always so simple for you, isn't it?" It was clear that Al would never share his reservations.

"You're just overcomplicating matters, as usual," Al answered. "And speaking of overcomplicated, you've got a visitor." He gestured with his cigar.

Looking up from the corn, Sam saw a figure crossing the field toward him. The man was bent, walking with a rough-cut crutch, his left leg stiff and useless. His clothing was little better than rags, and he had a shapeless hat rammed down over long, dirty hair. Rough stubble covered his dirty face. One eye was hidden beneath a patch.

Drawing close, the stranger looked up and flashed a gap-filled grin. "Hello, Samuel. It's been a while. Recognize me?"

Sam regarded the figure in dismay. Of course he didn't recognize the man, since he wasn't really Samuel. But if he admitted that, it was likely to cause severe complications. He glanced at Al, who shrugged and then whacked the side of the handlink again.

"Sorry, Sam," he grunted. "You're on your own here."

Now what? Sam stared at the unsavory figure. What could he possibly say to get out of this?

CHAPTER SIX

"You don't recognize me, do you?" the ragged stranger asked, cackling slightly.

What could he possibly say? Sam shook his head miserably. "No, I don't," he admitted.

The stranger cackled again, louder than before. "My best disguise ever, eh, Samuel?" he chortled. "It's Nathan—Nathan Durham."

What a relief! Sam almost felt like hugging the man. "Nathan?" he said, quizzically. "Is it really you?" He glanced at Al, who was tapping in a question on the handlink.

"Yes, Samuel." The cackling was gone, and the man's voice sounded stronger and younger. "I knew that if my best friend couldn't see through this disguise, then there was little chance that the British would do."

"What is it all for?" asked Sam, playing for time.

"What do you think? I'm off to spy on the British, and could hardly go as myself. I don't have to tell you how important it is for us to get up-to-date information on their movements. There's a battle afoot."

"That much I know," Sam admitted. "I've been asked to join Colonel Smith's militia."

"Bother." Nathan chewed at his lip with his few teeth. "Well, you'll have to postpone that for now, Samuel. I came mostly to tell you that you're to go to the Havens Inn as soon as possible. You'll be met."

As if matters weren't complicated enough! "What's it about, Nathan?" Sam asked.

"As if they'd tell me," Nathan said with a chuckle. "Just get along as soon as possible. They know you're pretty busy, so they won't be expecting you today."

"Ah . . . okay. I've just got a few things to clear up first."

"Good." Nathan lifted his eye patch and winked. "I'll be seeing you when I return, Samuel. Be prudent, and be sure to keep your counsel close. It's difficult to know who's a Tory sympathizer these days." Replacing the patch, he waved, then shuffled off, the way he had come.

"Jeez," muttered Al, "I hope his disguise really is as good as he thinks it is. Just because he fooled you, he thinks he's James Bond!"

Sam watched him for a few moments, until he was out of earshot, then turned to Al. "I hope you can explain some of that," he said grimly. "Just what was my ancestor involved with, anyway?"

"By the look of things, a heck of a lot," Al answered. "Okay, Ziggy's got some facts for you that should help. Nathan Durham was a kind of secret agent. . . ."

"That part I already guessed," Sam snapped.

"Don't get so testy. He worked for a fella called William Floyd. He was one of the signers of the Declaration of Independence. He has a big house out in the Moriches Bay area here on Long Island, but he's off with the

Continental Congress right now. Durham's obviously keeping track of the movements of the British while his boss is away. I guess Samuel was involved with him somehow.''

''You guess?'' Sam frowned. ''Why don't you just ask Samuel? He's right there in the Waiting Room, isn't he?'' Al didn't answer immediately, which raised Sam's suspicions. ''Al? He *is* there, isn't he? You didn't let him get away, did you?''

''No, no,'' Al replied, a little too glibly. ''He's there still, and he's in good shape.''

''So what are you not telling me?'' Sam demanded. ''I can tell when you're weaseling.''

''Weaseling? Me?'' Al tried to look indignant. ''It's not *my* fault—he's *your* ancestor. And a real suspicious so-and-so.''

''Meaning?''

Al studied the tip of his cigar thoughtfully. ''I guess Dr. Beeks has been asking too many questions. He's suddenly decided that we're probably British agents trying to pump him for information. He's doing the name, rank, and serial number routine right now.''

''Great.'' Why did things seem to be getting more complex instead of less? ''So, until Verbeena can convince him you're not the bad guys, he's refusing to cooperate? Why didn't you tell me this earlier?''

''I didn't want to worry you,'' Al replied. ''You seemed to have enough to think about.''

Sam sighed. ''Well, there's not much I can do to help you with Samuel. Is there anything else you *can* tell me? Like where this rendezvous I'm supposed to make is going to be?''

''I'm working on it,'' Al answered, tapping furiously on the handlink. ''The Havens Inn. . . . Ah, got it.'' He

54

raised an eyebrow. "You know, it still exists in our time. It's called the Ketcham Inn. At this period, it was a stagecoach stop, the end of the road from Brooklyn. It's in the Moriches Bay area—surprise—and owned by a...." He slapped the link. "Benjamin Havens. Ziggy can help with directions."

"That's something, at least." Sam tried to puzzle it out. "This meeting is obviously undercover work of some kind, if Durham is involved but has no details. Plus the militia I'm supposed to be joining. Then there's this Committee of Safety this afternoon.... Did you get anything about that, and John Kirk and George Townsend?"

"Ah, now there I can help you." Al did his sitting down in thin air trick again. "They were pretty busy guys, it seems. Starting this afternoon—August 12, 1776—the Committee takes it on itself to, ah, *persuade* Tories, Tory sympathizers, and suspected Tories to get the hell off Long Island. Pardon me, Nassau Island. To that end, they generally just roughed folks up, and made them realize that staying would be hell. On the other hand, that John Kirk is one nasty piece of work. He's using the Committee to get even with folks he has grudges against, or simply doesn't like." Al shook his head. "Boy, is he gonna get his come the revolution."

"But not today?"

"Nope. Right now, he and Townsend are in their glory. They're calling the shots, and making themselves pretty unpopular. Nassau Island will stay pretty much pro-British for a good part of the war, so they're really on the losing side right now. Once the Battle of Brooklyn is fought, though, Kirk is gonna get tossed into jail, along with his wife and kid. They'll rot there until they die of smallpox.'' Al snorted. ''Small loss, if you ask me.''

Sam couldn't help a twinge of pity, especially for the innocent wife and child. ''It sounds pretty cruel to me.''

''Trust me, he deserves it.''

''But until after the battle, he's pretty much in charge?''

''Yeah.'' Al scratched his chin. ''And he seems to have taken a dislike to you, from what you told me. I'd play it safe and not get on his bad side for now. Then again, I don't think this clown has a good side. Maybe you'd be better off just avoiding this meeting this afternoon.''

''Right,'' snorted Sam. ''And then *I'd* be on his hit list, along with Hannah and the baby. I don't think that'd be very smart. Besides, I'd rather be where I can keep an eye on him. Maybe the Committee is just going to throw their weight around, but I'd like to be certain that it stops there.''

Al grimaced. ''Maybe you're right, Sam. Maybe that's why you're here.''

Sam nodded. ''Wait a minute. You said that Ziggy figured out there's a fifty percent chance I'm here to save Samuel from something. What about the other fifty percent?''

''Oh, yeah. Almost forgot about that.'' Al looked worried for a moment. ''Look, we haven't got a whole lot of genealogical data on your family, like I said. Only that Daniel is gonna be your ancestor. Ziggy gives the other fifty percent odds right now that you're here to make sure he grows up to begat you. Or is that beget you? I always get my tenses confused.''

''What?'' Sam was distinctly worried now. ''You mean there's something wrong with Daniel?''

"No, not at all," Al replied hastily. "It's just that with you being a doctor and all, and kids in these ancient times being so prone to suddenly snuffing it for no apparent reason, the logic seemed pretty sound. Still does to me. So maybe you'd just better keep a good eye on the kid. Assuming you don't aim to commit a very bizarre form of suicide by allowing your great-whatever grandpappy to die."

Sam considered the idea for a moment. "You really know how to reassure me, don't you? Okay, I'll make certain to check him as often as possible." Sam glanced at the sun, which was almost overhead. "Starting about now, in fact. It must be about lunchtime. And I have to get over to that Committee meeting afterward." He rolled his eyes. "I don't know what Samuel Beckett was up to exactly, but it seems to be involving me in a great deal of work."

"Yeah," Al agreed, without much sympathy. "But there are some great perks to the job, if you get my drift."

"I already told you my viewpoint on that," Sam snapped. "Can't you just forget about Hannah?"

"How can I?" Al objected. "One look, and I'm gone. If I weren't a hologram. . . ." He let his voice trail off, then roused himself. "Anyhow, you won't need me to watch you eat lunch, so I'm going back. I'll see if Beeks has convinced your ancestor that we can be trusted."

"Show him a dollar bill," Sam suggested. "Would the British print money with Washington's head on it?"

Al's face lit up. "Great idea, Sam. See ya." The doorway opened behind him, and he vanished.

Heading back to the house, Sam tried to straighten out his thoughts. There was so much to think about. He still didn't have any real idea why he was here. Ziggy's two options made sense, but they were based only on what the hybrid computer knew of the situation—in other words, what she'd gleaned from Al's observations and what they'd learned from Samuel Beckett in the Waiting Room. Her projections were nothing more than guesswork—extremely educated guesswork. She was doing her best, but there were plenty of other possibilities that she obviously hadn't considered and couldn't consider yet.

Samuel Beckett was clearly a complicated person. He was married to the niece of Colonel Smith, the local militia leader and obviously a close friend of the family. The call to arms was obviously fairly important. Then there was this Havens Inn business. Samuel was involved in some kind of spy ring, it would seem. There was no use speculating as to what that meant until he kept the odd appointment that had been made for him. Then, finally, there was this Committee of Safety nonsense.

Kirk, Townsend, and some of the others were obviously in it not to protect their fellow countrymen but to pay back old scores and to bully when they felt they could get away with it. This was the dark face of patriotism, when a supposed love of one's country gave men like Kirk free rein to act like terrorists and to attack the innocent along with the guilty. Sam knew that there were thousands of true patriots laying their lives on the line even now to fight for freedom. Then there were the scum like Kirk, who, under the guise of patriotism, were nothing more than a bunch of thugs with a veneer of respectability.

So why had Samuel Beckett ever even considered joining such a group? Their aims had to be anathema to everything a Beckett would stand for. Unless, of course,

Samuel wasn't such a nice man. It hurt Sam to consider the possibility that his ancestor might have joined the Committee of Safety because he believed in its aims. How could any sensible man have joined such a bunch of thugs for any good purpose? Or was he simply judging Samuel by his own standards? While Sam didn't exactly believe that all moral values were relative, he did understand that it was wrong to judge the morals of one generation by the standards of another. For example, he knew that slavery was a vile practice and without question as degrading to the slave owner as to the slave. Yet many otherwise upright people in this day and age owned slaves—such as George Washington. He was thankful that his ancestor didn't own any. Many of the farmers in this period did.

All of this introspection was getting him precisely nowhere. There wasn't enough information yet to decide why Samuel had done anything—except, obviously, why he had married Hannah. He'd have had to be a complete fool not to marry such a prize. Sam couldn't help feeling anticipation as he returned to the farmhouse.

Lunch was bread and cheese, with corn cake afterward, washed down with what Hannah called "flip"—more of the thick cider, this time laced with a dollop of rum that gave it a pleasant kick. "To warm you on your way," she said with a laugh.

"I'm warm enough after a morning in the fields," Sam replied. "And the thought of coming home to you this evening."

That made Hannah smile even more. "Then perhaps you'll show your affection," she said lightly. "Our discussion of last night is not yet over, Samuel, so be warned. You know that I hate to take no for an answer."

"I had noticed," Sam agreed drily. He hoped he

could think of a better excuse to get out of his supposed marital duties—though a traitorous part of his mind wanted to batter his morals into senselessness. It was a disturbingly large portion of his mind.

"Well, at the very least, you'll have apple pie to come home to," Hannah promised him. "It's baking up now."

"I know," Sam said with a grin. "I've smelled nothing else since I came in the house. It's wonderful."

"Nothing else?" Hannah pouted. "I am deeply offended."

Sam pouted back at her. "Fishing for more compliments?" he mocked. "I thought you kept accusing me of flattery."

"But did I ever ask you to stop?" asked Hannah lightly. Then she kissed his nose. "But I know you love me, Samuel—even if you don't say it as often as I'd like. Now, you'd best be off with you, before I find you more chores."

Sam threw up his hands. "I'm going, I'm going. I hope I won't be too long, but I really can't be sure."

Hannah nodded, suddenly serious. "I wish you'd tell me what you're up to. Or, at the least, where you're going."

There could be little harm in that, surely. "I'll be in Oyster Bay. Isaiah Watts will be with me."

There was a flicker of interest at this news. "Isaiah is a good man, Samuel. But you know how easily led he is. He hasn't persuaded you to join him in another of his foolish schemes, has he?"

Now that sounded like a clue. Maybe that was precisely what had happened. If Isaiah had joined the Committee of Safety, perhaps Samuel had joined it to keep an eye on his weaker-willed friend. "I don't believe so,"

60

Sam answered. "Besides, you know how stubborn I can be. I promise I'll do nothing rash."

"And I'll hold you to your word." Hannah kissed his cheek again, sending a shiver of pleasure through Sam. "Take care for both of you."

"I will." Reluctantly, Sam dragged himself away from her. He smiled reassuringly at her, then hastily walked to the barn. He wished he had a cold shower handy, but he was way too far in the past for one of those. Why did Hannah have such an effect on him? He knew that his resolve was weakening with her every touch or kiss. He knew it would be wrong to do anything with her—but how much longer could he hold out against her? He turned his eyes to the skies. "If you want me to be good," he muttered, "you'd better make this a very short Leap."

Saddling Old Flighty took just a few minutes. Sam looked around for Al, hoping his adviser would arrive. There was no sign of him. "Must be having a long lunch hour," he muttered. "Well, I hope we can retrace our way, fella." He patted the horse gently, then led him outside. He saw Hannah in the doorway and waved to her. She waved back, lingering a moment before reentering the house. She was such a good woman, and a wonderful wife to Samuel. Sam couldn't believe that his ancestor could be unworthy of the love of such a good woman. Therefore, he had to have a very good reason for being part of this stupid Committee of Safety.

At least, Sam hoped he did.

He rode down the pathway to the main trail. It looked very different from the route he had taken the previous night. The trees were full, thick, and green, and the route was shaded from the burning sun. The horse ambled along at Sam's easy direction, heading toward where

Sam and Isaiah had parted company the previous night. Sam was fairly certain he could trace at least part of the route, but it would have been helpful to have Al with him to give directions.

What was keeping Al? He seemed to be having a lot of problems turning up on time for this Leap. And they were having more trouble with Samuel than they normally did with anyone in the Waiting Room. Perhaps it was simply due to Dr. Beeks's caution about contaminating the time stream. Or maybe there was something distracting Al. That happened from time to time, and it was generally to do with women. He'd looked startled when he'd first set eyes on Hannah, and then had gone into his usual lecher's overdrive. Maybe Tina was annoyed with Al, and he was suffering a lack of outlet for his sexual urges.

Sam couldn't help suspecting that Al was sneaking peeks at Hannah instead of doing his job. That thought brought a flash of jealousy with it. Damn it, if even he couldn't.... He refused to follow that thought any further. This was not the time to be thinking of pleasure, illicit or otherwise. He was here on a mission, not to have fun.

If only he knew what that mission was....

A short while later, Sam saw a rider ahead of him. It was the first person he'd seen since leaving home. This was obviously not a densely populated area. After a moment the figure waved, and Sam realized that it was Isaiah Watts, waiting for him. Sam gently urged Old Flighty to a little more speed, and drew abreast of his ancestor's friend.

"Are you that eager for this afternoon's activities?" Sam asked gently.

"Not at all," admitted Isaiah. "I've been wanting to

speak with you about it again, Samuel. That's why I'm here, instead of at my house.''

A good thing, too. Without help from Al, Sam would never have been able to find that farm. "Having second thoughts?'' guessed Sam.

Isaiah fell in beside him, and they rode on down the road together. "Many of them, Samuel,'' he confessed, his face downcast. "I'm sorry I dragged you into this Committee business in the first place, my friend.''

So that *had* been the reason Samuel had joined up! Sam felt a wave of relief in knowing that his ancestor hadn't joined from political convictions. "Didn't I say I'd keep an eye on you?'' Sam asked kindly. "You do tend to make decisions hastily, Isaiah.''

"Don't I know it,'' Isaiah agreed ruefully. "And Anne gave me a right time of it last night, I can tell you. She didn't speak to me for most of the night, and she blames me for dragging you into it, too.''

Marital strife on top of a guilty conscience.... No wonder Isaiah didn't appear too happy. Sam patted Isaiah's arm. "Look, what's done is done. Like I told you last night, I suspect that backing out now would bring the Committee down hard on you and your family. The best thing we can do is try to act as a moderating force today. I think that if he were unchecked, John Kirk would be a veritable devil.''

"Aye, Samuel, you're right there,'' Isaiah sighed. "But can just the two of us stand against him and George Townsend and the others?''

"I don't think that everyone on the Committee agrees with Kirk's extremist views,'' Sam pointed out. "With luck, some of them will back us—if we make a firm stand. Do you think you're up to it, Isaiah?''

"I'll try to be. I feel so foolish already. I have to make

63

up for what I've done. Not merely in joining these troublemakers, but for placing your life in peril."

Sam grinned. "I wasn't the one in trouble last night," he replied. "Kirk was the one who was eating dust."

"Aye," agreed Isaiah. "And he's not likely to let you forget that. He's going to want to pay you back for what you did to him. You'd best be watching your back today, Samuel. Or, better still, let me watch it for you. I owe you that, at least. If you think I'm up to the task, that is."

Sam patted Isaiah's arm. "There's no one else living I'd trust as much as you," he replied. "Except Hannah."

Isaiah smiled with pleasure. "Thank you, Samuel. I appreciate your trust. Mind you, I think Hannah would do a better job defending you than I would. A mother bear wouldn't get in her way if she was angry—not and live to talk about it."

Smiling, Sam nodded. "She's a good woman, Isaiah."

"The best," agreed Isaiah. "After my Anne, of course." Then he gestured. "You'd best stop thinking so fondly of your wife, Samuel—you almost missed the turnoff here."

Oops. "So I did." Sam hadn't almost missed it—he hadn't a clue as to where it was. Thankfully, Isaiah was here to correct him. "You're already watching out for me, you see."

They turned down the path to the house where the meeting had been held the previous evening. Sam had absolutely no idea where he was, and trusted to his companion to set him straight if he made any further mistakes. All Sam had to do was invent further excuses for his "forgetful" behavior.

As they approached the house where the meeting had taken place, Sam could see that they were among the last to arrive. There were already a dozen men at the small house. Horses were tethered to a rickety-looking fence. Sam and Isaiah tied their mounts' reins there and went to join the assembled men.

Sam recognized the faces from the previous evening. Kirk had a slightly mottled bruise on his right cheek, making him look even more unpleasant. Townsend had his dignified expression on, which didn't fool Sam for a second. The man's eyes were predatory. Morgan, Kirk's sidekick, scowled heavily at Sam.

Well, he hadn't expected a hearty greeting, so this wasn't a surprise. "Are we ready?" he asked Townsend quietly.

"Very nearly. Just two more latecomers, and then we'll be set." He looked around the assembled group. "Is everyone prepared?"

"Aye," Kirk growled. "And there'll be more than a few Tories who'll regret that this day ever dawned."

Sam regarded him with disgust. It sounded as if Kirk was ready to vent his spleen on any ready target. As Sam had feared, it was looking more and more likely that this would become a vigilante group.

CHAPTER

SEVEN

Townsend flicked a glance at Sam, then smiled genially. "John, John," he chided, gently. "I'm sure it won't come to any trouble. We'll simply . . . advise the men concerned, shan't we?"

Kirk's face lost none of its scowl, and he gave Sam a hard look. "If that's all it takes," he agreed. "But we know how to deal with traitors." There seemed to be a loaded message in this comment that Sam couldn't ignore.

Stepping forward, he asked mildly, "And how do you deal with fools? Be careful how you reply—your answer might demonstrate you to be one."

There was a general chuckle at this comment, and Kirk flushed. "Mind your tongue, Samuel Beckett," he advised. "You're too clever by half."

"Then that should make up for your lack, John," one of the other men called, causing more merriment. Kirk flushed again and turned away.

Sam was content. The mood of the group seemed to have swung to humor now, and that made the men less likely to do anything foolish. Also, since Kirk had lost out in the exchange, his opinion was less likely to carry weight. He turned back to Isaiah, giving his lanky friend a reassuring smile.

"Ah!" exclaimed Townsend, pointing. "Here come the last members of the Committee." Three riders were making their way down the road to join them. "To horse, my friends, and then off to Oyster Bay. We've a few Tories to educate before the sun sets today!"

Making sounds of approval, the men mounted up, then formed a loose group, Townsend at the head. One of the new arrivals fell in beside Sam and Isaiah. Sam remembered him from the previous evening as Joshua Cox, one of the more level-headed members of the group.

"How is the mood today?" he asked carefully, in a low voice clearly not meant to carry to Kirk.

Sam looked around and saw Kirk and his crony, Morgan, bringing up the rear of the straggling group. "For the most part, good," he replied. "But there's a dark cloud following us."

"Aye," said Cox, with a sigh, "I was afraid of that." He considered for a moment. "Samuel, I know we've not been the most sociable of friends until now, but I do feel that you're an honest and sober man. And I'll have you know that I respect your opinions."

Wondering what this was leading up to, Sam inclined his head slightly. "Thank you. I appreciate your faith in me."

Cox nodded slowly, obviously weighing his words. "Some of us feel," he said hesitantly, "that Kirk is a trifle . . . overenthusiastic with his views."

"A fanatic, you mean?" suggested Sam politely.

With a sigh, Cox nodded. "Aye, I suppose I do. We

don't feel that he's the best person to be leading this Committee.''

"But he isn't leading it,'' Sam pointed out. "Townsend is.''

"Theoretically, yes,'' agreed Cox. "But we don't feel that he'll do anything to oppose Kirk. He didn't stop the man from threatening you last night, did he?''

"Nor did anyone else.'' Sam gave the uncomfortable man a hard stare. "Only Isaiah spoke against him.''

Squirming, Cox said, "We *wanted* to. But we lack your courage, Samuel. That's why we want you to know that if you oppose Kirk again today, we'll be ready to back you up. We trust your judgment.''

Sam couldn't help wondering who this "we'' happened to be. He glanced at the other riders, but most were studiously avoiding looking in his direction. He sighed. "Look, Joshua, I appreciate your trust. But I think you're placing too much of it in me, instead of where it belongs.''

"You're a good man, Samuel . . . ,'' Cox began again, but Sam cut him short.

"Listen to me, Joshua. You can't go through your life looking to others to set the standards by which you'll live. No matter how good a man I am in your eyes, you can't live your life using mine as a model. You have to make your own decisions, and then have the courage to stand by them. That's what this war with England is *really* about—independence. We can't rely on the king and his officials to rule the Colonies in ways that are best for us. We have to take the power and the decisions—and the responsibilities—into our own hands. 'No taxation without representation,' remember? Well, that works well on a national level only if it works first on an individual level. We each have to listen to our own consciences, follow our own creeds, and have the courage to stand firm on our convictions. You can't look to me or anyone else for that, Joshua. If the fire and the strength don't come from within you, then they're not yours at all. Don't wait for me to set an example and follow; be prepared to set an example of your own.''

Cox looked appalled. ''But . . . I could be wrong!''

''That's one of the drawbacks to independence. We could any of us be wrong. But we could be right, too, and that's what counts. If you're wrong, you'll soon be set straight. You can count on that. When every man has the power to vote and the right to his say, then ideas and ideals can be exchanged. When any one of us gives up those rights—either to a king in some far off country or to one of our neighbors next to us—then we lose the very thing we're fighting this war over: our freedom.'' He reached out and clasped Cox's arm. ''Examine your conscience, Joshua,'' he urged. ''And then do what you know is right.'' He grinned. ''Even if it's not what I believe in. Stand up to me when I'm wrong, too.''

Cox was clearly troubled by Sam's advice. He nodded curtly, then spurred his horse forward to join other riders. What was he going to tell them? That he'd broached Beckett about being their leader, and been turned down? Or that they had to make their own stands?

''That was hard advice you offered him, Samuel,'' Isaiah commented.

''But heartfelt,'' Sam answered. ''And it goes for you, too, Isaiah. I can't be constantly offering other people my opinions on how to run their lives.''

Isaiah had the grace to blush. ''Aye, I figured that much out,'' he admitted. ''I'm not that dim-witted.'' He sighed. ''But this independence of ours is going to take some getting used to, isn't it? If we have to each of us

69

make decisions and then persuade our neighbors to support us. . . ." He shook his head. "It sounds like chaos in the making to me."

Smiling, Sam replied, "It's called democracy, Isaiah. It's on its way, and nothing can stop it. In a few short years, this country is going to have a government unique in world history, and each and every one of us is going to be a part of it. It will be the envy of the world—even if it isn't going to be the easiest thing in the world to control. And I'm sure that sometimes it'll look a lot more like chaos than a system of government. But it's a force that's unstoppable. Not the Tories, not the likes of Kirk, can prevent it from happening. This revolution under way today is one that will alter the shape of history—and we're all a small part of it."

Isaiah chuckled. "You make it sound so inspiring."

"Yeah," said a familiar voice off to Sam's left. "You should think about entering politics, maybe."

Sam glanced at the trees beside the road. Floating along, keeping perfect pace with the horses, was Al. He'd obviously had Ziggy lock his projection in on Sam. It was quite eerie watching Al float effortlessly through projecting branches of trees.

Once again he'd picked a terrible time for his entrance. Sam could hardly talk to him right now, with Isaiah and the others watching. They'd think he was crazy, or possessed.

"I try to tell it as I see it," Sam answered Isaiah. "I don't always know what's going on." He gave Al a pointed glare.

"Maybe not," Isaiah said. "But you always *appear* to know."

"Was that snipe at me?" asked Al with a scowl.

70

"'Cause if it was, let me tell you that the reason I'm late is that *you* screwed up."

"Appearances can be deceptive," Sam said, desperately trying to cover both conversations with a single reply.

"Then you put on a good show," laughed Isaiah. "Honestly, Samuel, there's no need to be so modest."

"That idea of yours with the dollar bill!" Al rolled his eyes. "Oy, what a mistake! I fought with Beeks about it, and she finally let me do it. Only because it was your idea. Boy, did it backfire. He got it into his head that it was some kind of British stunt. Bounty for anyone who delivered the head of Washington, that kind of thing. It was all too much for him. He thought the United States line was a sarcastic crack, and that the Washington, D.C., mentioned was some kind of a death warrant against good old Georgie boy. I tried explaining that it's gonna be the capital of the U.S., but by then he was already convinced that I was lying. Now Beeks says I can't talk to him again. We're gonna get zip from him unless we can figure out a better strategy."

"I'm not here to try and solve everyone's problems," Sam said, watching both Isaiah and Al. "People have to figure out their own solutions to things."

"You're a great help," Al grumbled. "Well, I'm outta here. I'd better go figure out solutions to problems you caused. I'll catch you around." He tapped the handlink, then exited through a door that matched his velocity before vanishing.

"I understand," Isaiah said. "And I promise to try my best."

"None of us can do more than that," Sam replied. He was almost relieved that Al had vanished. Sometimes it was too much of a strain trying to figure out ways not to look crazy when he was around. He just hoped that his friend would return at a better moment.

The rest of the journey was carried on mostly in silence. Sam wasn't the only one occupied by his thoughts. Isaiah was clearly trying to reach decisions, and Sam hoped that Cox and his friends were, too. He was all too afraid that Kirk and Townsend had long ago reached their own decisions. He was certain that whatever they had chosen would not be good.

And what was he to do? He was still no clearer on the reason why he was here. Ziggy believed it was to save either Samuel or Daniel—but was she correct? She was only working on probabilities, and even then only on avenues that had occurred to her as being important. He could be here for a very different reason, one that Ziggy had completely overlooked. It wouldn't be the first time that had happened.

Most of the path to Oyster Bay was fairly clear. It was barely more than tree-cleared dirt, compacted by horses and carts that had traveled before them. Signposts were infrequent and hardly helpful, since most didn't give distances. They passed a number of other travelers on the road, mostly farmers taking their produce to towns or returning with the goods they had obtained. Most of them ignored the riders completely. One or two smiled at them, and just as many scowled openly. All seemed suspicious of a band of a dozen able-bodied men riding together, and relieved when the riders passed them by without incident.

Oyster Bay, when they reached it, proved to be a smallish village by Sam's experience, but undoubtedly a fairly populous one for this day and age. They passed several farmsteads on the way to the town itself, all very similar to the Beckett farm. Once in Oyster Bay, it was quite clear where the town gained its name: the bay was visible from almost every point, and there were many vessels either at anchor or moving slowly on the still waters.

Ominously, one of them flew the Union Jack. Many flew no flags. Several had a roughed-out flag that reminded Sam that the familiar Stars and Stripes had not yet been designed.

"So," asked one of the riders, obviously in anticipation, "who's first on your list? I only pray that it's William Bradford! I'd like to show that traitor my fist—very close up." He laughed.

"Bradford's on our list," Townsend said smoothly. "But not for today. He doesn't live in Oyster Bay, so we can't get our hands around his scrawny neck this day. John has the list of who we'll deal with on this journey. Who's the first?"

"Vandergriff," Kirk growled. "And he's asked for it almost as much as Bradford."

"They don't much like this William Bradford," Sam muttered to Isaiah.

"Few patriots do," Isaiah answered. "He's been so loud-voiced in his praise of the British. There's no doubt that he's one of the worst traitors unhung. But you know that, Samuel, surely?"

"Just a joke," Sam replied, hoping that Isaiah would accept this weak explanation.

"This way," Townsend ordered, gesturing down a side street. The town consisted of no more than three or four streets. Most had moderate-sized houses or stores. Most of the latter seemed to be chandlers and were concentrated by the bay. Apart from the few streets, there were scattered houses that seemed to have accumulated about the main blocks without much planning. It was

73

toward one of these that Townsend led the Committee members.

It was a small, single-storied house that looked as though it had only two or three rooms. To one side of it was a forge, and the sound of hammering was audible from a distance. One man stood outside, holding the reins of a skittery horse. He glanced around as Townsend stopped and stared down at him. The man blinked nervously as he saw several grim faces and the dozen riders.

"Maybe I'd better come back later," he stammered.

"Maybe you'd best not be back at all," Kirk growled, "seeing as how Vandergriff is a Tory sympathizer. You wouldn't want to support a traitor, would you?"

"Uh, no, of course not," the man muttered. "Uh, I had no idea." He danced nervously from foot to foot.

"Well, now you do," Kirk snapped. "And what will you do about it?"

It didn't take the man more than a few seconds to make that decision. Gripping the reins tightly, he bolted down the street, casting an occasional wild-eyed look over his shoulder.

"Vandergriff!" Kirk yelled loudly over the sound of hammering. "Out with you!"

The noise ceased. A moment later, a tall, muscular man stepped out of the blacksmith's shed. He wore no shirt, but a leather apron tied about his waist extended to his neck. His sweaty body was encrusted with dirt. He scowled up at Kirk.

"What is it you want?" He had a pronounced Dutch accent. "I am quite busy right now."

"No, you're not," Kirk said softly. "Business is over for you. You're a damned Tory sympathizer, and we

74

don't want your sort around here. You're leaving town today.''

Vandergriff's face became redder. ''And who are you to give me such orders?'' he snarled.

''We are the Committee of Safety,'' Kirk replied. ''We are making this island safe for loyal Whigs. Now, either start moving, or we'll help you on your way.''

''This is my home,'' Vandergriff replied. ''It is my business, and I am staying. You have no right. . . .''

''No right?'' Kirk spat on the ground at the blacksmith's feet. ''You support the English, and you talk to me of *rights*?'' He pointed a shaking finger at Vandergriff. ''Either get out now, or we'll show you what rights we have! We are a jury of your peers, and you've been found guilty of treason. Now, move out, or we'll show you a taste of real justice.''

Vandergriff stood where he was, his fists clenching and unclenching, as he stared at the twelve riders. Kirk, Morgan, and Townsend were glaring back. Cox and Isaiah looked troubled, as did a couple of the other men. Most, like Sam, kept their faces impassive, waiting to see what would happen.

What happened was that the blacksmith crossed his arms and spat in the dust at Kirk's feet. ''You have no right,'' he repeated. ''I shall not leave.''

''You'll leave, all right,'' Kirk promised. ''Either on your feet or in a pine box.'' Reaching down to his saddle, he jerked free a length of rope. Sam gave a start as he realized that it was already knotted to form a hangman's noose. ''Decide now which it'll be.''

CHAPTER

EIGHT

Sam tensed, ready to move if the situation deteriorated. Once again, it looked like it was going to be up to him to be the conscience of the group.

Then Vandergriff simply collapsed inward. His eyes fixed on the noose, his muscles went limp. "All right," he said, slowly and clearly. "You win. I'll go." A brief fire returned to his eyes. "I'll get better customers in Connecticut, I'm certain."

Kirk sneered, obviously disappointed that this had been so simple. "Unless they run traitors out, too," he snapped.

Townsend reined up his horse. "We'll be back," he promised the blacksmith. "But you had better not be."

The Dutchman shook his head. "I won't share the same soil with men like you," he vowed, glaring at the group. "And I won't forget this."

Sam's conscience flinched, but there was nothing he could do. This clearance of Tory sympathizers was historical record. It was pointless to try and stop it, but at least he might be able to act as a brake on its worst excesses.

"Come on," Kirk said loudly. "There are nineteen more names on our list!" He wheeled his horse around, heading for the next victim. With a heavy heart, Sam followed.

The next three people proved just as simple to evict. One look at the dozen riders was enough for them. It was intimidation and witch-hunting at its worst, but it was effective. There was absolutely no evidence against any of the men on the list that Sam could see, but it made no difference to the members of the Committee. Each man was warned to leave, and leave fast, if he knew what was good for him. It was very short and simple, despite the hatred and fear burning in the eyes of their victims. Sam was sick at heart.

And it was obviously far too easy for Kirk's tastes. He was getting more and more tense with each "social call" they paid. Sam didn't have to be psychic to know that the bully was hoping someone would resist, presenting him with an excuse for violence.

That someone was the fifth man, Toby Morton. Morton, one of the small shopkeepers down by the dock, was a wiry, middle-aged man with a slight squint in his left eye. He looked as though he should have caved in and gone, but when Kirk presented him with the ultimatum, Morton simply stared back at him.

"This is my shop," he said mildly. "If you're not here to buy anything, then leave."

"Nobody will buy anything from you ever again," snarled Kirk, glaring at the few passers-by who hadn't fled. "Not if they know what's good for them."

"That's their decision to make," Morton replied. "Not yours to impose on them. I've been here for five years, and nobody tells me to leave. Nobody.''

"Maybe there's a problem with your hearing," Kirk suggested. "We just told you exactly that."

"Maybe there's a problem with yours," answered Morton. "Buy something, or go away." He turned his back on his tormenter, and made to reenter his store.

"By God!" swore Kirk, leaping down from his horse. "Nobody ignores me!" He cuffed Morton hard across the back of his neck, sending him to his knees in the dirt of the road. "Now, get moving!"

Morton shook his head to clear it, then looked up at Kirk. "One moment," he said, rising to his feet a little groggily. He leaned on one of the barrels beside his door. "That was not a fair blow."

"Any man who turns his back on his country and me doesn't deserve warning!" Kirk yelled.

"I'm no traitor," stated Morton. "I'm loyal to my king. It's the likes of you who are traitors. And when the Royalists beat your precious General Washington and restore order, then it's the likes of you who'll be in trouble, not me."

"From your own mouth," growled Kirk. "You deserve no mercy." He stepped forward, ready to beat the man again.

Before Sam could act, Morton came to his feet. He now held a marlinespike in his hand like a club. It obviously had been hidden behind the barrel in case of emergencies. "Then show me none," Morton suggested mockingly. "Try me now, if you dare."

With a roar of rage, Kirk leaped for the storekeeper. Morton was still groggy from the blow he'd suffered, and didn't move quite fast enough. Still, he managed to bring the club down on Kirk's left shoulder as the burlier man slammed into him. Kirk's rage was now mingled with pain.

Sam leaped down from his horse, worried that the situation was getting way out of hand. The two men were rolling in the filth, neither of them able to get a good blow in, but both trying hard. Seizing his moment, Sam dived in and grabbed Kirk's upraised hand before he could punch Morton in the face.

"Enough," Sam snapped. "Let him up."

Then the world went black for an instant. Pain exploded in the back of Sam's head, and the ground came up to smack him in the face. There was a weight on his back, obviously another man, and then it was gone. Groggily, Sam tried to focus on what was happening.

Morgan, Kirk's thug, had jumped him from behind. He'd obviously had orders to keep an eye on Sam in case of trouble. Sam staggered to his knees, and saw that Morgan was now standing by, his fists clenched. Beside him stood Isaiah, his face red with anger.

"Leave Samuel be," Isaiah snapped. "I'll not see you ambush him again."

"You little runt," growled Morgan. "I'll break every bone in your scrawny body for this!"

Then Townsend, still on his horse, pushed between the men. "I'll have no fighting amongst ourselves! We're here to evict and punish traitors, not to squabble between ourselves. Stop this immediately."

This exchange had given Sam time to clear his head, and then to get, wavering, to his feet. Ignoring Morgan, he turned back to the original brawl. Morton was down, blood streaming from his nose and mouth. Kirk stood over him, ready to kick him in the ribs. The marlinespike was several feet away, blood staining its end. Blood from a small cut trickled down Kirk's temple.

"That's enough," Sam said. "Kirk, there's no need for further violence."

Kirk whirled to face Sam. "Who are you to say what's needed?" he snarled. "Whose side are you on, anyway?"

"I'm on the side of sense and decency," Sam retorted. He was almost recovered now, and the world had stopped whirling. "You've beaten the man. There's no need to kill him." He shoved past Kirk and bent to examine Morton.

The storekeeper was battered, but there was obviously still some fight left in him. "Let me be," he said thickly, wiping at his mouth with his sleeve and leaving a red trail on his shirt.

"It's enough," Sam said gently. "You can't win this fight. See sense, and just leave town. It's the simplest solution. And the safest. If you provoke him further, he'll do you serious damage."

"That's easy for you to say. This isn't your store."

"And it won't be yours much longer," Sam informed him. "This is a fight you can't win. The best thing you can do for your own safety and that of your family is to give in quietly."

Kirk had listened enough. "You've got two hours," he told Morton. "If you're not under way by then, we'll be back. And when we are, we'll burn down the whole damned store—and you with it if you're still here." He glared down at Sam. "And you with him, if you get in my way again."

Straightening up, Sam stared Kirk in the eye. "I'm simply trying to prevent needless violence," he replied. "I'm sure that Morton will see sense and move out. There's no need to hurt him further."

"Is that the *real* reason for what you say?" asked

Kirk. "Or do you speak like that because you're secretly on his side?"

Sam scowled. "Are you just opening your mouth to see what falls out of it? Or are you accusing me of being a Tory, too?"

There was even more tension in the air now. Kirk glowered at Sam. "I think you're just as much a traitor as he is," he replied, spitting on the ground by Sam's feet. "I heard what you told your wife last night. You said that you hoped the British would win the upcoming battle."

"That's a lie," Sam said coldly. "If you really were listening to me last night, then you know it's a lie. And if you *were* listening to my private conversations, let me warn you that if I ever catch you at it, you'll be worse off than Morton there. *Never* do that again."

"You're a damned traitor and a scoundrel, that's what I say!" cried Kirk. "I know what I heard!"

Sam clenched his fists, ready for whatever might develop. "And you're a liar and a coward," he replied evenly. "Skulking in the darkness, spying on me, and then lying about what you heard."

One of the Committee members called, "You deny what John says, then? This is a serious matter, Samuel Beckett!"

"This is hearsay," Sam answered, not taking his eyes off Kirk. "And he's lying. You all know that he has been trying to pick a fight with me for a long time."

"That's true enough," agreed Cox hastily. "Then what *did* you say that he overheard?"

Sam shook his head. "What I say to my wife is nobody else's business," he answered. "I don't owe you a reply." There was a mutter of discontent. "But," Sam added, "because I'm no traitor and because we're in this

81

together, I'll tell you what I said that Kirk is misrepresenting. I said that I thought that the British were likely to win the upcoming battle.''

''What?'' Townsend glared down at him from his horse. ''Are you on their side?''

''No,'' Sam replied coldly. ''They are better armed and are well led. We are not so well off. But I am ready to do my duty. Ask Colonel Smith—I've joined his militia, and stand ready to fight for our freedom. Whatever way the battle goes, I'll be there, fighting for the freedom of our country.'' He nodded his head toward Kirk. ''That's what he heard last night. And I'll wager that *he* hasn't agreed to join the militia. He prefers to do his fighting with simple shopkeepers, not Redcoats who can fight back.''

Townsend considered for a moment. ''If what you say is true,'' he decided, ''then you can hardly be called a traitor, Samuel. Any man who takes up arms to fight for freedom is no enemy of mine. Or of yours, John,'' he added pointedly to Kirk. ''Stand down.''

''We only have his word for it,'' Kirk objected.

''And only yours against him,'' Cox broke in. ''And it is not sufficient for me.''

''Nor me,'' agreed Isaiah. ''Your grudge against him is well known.'' There was a mild chorus of agreement at this remark.

''I'll not have bickering and fighting amongst ourselves,'' Townsend repeated. ''Stand down, John. Now!''

Glaring at Sam and then at the rest of the Committee, Kirk whirled about and returned to his horse. ''This isn't over,'' he promised. ''I shall get proof that Beckett is a traitor.''

''And if you do so,'' Townsend promised, ''we shall

heed it. But until you have proof, this matter is over. Is that understood?''

''Aye,'' Kirk agreed reluctantly.

''Samuel?''

''I'm willing to forget it,'' Sam said, relieved. He knew that he could take Kirk in a fair fight. But he doubted that a fair fight was what Kirk had in mind, especially since there was Morgan to back him up. Sam bent over Morton again. ''Be smart,'' he said gently. ''Get out of town while you can.''

''You're all scum,'' Morton moaned. ''But you're right. I can't fight you all. I'll go. And I'll pray that you all burn in Hell for what you're doing.'' He staggered to his feet, shaking off Sam's hand to help. ''I'll take nothing from any of you. Certainly not a hand.'' He stumbled into his shop.

''He's going,'' Sam said, returning to his horse, ashamed of what they were doing.

''Then so should we,'' Townsend decided. ''The afternoon is waning, and there are more traitors to move on.''

Sick at heart, Sam mounted and followed the Committee as they headed for their next victim. Isaiah moved beside him again.

''I'm sorry I wasn't more help,'' he apologized.

''You did your best. And next time, you'll discover that it's easier to do the right thing. Acting bravely is a habit; once you get used to it, you'll discover that you can't stop.''

''I hope so.'' Isaiah grinned. ''It would be the first good habit I've ever acquired.''

The rest of the afternoon was a sick blur to Sam. After Morton's resistance, most of the others complied pretty meekly with the Committee's instructions to get out of town. Word undoubtedly had spread of their activity—and the likely consequences of trying to stand up to them. There was no such thing as a police force, and nobody was likely to try and stop the Committee in its work. In fact, Sam suspected, most of the locals probably supported the group's work—or, at the very least, had no strong opinions either way. And the Tory sympathizers who weren't selected this time around were probably staying low, hoping they would be overlooked. It was the way of intimidation in every day and age, and it was no less nauseating because it was being done in the name of freedom from tyranny.

"It leaves a foul taste in the mouth," Isaiah observed at one point, as they watched another terrorized man agree to leave his home and neighbors.

"It should do," Sam replied. "The only crime these people have committed is to back the wrong side in a war. They're no danger to anyone at all. When we win, they'll gladly convert to our cause. All this is doing is creating a vast amount of ill will. It's going to have serious effects soon enough."

"How can you be so sure?"

Sam considered for a moment. He could hardly tell his friend the truth—that he was from the future, and knew everything that would happen. Isaiah wouldn't believe him. "It's the obvious course of events," Sam said sadly. "Violence and oppression beget violence and oppression. Right now, the Whigs are in control, but wh—*if* that changes, then the Tories will be the persecutors, and we will be the victims. And in the fortunes of war, that could happen at any time. We should be trying to win these people to our cause, not attacking them and expelling them from their homes."

"It's too late for that," observed Isaiah.

"Yes," agreed Sam with a sigh. "It's far too late for that."

There was only one other man who stood up to the Committee, a merchant named Gentry. He was a thick-set man, running to fat, with a balding, Ben Franklin style haircut and a harried expression. When he was told to pack up and leave, he pulled off his tricornered hat and threw it to the ground.

"By Heaven, the only way I'll leave my home is to the grave," he swore. "I've heard what the lot of you are up to, and I'm not going to go along with you like the rest of the sheep you've picked for fleecing." He glared at Kirk and Townsend. "You're hiding your personal grudges under the guise of patriotism, but I know better. I'm not budging from my home, and I defy you to do your worst."

"Now that sounds like a fair invitation to me," Kirk growled happily, and started to dismount from his steed. "I'll be more than happy to show you the errors of your ways."

"Will you indeed?" asked Gentry. Until now, his right hand had been hidden behind his back. He swung it around, and there was a musket in it. "And, pray tell, what error have I committed?"

Kirk halted in midswing and stared down the barrel of the musket. It couldn't be a very accurate weapon, but it was leveled at him at almost point-blank range. There was no way Gentry could miss him if he pulled the trigger. Sweat broke out on Kirk's forehead, and he licked his lips.

"What?" asked Gentry mildly. "Cat got your tongue, John Kirk? Well, that's not something men witness every day. You normally prattle on at great volume."

A flicker of movement caught Sam's eye. It came

from Morgan's direction. As he glanced that way, Sam saw something flick through the air in Gentry's direction.

It was the tip of a whip, weighted with a small piece of lead. Morgan had cracked the whip, and the sound startled Gentry as the lash hacked across his arm. Even his coat couldn't protect him from the sting of the metal-tipped whip. The lead weight sliced through the layers of clothing and flesh in a spray of blood. With a scream, Gentry let his arm fall. The musket discharged into the ground, sending up a cloud of dust and soil.

Then Kirk was on him, leaping from his stirrups and bearing his opponent to the ground. He punched hard, then threw the empty musket aside.

Sam leaped from his saddle, but he was slower than Isaiah, who streaked across the intervening space and grabbed Kirk firmly by the shoulders, putting all his weight into throwing him aside.

Changing his own direction of movement, Sam whirled to face Morgan. As he suspected, the man had reeled in his whip and was preparing another crack. The target for this blow was obviously going to be Isaiah.

Sam yelled ''Hai!'' and threw his hands up in front of Morgan's steed. Startled, the animal reared. Dodging aside, Sam dived past the animal's flailing forelegs and gave the yelping rider a boost with his fist. Morgan, howling, toppled backward from his saddle, his whip flying aside.

Looking round, Sam saw that Isaiah and Kirk were facing off against one another. Kirk's face was filled with fury, Isaiah's with grim determination. Sam hesitated, reluctant to interfere while Isaiah was finally making a stand of his own. On the other hand, he doubted that the wiry farmer could stand up to Kirk. While he hesitated, Townsend moved.

Using his horse again, he pushed between Kirk and Isaiah. "Enough!" he roared. "Haven't I just finished telling you that we must present a unified front against our foes? I will not countenance another public brawl. Cease, this instant."

"I will," Isaiah agreed doggedly, "as long as Kirk and Morgan let this man alone. He's injured already, and that is not what I joined this Committee to do."

"I'll not let up on him until he leaves the area," Kirk growled. "I'll suffer no damned traitors in my town."

"It's not *your* town," Sam broke in, brushing past Kirk to head for where Gentry lay in the dust. "It's *our* town, and we want no unnecessary violence." He bent over Gentry. "Easy," he said. "I'm. . . ." Then he recalled that he was supposed to be a farmer, not a doctor. "Let me have a look at that."

Gentry started to protest, but his heart wasn't in it. He was pale, his features pinched by pain. Sam eased open the torn and bloody shirt, and winced when he saw the cut that the lash had left. It was deep, and bleeding badly.

"He needs medical attention," Sam said firmly. "Otherwise he's in danger of bleeding to death. Stop your bickering, and someone fetch a doctor."

Cox shook his head. "There isn't one, Samuel," he replied. "Doctor Grace is out of town today, seeing to a difficult birth."

"Besides," grumbled Kirk, "what difference will it make if one Tory dies now, rather than later?"

Furious, Sam rounded on the man. "If he dies," Sam promised, "then I'll make certain that you and that lap-

87

dog idiot of yours are punished for it. There is no need for this kind of violence.''

''As I suspected,'' Kirk snapped, ''you're a Tory sympathizer after all. We don't need the likes of you on the Committee.''

''And you won't have the likes of me, either,'' Isaiah interrupted. ''I'm ashamed to be seen in the company of vermin like you. I'll not be a part of this anymore.''

''Nor I,'' agreed Cox firmly. ''There's no call for this.''

''So,'' Townsend said slowly, scanning the assembled men. ''Are there more of you who feel this way?'' Two more of the riders reluctantly nodded. ''Well, then, we'll not keep you with us if that's how you feel. But we will all remember this day, and the way that you men voted. You'd best keep one eye looking over your shoulders. One of these days, you may be the ones we roust from our company.'' Wheeling his horse, he cried, ''All those loyal Whigs—after me!'' He started off down the street.

Most of the Committee followed him, including Kirk and Morgan, who both spat as they passed Sam and the fallen Gentry. A moment later, only Isaiah, Cox, and the other two men were left with Sam.

Grimly, Sam looked at them. ''If there's no doctor,'' he said, his voice tight and angry, ''then it's up to us to help him.''

''Dammit, Samuel,'' growled Cox, ''I'm a merchant, not a doctor. What can I do?''

''Go into his house,'' Sam ordered. ''I'll need needle and thread. And hot water, bandages. You two, go with Cox and help him. Isaiah, give me a hand with Gentry.'' Sam had torn the man's sleeve to create a tourniquet and stop the bleeding. Gentry was ashen now, breathing in short, gasping bursts. ''We have to get him inside. Then

88

I'll need light to work with." Together, they carried Gentry inside.

A scared-looking young girl hovered there, staring in horror at the merchant, and then at the strangers in her house.

"Are you his daughter?" asked Sam gently. The terrified girl nodded. "Then you'd better tell your mother that your father's been injured."

"She . . . she's dead," the girl replied, squeakily. "Two years ago, in childbirth."

"I'm sorry." Sam gestured with his head for Isaiah to help him take Gentry into the kitchen. The large windows there made it the brightest room in the house. "Then you'll have to help me with your father. What's your name?"

"Betsey, sir."

"Okay, Betsey," Sam said, as he and Isaiah laid Gentry on the large kitchen table. "Are there any other children?" She shook her head. "Fine. Now, the other men are looking for needles and thread. Can you help them?" She shot out of the room without replying. "I'll take that as a yes," Sam muttered. He looked again at Gentry's wound. At least it seemed clean. "This is going to take a while," he told Isaiah. He winced as he realized how primitive the equipment would be. Still, he had to do everything he could to save Gentry's life. "Well, here goes. . . ."

CHAPTER NINE

"Good night, Samuel."

"Night, Isaiah. I was very proud of you today. It took a lot of courage to stand up to Kirk that way."

"I was inspired by your example," Isaiah answered simply.

"Take Townsend's warning seriously," Sam urged him. "Watch your back. I wouldn't trust Kirk not to pay you back when he thinks you're not looking."

"I'll be careful, Samuel. Thank you again. I'm still astonished at your skills. Is nothing too difficult for you?"

Sam snorted. He'd managed to save Gentry's life and to stitch up his wound, even though the man had lost a lot of blood. Doctor Grace, who had returned late in the afternoon had complimented Sam on his work, promising to take over the man's care. Nevertheless, Sam still felt guilty about his part in the day's work. "Going home would seem to be," he replied. "Take care." Waving to Isaiah, he set off down the road toward the farm.

Al popped into existence a moment later, wavering his cigar theatrically. "I thought he'd never go. We have to talk."

"It's about time, Al," Sam said. "What *have* you learned?" Anything at all of use?"

"Maybe. I did some background checking on all the names and places you've been involved with since you got here. The main thing that's come up is that Isaiah Watts seems to die pretty soon."

"What?"

"Well, records for this time are pretty hazy. Especially since there's a war going on. But Ziggy can't find any records for an Isaiah Watts after the middle of September. She's run her calculations, and now thinks there's a forty percent chance that you're here to save his life."

That made sense. "Isaiah does seem to have a habit of getting himself into sticky situations," Sam said slowly. "Any idea how he's likely to die?"

"Nope," Al replied. "Like I said, he just vanishes from the records. I've had Ziggy try and trace his living ancestors, but there's an awful lot of Wattses. We're hoping that one or more of them might be into genealogy, and able to tell us what happened to him, but it's slow going. It's a bit of a crapshoot, Sam."

"Great." Sam considered the problem. Isaiah had just made a definite enemy out of John Kirk. "Maybe Kirk's involved."

"Possible," agreed Al, shrugging. "As far as the records go, there's no indication that he ever killed anyone. He was more of a bully and an opportunist than a murderer. On the other hand, there's no indication that he didn't. And we can't find this clod Morgan anywhere

91

in existing records. Like I said, this isn't the best-documented era. And Ziggy can't dig up what no longer exists. And Samuel is being less than no help at all. Verbeena's been trying to get him to trust her again, but it's slow going."

"You're not making this Leap any easier, Al," Sam said with a sigh. "Still, it looks like I've got one less problem to deal with. Isaiah, Cox, and Samuel were just booted off the Committee."

"What?" Al winced. "Sam, why don't you tell me things like that? It could change everything. Ziggy's gonna have to do a lot of rethinking now. That could affect all kinds of probabilities. Okay, I'll leave you to it now, and try and run some of this stuff past Ziggy and see what she says." He yawned. "Besides, I'm beat. I really got to get some rest." He grinned. "You planning on sleep or a little horizontal action first?"

"Get!" snapped Sam.

"Sayonara," Al answered, grinning wickedly as he vanished.

Sam sighed. Al had just reminded him of his other major problem—Hannah. Trying to make some sense out of everything, Sam allowed the horse its head and plodded on home.

It was getting dark when he arrived and stabled Old Flighty. As he was feeding the horse, Hannah rushed over to him. She kissed his cheek and smiled. "I've missed you so much, Samuel. Come along, dinner's ready and waiting for you. You can tell me what you've been up to then."

Almost overwhelmed by his greeting, Sam allowed himself to be dragged into the house. Once inside, Hannah started to get dinner ready for him, then gasped.

"Samuel! What have you done to yourself? Are you hurt?"

Sam frowned, then looked down. There were patches of blood on his shirt. "It's not my blood," he told her gently. "I had to help an injured man today. I didn't notice the stains. I'm sorry."

"Oh, I'm only glad it wasn't your blood!" She laughed in relief. "That's so like you, Samuel, always helping others. But you'd better have that shirt off you. It'll take some soaking to get that right—if I ever can. I'll fetch you a clean one."

"It's all right," he told her. "I can do it. You were fixing dinner, remember?" He stood up and headed for the bedroom. "I'll just be a minute." Inside, he pulled a fresh shirt from the chest of "his" clothing, and removed the bloodied one. Then he was aware he was not alone.

He glanced around to see Hannah watching him. "Didn't believe me?" he chided her, turning around. "See—no wounds."

"I see." She crossed to him, running her hand over his chest. It was a shock and a thrill to feel her touch on his naked skin. "And I like what I see." She moved to kiss him again.

Sam sidestepped quickly, trying to recover his poise. "Ah . . . we were talking about dinner," he said gently.

"Dinner could wait, Samuel. It's waited for you an hour or more already. Another wait won't ruin it." She pulled him to her, fiercely. "I'm not sure I can wait."

Terrific! Sam struggled with his conscience. He couldn't do what she wanted him to . . . and what *he* wanted him to. It wouldn't be right. She was a married woman, and his ancestor. It was wrong of him even to find her this damnably attractive. He couldn't deny that

93

he did, especially when he felt the softness of her hand. He quickly pulled free, his resolve shaking badly.

"What is it, Samuel?" she asked, concerned. "Don't tell me you aren't in the mood." She grinned. "I know better."

"Uh . . . ," Sam muttered, flustered. "It's just that I'm really hungry," he said lamely.

"Then we'll have to be quick," Hannah answered, eyeing him again. "We can take our time later."

"*Really* hungry," he said quickly, afraid she'd attack him again.

Hannah stared at him, puzzled and hurt. "What is wrong with you, Samuel? You've never behaved like this before. And I've certainly never had to invite you so often in the past."

"I have a lot on my mind," Sam said, struggling into his fresh shirt while he still could. "I'm sorry, Hannah."

"So am I," she replied, more than a little peeved. "Well, if you're so hungry, we'd better eat, hadn't we?" Whirling on her heel, she stormed back into the main room. Sam heard her clattering the dishes.

"Why me?" Sam muttered, raising his eyes to the ceiling. "Why couldn't you have made her seven feet tall and bald and made this easy on me?" There was, of course, no answer.

Dinner was very silent. Hannah was clearly confused and hurt. Sam couldn't blame her, and he couldn't think of anything to say that might ease the tension. She was feeling very affectionate and wanted to make love to her husband. There was no way she could know—and no way Sam could tell her—that the man she thought was her husband was actually another person in his guise. And the fact that Sam was so attracted to her and turned on by her didn't help in the slightest. It was hell on both

94

of them, but doing what came naturally would be a dreadful mistake.

Sam was sure of that. But he was getting less sure by the minute. His moral certainty was being eroded slowly but certainly by his desires. Why had he been placed in this terrible dilemma? It simply wasn't fair.

Hannah's bad temper lasted through their dinner of chicken and corn, but didn't make it through dessert. She'd made a fresh apple pie that smelled heavenly, and as she saw Sam's obvious appreciation, she managed to crack a smile.

"If all you want me for is my cooking," she grumbled good-naturedly, "at least you know how to appreciate it."

"You're the best cook in the world," he assured her, around a forkful of pie. "I don't know how long it's been since I tasted anything this good."

"Since my last pie a week ago."

"That long? It seems much, much longer."

Hannah shook her head. "Samuel Beckett, I don't know what I'm ever going to do with you. You really do have a glib tongue."

"And it's one that appreciates your culinary efforts," he assured her. He rose to help her clear the table. "You're a marvel, Hannah Beckett. I don't know what I'd do without you."

"I know what you won't do with me," Hannah replied, a flash of fire in her voice. "And I don't think your reasons are adequate."

Ouch. "The man I helped today," Sam said slowly, "his wife died a couple of years ago in childbirth."

"Oh. Is *that* it, now?" Hannah glared at him. "You're trying to tell me that you're afraid I'll do the same?" Her eyes narrowed. "I don't believe you, Samuel. I'm sorry to say that, but I don't. There's some other reason behind your odd behavior that you refuse to tell me. All these excuses are just words.''

''It's. . . .'' Sam struggled to find something to reassure her, but he couldn't.

''You'd better finish your chores,'' Hannah said mildly, apparently dropping the subject when she realized she was getting nowhere. ''I'll do the washing up.''

Seizing his chance to escape, Sam bolted. Darkness was descending, but there was enough light for him to finish the few remaining tasks about the farm and to plan the morning's work.

Anything to keep his mind off Hannah.

He had to find the time to go to Havens Inn, as he'd promised. Still, the messenger had implied there wasn't a great rush. The most urgent task that Sam could see was getting some of the surplus corn into town for sale and trade before it spoiled. He'd gathered several barrels, which should be plenty for the moment. He knew that there had to be quite a lot that Hannah would need in town. Perhaps a trip into Smithtown the following day would do them both good. And it might distract Hannah a little. It couldn't be much fun for her, stuck here on the farm all day, alone with the baby. No wonder her thoughts kept turning to. . . .

Forget that! Sam was struggling with his own thoughts on the matter. If only she wasn't so damnably attractive! And such a lovely person, too. She was sweet-tempered, bright, and very loving. The perfect woman—if she wasn't married to another man, and Sam's ancestor at that. Some Leaps just didn't play fair!

Finally, realizing that he was simply idling in the gathering gloom to avoid Hannah, Sam returned to the house. At least bedtime was early in this era, to save on

96

precious candles and oil. On the other hand, spending another night celibate beside Hannah was definitely going to strain his self-control.

He had no idea just how much until he closed the door behind him and turned around.

Hannah was seated in a large tin tub in the center of the kitchen, sponging her arms and staring at him innocently. She smiled when she saw his expression. "Surely you haven't forgotten that it's bath night, have you, Samuel?" she asked coyly. "It's been a week, you know."

Trying hard not to stare at her, Sam shook his head vigorously. "Um . . . it slipped my mind."

"Well, now I've reminded you," Hannah said. She held out the sponge. "Come and wash my back for me, will you?"

Sam had no idea what to do. He was almost drowning. Maybe this was the Becketts' weekly bath night, but he suspected that Hannah was definitely using that fact to her own advantage. She clearly had not given up her attempts to make love to her husband.

If only it was her husband who was here!

What should he do? If he refused her, she'd get suspicious and angry. But if he accepted. . . . How could he avoid being more and more aroused by touching her? He hesitated for a moment, then moved forward to take the sponge. He tried to avoid staring at her breasts as he moved behind her.

The soap was hard and dirty brownish-white, but lathered up. He sponged Hannah's back, carefully staying above the water. Touching her like this was another refinement in the hell Sam was going through, and he had no idea how long he could keep this up without succumbing to the temptation that was raging throughout his body.

"That feels so nice, Samuel," Hannah murmured happily. "Your touch is always so gentle."

Oh, great. It sounded like she was getting aroused. That was all Sam needed. *Help!* he muttered to himself and anyone who might be listening.

For once, with almost perfect timing, Al walked through the wall. His eyes bugged at what he saw, and his cigar flopped from his mouth, vanishing as it left the imaging area. "Jeez," Al muttered, his eyes firmly fixed on Hannah. "Maybe I should come back later."

Not daring to say a word, Sam shook his head swiftly. Why had Al showed up now? And was he here to help or to complicate matters?

"Why don't you wash my front now?" Hannah suggested.

Al almost had a heart attack. "Boy, some guys get all the luck," he grumbled. Then he caught Sam's agonized glare. "Oh, yeah." He tapped the handlink. "Ziggy says there's somebody lurking in the bushes outside. Ten'll get you a hundred it's that creep, Kirk."

Sam felt tremendous relief as well as anger. So Kirk was back spying again? He handed the sponge back to Hannah. "There's someone outside," he said softly. "Stay low, and stay quiet."

She stared at him in astonishment. "Are you certain?" she asked quietly. "Or is this another in your series of strange behaviors?"

"I heard a sound," Sam told her, not strictly lying. "And there was someone here the other night, spying on us." He gave her a reassuring smile. "I don't want him to see my wife like this."

"No do I," Hannah said, shocked. "Pass me a cloth, Samuel."

Sam moved to the cupboard and got her a rough sheet. As he did so, he spotted something that could be very handy—a slingshot. With a grin, he tossed the sheet to Hannah. "I'll be quick," he promised. Then he slipped out the door.

It took Al a moment to slide through the wall after him. His eyes were still wide, but he'd recovered his cigar. "Jeez, what a sight," he said admiringly.

"The intruder," hissed Sam, staring around in the darkness. "Where is he?"

"Oh, yeah." Al swallowed, and slapped the handlink. "Okay, he's in the bushes over there. Hang on." He tapped in a code, vanished then reappeared a second later in the middle of one of the small bushes. "I'm standing right behind him," he called. "It *is* that creep Kirk. Aim for me, and you'll hit him."

It would have been difficult to miss Al. He was almost glowing in the night. Sam scooped up a fist-sized stone and slipped it into the slingshot. Then he whipped it back, and let fly.

There was a howl of agony from the bush, and a clattering of disturbed branches.

"Next time, it'll be buckshot!" Sam yelled. "Stay away from me and mine, John Kirk! Do you hear me?"

There was no reply, but the sound of the man retreating in a haste was unmistakable. Al popped back beside Sam.

"Nice shot," he said, grinning. "Dead on his right shoulder. He'll have a bruise there for a week."

"And he won't dare come back," Sam said with satisfaction. "Thanks for the warning, Al." He turned back to the house. "Goodnight, Al."

"What? That's all the thanks I get?" The hologram shrugged his shoulders. "Just one more. . . ."

"No," Sam said firmly. "You've seen more than enough."

"There's no such animal as more than enough," Al grumbled. But he triggered the doorway anyhow. "Spoilsport!"

"Go back to Tina," Sam advised. He reentered the house, half dreading what he might see.

Thankfully, Hannah had the sheet wrapped about herself. It wasn't much covering, but it was enough not to distract Sam too much. "Are you all right, Samuel?" she asked. "I heard the noise."

"I'm fine," he said, laying the slingshot on the table. "And I'm sure he won't be back."

"I heard you address him," Hannah said. "It was John Kirk." Her eyes narrowed. "Why would he be here, spying on you?"

Sam weighed his options, and decided that at least some of the truth was best right now. "Because he thinks I'm a British sympathizer. He's attempting to denounce me as a Tory."

"What?" Hannah was half angry, half shocked. "How could *anyone* think that of you? That Kirk has always been nasty and suspicious. I've half a mind to take a paddle to the man!"

"Not dressed like that, you won't," Sam answered. "You'd catch your death of cold."

Hannah giggled slightly. "Aye, that I would." Her eyes sparkled. "Is he gone for now, though?"

"Gone for good, I hope. I hit him hard in the shoulder. He won't want to be back for more of that."

"Wonderful." Hannah moved closer to him. "Now, I do believe it's your turn for a bath, Samuel. And I'll brook no arguing from you. You're starting to get more than a little ripe, my dear.''

Oh, wonderful! She still had only one thing on her mind. On the other hand, she was partially right. Sam wasn't used to skipping his morning shower, and he really could do with a bath.

And he could really do without her help, because he could see how *that* would work out. . . .

For the second time that evening, Sam was saved at the last second. Just as she was about to help him off with his shirt, Daniel started to cry.

Hannah frowned, staring over her shoulder in irritation. ''Why is everyone in this house hungry at the most inappropriate times?'' she complained.

''He must take after me,'' Sam guessed, relieved.

''In some ways at least,'' Hannah agreed. ''Then I suppose I'd better feed him.'' She could hardly miss the look of relief on Sam's face. Instead of being angry, she managed one last shot before she left for the bedroom. ''You'll be needing this.'' And she dropped the sheet.

Sam tried to avoid staring as she walked across to the bedroom, then turned in the doorway. ''I won't be long,'' she promised.

''Nor will I,'' Sam muttered. He stripped and plunged into the tub quickly. The water was getting a little chilly, and that helped him speed through his bath almost as fast as the fear of Hannah returning. By the time she did so, he was dry and dressed again.

Hannah was in her nightshirt now and carrying the baby, bouncing him slightly and crooning to him. She glanced up and sighed. ''Finished already?''

Sam nodded. ''How's Daniel?'' He stared down at the burbling infant, who held tightly to one of Hannah's fingers with a tiny hand. ''He's a handsome boy.''

"He takes after his father there, too," Hannah replied with a smile.

"And he's very gentle and bright," Sam added. "That's what he gets from you." He gently eased the baby from her grip. "Let me have some fun," he said. He wanted to check the boy out, mindful of Al's warning that there was still a good chance he was here to stop Daniel from dying prematurely.

"Fun?" Hannah asked as she relinquished her grip. "I've been offering you that for days, Samuel, and you keep declining." She watched him carefully as he held the baby. "But you do seem to enjoy your son."

"He's a wonderful child," Sam answered. He carefully checked the boy out as well as he could without instruments. "And he certainly seems healthy and contented," he added thankfully.

"After all the milk he's taken, he should be," Hannah replied. "It's left me more than a little sore, Samuel, so you needn't worry about having to avoid me for the rest of the night."

Sam wished he could deny the accusation, but he knew she would never believe such a denial. Instead, he crooned gently at the baby, who slid into sleep again. "I'll return him to his bed," Sam offered. "He should be fine for a while."

"It's about time for us to follow him," Hannah said. "Unless you've anything else to do first."

"No, the chores are finished. I did think we might go into town tomorrow, though. There's plenty of corn to trade."

That made her smile. "And plenty of things to get. I'd like that, Samuel. I've been here alone long enough. Daniel should be sturdy enough for the trip now. It'll do us all good."

Well, at least he'd managed one thing to please her, Sam reflected. And Daniel's appetite had rescued him from another dilemma. But how much longer could he keep this up? And how much longer would this Leap last?

CHAPTER
TEN

As soon as the chores were over the following morning, Sam hitched Old Flighty to the cart. It was barely large enough for two people on the high seat, but there was room in the rear for all the barrels of corn Sam had prepared, plus other vegetables that Hannah decided they could spare. When he was ready, Hannah emerged from the house with Daniel wrapped carefully in several layers of clothes.

"I hope he's not going to be too warm," Sam remarked.

"I don't want him catching anything," Hannah replied tartly. "He's only six months old, Samuel, and very vulnerable."

"I know," Sam agreed gently. "You're being very careful."

That mollified her, and she allowed him to help her to the seat. Then he clambered onto the other side of the cart, caught up the reins, and urged the horse into unwilling motion. It felt odd not locking the door to the house, but it was not customary for farms to have doors that locked in this period.

The ride into town was fairly straightforward, and Sam didn't even need directions from Al. He discovered that Smithtown was about the size of Oyster Bay, with just a few main streets and then the outlying houses and farms. There was another harbor off to the north of the main settlement, which they didn't need to visit. Sam reined the horse in front of the general store. It was a guess on his part, but a pretty safe one, since there were only two such stores, and the other was farther into town.

The owner—Jacob Bramley, according to the sign over the door—emerged from the store and smiled. "Good to see you again, Samuel," he said. "And I can certainly use your produce. I'll give you a hand in with it while Mrs. Beckett does her shopping."

"Thanks, Jacob, I appreciate that." Sam helped Hannah down from the wagon.

Bramley peered at the baby. "So that's the next generation, eh? A handsome child."

"Takes after his father," said Hannah.

"And he's good-tempered and lovable," Sam added. "He got those qualities from his mother."

"Flatterer," said Hannah with a smile. She entered the store.

Sam and Jacob spent the next fifteen minutes unloading the supplies and moving them into the store. When that was done, Jacob wiped his brow. "Time for lemonade," he decided. "Then we'll reckon up the tally, and see how much of your hard-earned sweat your wife has already spent, eh?"

"Sounds great," Sam admitted. He was feeling more than slightly thirsty, and accepted the mug of cold drink with appreciation. The tallying of accounts didn't take long, and Sam was relieved to see that he'd managed to end up with a slight balance owing him against their next trip into town. Hannah looked quite pleased, and she had a small package of items, tied up in brown paper and string, as well as sacks of salt and sugar. When Sam had transferred these to the wagon he asked Hannah, "Anything else we need?"

"Yes. You might check at Hammer's to see if there's any mail for us."

"Oh, right. Almost forgot." Sam grinned. Hammer's must be the store down the road. "I won't be long. Be good."

"I'll try," Hannah promised with a smile. Then she nodded. "Here's Elisa West, probably with some of her gossip, as usual. At least I'll be kept busy until you return."

Sam headed down the street. He passed Elisa West and nodded amiably at her. To his surprise, he received a snort and a toss of the head in reply. Oh, well, maybe Samuel had done something to upset her. There was no point in worrying about it now. Sam passed several other people on his way to the store, but none of them greeted him by name.

Hammer's store was along the same lines as Jacob's, but slightly smaller. It contained much the same barreled and boxed goods, plus a small section of imported crockery and American-made pans. The man behind the counter waved a greeting.

"Anything I can get you, Samuel?"

"Just mail, if there is any."

"Right." The man looked under the counter, obviously the site of the local post office. There was no mail delivery in this period, of course. It was up to everyone to collect their mail from the store. "Sorry, Samuel," he reported, straightening up. "Nothing this time. Maybe next week."

"Maybe," agreed Sam. "Thanks, anyway." He headed back to Hannah. She was still listening to Elisa West. Well, at least she'd not been alone. The woman glanced around, said something hastily to Hannah, then hurried off in the other direction. Sam smiled to himself. Obviously gossip he wasn't supposed to overhear! Not that he wanted to—and he doubted if he'd know any of the people it was about, anyway, even if Samuel would have.

"Not too dull, I hope," he said to Hannah as he drew closer.

"Let's go home, Samuel," she replied coldly.

Sam stopped and stared at her, puzzled. "Is something wrong?" She didn't sound like her normal self.

"Let's go home, Samuel," she repeated. Her face was impassive, but there was something burning in her eyes.

Confused, Sam helped her onto the wagon. She was stiff and didn't look at him. What was going on here? What had gotten into her? She seemed to be almost biting her lips to stop from saying anything. Sam finished loading their purchases into the wagon, then took his seat. As he flicked the reins to get Old Flighty into motion, he stole a glance at Hannah. She was staring determinedly ahead.

A few minutes later, they were out of Smithtown and on the road to their farm. Sam chanced a gambit. "What's wrong?" he asked. "Is it something I can help with?"

"We'll discuss this at home," Hannah snapped. She refused to look at him.

Confused and hurt, Sam allowed the horse to plod

homeward, trying to figure out what could possibly have gotten into her. As the silence between them stretched, it was broken by Al's voice from behind him.

"Jeez, what a morning. Your ancestor is as stubborn ... well, as stubborn as you. Verbeena still won't agree to my talking to him again. She seems to think I'll say something wrong. Me!"

Sam glanced back, and saw Al apparently standing in the back of the cart. He was dressed in a bright yellow suit and hat, with a green shirt, red tie, and green loafers. He looked like a canary on drugs. Sam nodded his head slightly at Hannah, then rolled his eyes.

Taking the hint, Al bent around to peer at Hannah's set features and grim poise. "Uh-oh," he muttered, straightening up. "The silent treatment, eh?" Sam nodded slightly. "Yeah, my ... second wife ... or was it my third? Oh, well, either way, she used to give me that 'to you I'm not speaking' routine. It always meant that an hour later, she was gonna start ranting and screaming and throwing things. Better get set to duck a lot. This one," he waved his cigar at Hannah, "is so goody-goody that when she explodes, it's gonna be a doozy."

That was hardly a comfort, but Sam suspected that Al was right. Obviously something Hannah had heard from Elisa West had set this off. Until Sam knew what it was, there was nothing he could do to heal the wound.

The trip back was punctuated only with comments from Al about how difficult Samuel was being, and how much Sam was going to get it when Hannah finally exploded. At last they reached the farm. Sam jumped down, and Hannah unbent enough to pass Daniel down to him and then allow him to help her down from the cart.

"We'll talk when you've unloaded the cart and I've

108

put Daniel to bed," she said, then stormed into the house.

"What did I tell you?" asked Al. "She's gonna blow so loud, it'll make Krakatoa sound like a firecracker."

"You don't have to hang around to witness it," Sam pointed out, unloading the supplies.

"You think I'd leave my best friend in the lurch?" asked Al indignantly. "Besides, this could be fun, watching someone other than me on the receiving end of a hissy fit. What set her off, anyway?"

"I've no idea. She was talking to some gossip in town."

"Oh." Al waved his cigar philosophically. "Maybe Samuel has been a bad boy. Maybe the old biddy saw him smooching with some barmaid or something. That sort of thing always sets a wife off."

Sam decided that he didn't want to know any more details about Al's arguments with his second (or third) wife. "Let's just wait and see." He finished stowing the cart in the barn. "She'll let us know in a minute."

"It's time to face the music," Al sang off-key. "Some guys are gluttons for punishment. This I gotta see."

"Big help," muttered Sam as he entered the house. He closed the door behind him, and Al walked through it, a wide grin on his face.

Hannah had put Daniel in the bedroom and closed the door. She was waiting, a dark scowl on her pretty face. As soon as Sam stepped into the room, she said, "Elisa West tells me what you refused to do, Samuel: where you were these past few days."

Oh-oh. "And what did she say?" he asked cautiously.

"That you were one of a group of riders who beat up

and terrorized several poor citizens of Oyster Bay. That you accused them of being Tory sympathizers and forced them out of their homes, and made them take their families to Connecticut or face worse.'' Her eyes were spitting fire. ''And now I'm waiting to hear you deny the charge.''

Sam took a deep breath. ''I won't lie to you, Hannah,'' he began. ''I was one of the Committee, but. . . .''

''You *admit* it?'' she yelled. ''You *did* do that? Samuel Beckett, never since the day I met you have I ever been ashamed of knowing you—until today!'' As he tried to protest, she cut him off. ''I'll hear none of your excuses and evasions. I'm disgusted with you for such behavior toward our friends and neighbors, whatever political allegiances they may hold. And I am not speaking with you any further!'' She whirled on her heels and stormed into the bedroom, slamming the door hard behind her.

''Hannah!'' Sam cried, going to the door. ''Please, let me explain!''

''If you try and come through that door, Samuel Beckett,'' she shouted, ''I'm leaving this house forever, and taking my baby with me! You've got chores to do— so do them!'' There was a loud thud from inside the bedroom.

There was obviously no point in even attempting to talk with her right now. ''All right,'' Sam agreed reluctantly. ''I'll be outside if you change your mind.''

''If I change my mind, it'll be to go back to my father! Get out!''

With a heavy heart, Sam did so. Perhaps a little physical work would make him feel better. Al walked through the wall to join him outside.

"Well," he said, "that solves one of your problems, at any rate."

Sam scowled at him. "What do you mean? She's not even talking to me."

"Right. So that makes your moral dilemma redundant. There's absolutely no way she's gonna want to have her way with you tonight. You're safe."

Trust Al to think of that. "Gee, thanks. Look, that isn't uppermost on my mind right now."

Al shrugged. "It's always uppermost on my mind. And I was trying to find the silver lining inside that great cloud of doom in there."

"Just what I needed," Sam sighed. "Maybe this would be a good time for you to vanish. I'm going to get some work done in the fields. I know how the sight of someone working his butt off makes you ill."

Al grinned. "As a wise man once remarked, 'I love work. I can sit and watch it all day.' Still, when a man's had an argument with his wife, he probably wants to be left alone."

"She not *my* wife," Sam pointed out. "She's *Samuel's* wife."

"Ah," said Al, taking a long draw on his cigar. "That's the nub of the problem, isn't it? You wish she *was* your wife."

Sam considered the idea for a moment. "Yes," he finally said, somewhat reluctantly. "Al, I can't explain it, but I really do think I'm in love with her."

Al snorted. "Even right now, when she's all set to crack a dish over your head?"

"Yes, even right now. She thinks she has a good reason to be angry, and I guess in one way she has. She's exhibiting moral indignation."

"Whose side are you on? Look, she's just being

prissy, and not giving you a chance to explain. She's grouchy and judgmental. Okay, she's got a nice bod. . . . No, a *great* bod, but is that enough to think you're in love with her? Or is there something you're not telling me?''

"It's not that," Sam said, trying to probe his own feelings. "There's just something about her that reverberates inside me. Like Hannah is a part of me. I can't explain it because I just don't understand it myself." He chewed on his lower lip a moment. "Maybe it's some kind of leaching effect—you know, something that Samuel felt that's left in me when I Leaped in. That sort of thing's happened before."

"Could be," agreed Al, without much interest. "Personally, I think you're just going flaky on me. It's the effect of being cooped up with this babe and your refusing to even touch her. I figure that one good roll in the hay with her would get it out of your system."

"That might work for you, Al," Sam snapped, "but not for me."

"I *know* it would work for me," Al replied, grinning.

"No wonder you had problems staying married," Sam snapped. "Anyway, I *can't* make love to Hannah. It would be adultery, for one thing, and incest for another."

Al rolled his eyes. "You keep harping on that," he complained. "How often are you going to wallow in this guilt trip of yours? Just do it, and let the moral questions go beg."

"Is it really that simple for you?" asked Sam. "Do you mean to tell me you have no moral standards at all?"

Al looked offended. "Of course I have moral standards," he huffed. "There's a lot of things I would

112

never do. On the other hand, I'll admit I have a kind of moral blind spot where woman are involved. It's just something in my psyche, I guess. When temptation comes along, I give right in.'' He thought for a second. ''That was what my fourth wife always complained about.''

''All right,'' Sam sighed. ''This isn't going to get us anywhere, I can see. Besides, as you said, Hannah's in no mood to fool around right now, anyway.''

''Not right now,'' agreed Al, studying the end of his cigar. ''But when she gets over this snit of hers, she's gonna want to make up.'' He grinned widely. ''Then I don't think she'll take no for an answer from you. Maybe you should think about making yourself a chastity belt or something. You may need it.'' He waved. ''On which thought, I gotta go see Tina. Bye.''

Sam snorted as Al disappeared again. Then he set to work on the chores, hoping to distract himself from his grim thoughts. It did keep him occupied physically, but his thoughts kept returning to Hannah. In one way, he couldn't blame her for her anger: it proved that she was passionate about justice. On the other hand, she was hardly being fair, not allowing him to explain or defend himself.

He still had nothing really resolved in his mind when he went cautiously back to the house at the end of the day. He peered around the door, half expecting to be greeted by a flying plate. Instead, he saw Hannah busying herself with dinner.

''Does this mean you're calmed down a little?'' he asked her.

''No. It means I'm not about to let you starve to death. That's all.'' She glared at him. ''And I don't want to hear another word from you.'' She handed him a plate of chicken and corn chowder, and took one of her own into the bedroom, closing the door behind her.

Sam ate slowly, his eyes constantly on the door, hoping she would reappear. She did, but only to wash the dishes. When Sam helped, she ignored him.

The treatment was wearing Sam down. ''Why won't you let me explain?'' he demanded.

She glared at him, then ignored him again. Obviously, she wouldn't listen, so there was absolutely no point in attempting to talk to her. When the dishes were done, she headed back to the bedroom.

''Shall I sleep in the barn tonight?'' Sam asked bitterly.

She turned to glare at him again. ''I'll not deny a man the comfort of his own bed,'' she replied coldly. ''But that's *all* I shan't deny you.'' She left the door open behind her.

She had her back turned to him when Sam clambered into bed. He sighed. It was going to be a long night, and it didn't look like things were going to be any better in the morning. Until Hannah relented, there would be no talking to her.

It was another long, rough night for Sam. He got very little sleep. The only slight consolation was that Hannah didn't seem to fare any better. She tossed and turned all night. Obviously she was very disturbed with this breach between them, but too angry to try and resolve it.

In the morning, Sam made a decision. Hannah might cool down faster if he weren't around to provoke her anger. ''I have to make a trip,'' he told her. ''I shouldn't be gone too long. Probably no more than today.''

''Good.'' She turned her back to prepare breakfast. Well, her mood hadn't improved overnight. She didn't even want to know where he was going, so that saved Sam the trouble of being evasive.

After breakfast, Sam saddled up the horse and rode away. There was no cheery farewell from Hannah. She didn't even emerge from the house to watch him leave. This left a burning hurt inside Sam. Okay, she wasn't technically his wife, but he really felt bad about this rift between them. But as long as she wouldn't let him talk, there was no way to heal things over.

He couldn't help suspecting that he was making a real mess of this Leap. Whatever he'd come here to do, he was certain that it wasn't to create the first divorce in his family's history.

Al emerged from the trunk of a large tree on the side of the road, then floated along beside him. He was back in his mix-and-match state of dress, with a paisley shirt, yellow vest, and red trousers. Behind the cigar was a wide grin.

"You're looking particularly smug today," Sam commented bitterly. "I'm glad to see that one of us is having a good day."

Al raised an eyebrow. "Things not improved between you and the luscious Hannah, hey?" he asked without much sympathy. "Tough. But we've finally started to hit paydirt. Verbeena got your ancestor to start talking again."

"That's good news." Sam stared at Al. "It *is* good news, right?"

"Oh, yeah." Al waved his cigar airily. "He said enough that we know that he never would have joined the Committee of Safety."

"Ah." Sam grinned. "So I saved his life when I Leaped into him, then?"

"Without a doubt," Al agreed. "Ziggy says it's a

115

hundred percent certain that if Samuel had refused the Committee, Kirk would have slit his throat. And Samuel doesn't have a clue how to do that kung fooey stuff of yours, so he'd have been butchered."

Frowning, Sam said, "But that can't be the only reason I'm here. Otherwise, I'd have Leaped a long time ago."

"Right," agreed Al. "But it's a start. And now we've got Samuel talking about that, maybe he'll open up on the other stuff." He paused. "So, where are you going, anyway?"

"If you recall," Sam answered, "I was supposed to head out to the Havens Inn to make a contact. That's where I'm going now."

"Oh." Al frowned. "You know the way?"

"No," Sam replied patiently. "I was expecting you to direct me."

"Right." Al tapped in commands on the handlink. "In that case, you're heading in the wrong direction. It's out in the Moriches Bay area, not off toward Smithtown. Better turn around.

"Thanks for telling me," Sam grunted, turning Old Flighty around. "Keep me up to date, will you?"

"No problemo." Al scratched his nose. "Any idea what's going to happen when you get to this inn?"

"None at all," Sam admitted. "I gather Samuel kept whatever he was up to, concealed from his wife. I don't have a clue as to what's going on. It would be really helpful if he opened up a bit, so I don't make a hash of this."

"So far, zip on that score," Al reported. "It looks to me like this is some undercover stuff he was involved in. According to Ziggy, the owner of the Havens Inn, Benjamin Havens, was notoriously anti-British. They used to raid his place and confiscate his stuff on a pretty regular basis. And a lot of American spies and agents used to pass by his inn.''

"Sounds like something out of James Bond 1776,'' Sam joked.

"It probably was. The British kept a wary eye on this guy, and he had to dodge their troops more than once.''

"So if Samuel was involved with him, it was probably to do with espionage,'' Sam realized. "Can't you convince Samuel that we're not trying to disrupt what he was up to, but just trying to change whatever went wrong?''

"He's *your* relative,'' Al pointed out. "And as such he's kind of skeptical.''

An idea occurred to Sam. "Has Ziggy run a probability check on what would have happened to Isaiah Watts if Samuel Beckett had been murdered?''

"Nope.'' Al grinned. "But it's worth a shot.'' He tapped in commands and waited a moment. "Oh, take that side road, there.'' He gestured with his cigar. As Sam obeyed, Al gave a chuckle. "Got it. Ziggy estimates a ninety-five percent chance that Watts would also have been murdered by Kirk to stop him from talking about the first murder. So it looks like you saved his life as well. Busy little boy, aren't you?''

"And how about Hannah and Daniel? If Samuel had died, then what?''

Al ran this one past Ziggy. "She estimates a sixty percent chance that Hannah would have gone to Josiah Smith for help, and then been evacuated for the duration of the war. A thirty percent chance she'd have stuck it out and faced serious trouble when the Brits win the battle. And a ten percent chance. . . .'' He raised his eyebrows. "Uh-oh. A ten percent chance she'd have been raped and murdered by Kirk or Morgan. It seems that you may have saved her life as well.''

Sam nodded happily. ''Then surely even Samuel should be able to see that I've already done nothing but good for him, his friend, and his family. Maybe if that's explained to him properly, he'll be a tad more cooperative.''

''Optimist,'' muttered Al. ''But it's worth a shot. I'll suggest it to Verbeena. Maybe I'll have some news for you later. Meanwhile, take that road to your right. It'll bring you down to the main Sag Harbor to Brooklyn road. Once you get there, just follow the road east for about thirty miles. You can't miss Havens' place. It's a pretty large inn, and the stage stops there overnight.''

Sam frowned. ''That sounds like you're off again.''

''Right.'' Al waved his cigar airily. ''I thought that since you've left Hannah all alone, I'd better stop by from time to time to check up on her. I'll see you later.''

Before Sam could argue, Al had vanished, obviously having Ziggy relocate him on Hannah. Sam sighed. He suspected there was more to Al's departure than a wish to be certain Hannah was safe. Still, for the moment there really wasn't anything that Al could do for him. He had nothing to do but travel for several hours. What could go wrong in that time?

Morgan reined his horse in, making certain that he stayed far enough back from the traveler on the road ahead of him. It wouldn't do to be spotted by Beckett at this stage of the game. Morgan had very clear instructions to follow Beckett wherever he went, and to report back on anyone he met with. Kirk was quite certain that Beckett was a Tory sympathizer at best, and more likely a double agent for the British. All he needed was proof, and then the Committee would take action to dispose of a traitor.

And Morgan was quite certain that he'd get the necessary proof—even if he had to manufacture it. . . .

CHAPTER
ELEVEN

The trip wasn't too bad, though it was past noon by the time Sam arrived at Carman's River. Crossing over, he was in the Manor of St. George, close to the Havens Inn. There had been little traffic on the road, only an occasional cart and driver, and several horsemen. Most had nodded a greeting to Sam, though some had regarded him with obvious suspicion. This wasn't too surprising, since a war was on.

What astonished Sam the most was that there was so little evidence of fighting. Two of the riders Sam had seen had carried muskets, and one a sword, but other than that, everyone seemed to be conducting their lives as usual. Probably most of the folks in these parts were not strongly committed to either side in the conflict, and were willing to wait and see what would happen. And most of the able-bodied men who were on one side or the other were probably getting ready for the upcoming battle to be fought in Brooklyn. Sam realized with a start that it was only a week away. And he still wasn't certain whether he should really be involved in the fight. He had already saved Samuel's life once, but if he became embroiled in the battle, then he could get Samuel—and perhaps even himself—killed.

If only Dr. Beeks could get Samuel to talk! Knowing what his ancestor had planned might give Sam a clue as to what he should do.

The inn was another half-hour's ride. It was very pleasant in this area, with plenty of forests still standing. Houses were few and far between, mostly scattered farms. William Floyd—a signer of the Declaration, and the man who employed Durham—had his estate just off the road around here, but Sam wasn't sightseeing. He kept to the road until he entered Moriches, and then asked directions from the first man he saw to the Havens Inn.

"Straight down the road, about a half-mile," the man replied, gesturing. "It's on the left. You can't miss it."

Sam thanked him and rode on. The town had just the one small road, with the usual scattered houses on either side. He passed a couple of larger farms, and then saw a sizable structure ahead that was clearly his destination. About time, too, as he was getting very hungry.

The inn was a two-story structure, one of the few Sam had seen so far. At the back was a stable for the horses, where Sam left Old Flighty to be looked after. He entered the inn.

It was quiet, and not too well lit, despite the large windows. Sam saw several rooms off to the side, and stairs leading up to more guest rooms. There were several people about, including two travelers resting and smoking by one window. One of them was reading a pamphlet of some kind. Most likely an opinion sheet for one side or the other in the war, Sam guessed. Neither man paid him any heed.

A young girl came out of one of the back rooms, and stopped when she saw Sam. She was carrying a pewter mug filled with foaming ale. She wore a simple dress, topped by an apron. Her bonnet covered a thatch of corn-colored hair. "I'll be with you in a moment, sir," she promised, and hurried to one of the men. Then she returned. "Can I be of service?"

"Yes," Sam said. "I'm here to see Benjamin Havens. My name's Beckett." He hoped that he was supposed to ask for the owner. Durham had merely mentioned that he'd be met there.

"Yes, sir," the girl replied. "I'll let him know that you're here." She gave a brief smile, then vanished to the back again.

Sam waited uncertainly, glancing about the room as he did so. The other men didn't seem to be interested in him at all, which was a comfort. He wished he knew what all of this was about.

The door opened again, and this time a stout man emerged, wiping his hands on a cloth. He was simply dressed in shirt and vest, but there was an air of prosperity about him. He was obviously in his fifties, with thinning, iron-gray hair and deep-set eyes. "Samuel!" he exclaimed. "It's good to see you again." He clasped Sam's hand and shook it fiercely. "Ah, it's been too long since you were here." He snorted good-humoredly. "That pretty wife of yours is keeping your days and nights busy, no doubt. Well, I can't blame you."

Since he was obviously supposed to know the man, Sam grinned back. "You know how farms can be, Benjamin," he answered. "Work, work, work."

"Aye, but the nights must be fun, eh?" Havens winked, and laid his arm about Sam's shoulder. "Well, don't stand out here, man, as if you're a stranger. Come

LIVE THE 3-D VIRTUAL ADVENTURE!

T2 NEW
TERMINATOR 2
3-D™

UNIVERSAL STUDIOS FLORIDA®

For Travel Packages call: 1-800-224-3838.
For more information call: 1-407-363-8000
or visit our web site at http://www.usf.com

JURASSIC PARK™
THE RIDE
UNIVERSAL STUDIOS HOLLYWOOD™

For more information on Universal Studios
Hollywood Vacations call (800) 337-5072

THIS SUMMER
YOU'LL WISH IT WAS JUST A MOVIE!℠

in, come in.'' He led Sam into the back room, which was, unsurprisingly, the kitchen. "Mary—where *is* that girl? Ah, there you are!'' He gestured to the young girl Sam had already met. "Don't stand there like a petunia taking root, fetch Samuel an ale!'' He punched Sam's arm gently. "And no doubt you'll be wanting a slice of Martha's game pie, too, eh? I know it's your favorite.''

"It's too long since I've tasted it,'' Sam answered, trying to match his host's mood.

"That's true,'' agreed Havens. "Well, I'll have a large piece heated up for you. Now, where's Selah? Is he skipping his chores again?'' He looked around the workers in the kitchen. "Josh, go find my son, will you?'' The boy nodded, and shot out the door. Turning to Sam, Havens added, "You'll hardly recognize him, Samuel. He's quite grown up since you were last here.''

I won't recognize him all right, Sam thought. But not for the reason Havens believed. "How old is he now?'' asked Sam. A pretty safe question.

"One and twenty,'' Havens answered proudly. "And just as anti-British as his father. Where the dickens is that Mary?''

She appeared from the back room with a tankard of ale, and hurried across with it. "Here you are, sir,'' she said, smiling broadly at Sam.

"Less of that,'' Havens said, slapping her rear. "He's a happily married man, young lady. Don't you go flirting with him.'' He winked at Sam. "Unless you're no longer so happy, of course.''

Sam accepted the tankard, and smiled back. "Very happily married,'' he replied. If you overlooked the past day, of course. . . .

"See, Mary, you'll just have to find another handsome to make those eyes at.'' Havens glared around the busy

123

room. "What's keeping that son of mine? Mary, get a piece of the game pie heated up for Sam. A *large* portion, mind, not the usual size you serve our customers."

"Aye," answered Mary, with another cheeky grin. "As large as you normally eat?"

"Not *that* big," Havens replied, matching her smile. "Be off with you, and stop bothering us. Samuel and I have a lot to discuss."

Mary disappeared among the other workers, and Havens drew Sam toward the back door. "Come along," he said cheerily. "A little fresh air away from all this work will do the both of us a world of good. And drink up that ale, man—there's no shortage of that for the moment. At least the British haven't put a stop to my shipments yet."

Sipping as he went—the ale was strong and bitter, but very refreshing—Sam followed his host into the yard. Havens bustled him across the yard, then into the quiet vegetable garden beyond. He obviously grew a great deal of the produce for his tables here, as well as buying from the neighboring farmers.

"It's a little quieter out here, Sam," he said. "And the only ears belong to the corn and the damned crows."

Sam smiled over the rim of his ale. "I'd begun to think you'd called me out here only to eat and drink."

"Hardly," Havens replied with a laugh. "Though you're more than welcome to do your fill of both, of course. You know that your money's no good here, so take advantage of it." Soberly, he added, "There's more trouble coming than even you might think, Samuel."

I doubt it, Sam thought. Knowing how the war would turn out gave him a clear advantage. "What do you mean, Ben?"

"The British have a number of plans for the island,

and none of them includes losing the impending battle. I'm not sure of what is going on, but you're to be met here tonight. Durham's on his way back with a special contact, and whoever he is, has asked specifically to meet with you. He'll be on the coach, so you may as well enjoy your wait. I'll have a room made ready for you overnight. You timed your visit perfectly."

Apparently he had. Things were getting more complex by the minute. As he'd suspected, Samuel was in some kind of spy ring here on the island, working for the Rebels. But what would this lead to? Well, one thing was obvious—he wouldn't be getting back to Hannah tonight. Though, given her current frame of mind, perhaps that was no bad thing. He didn't want another strained night of hostile silence.

There came a cheery hail from the yard, and they looked around.

"Selah!" exclaimed Ben as the young man approached them. "About time. Come and say hello to Samuel!"

Grinning from ear to ear, Selah pumped Sam's hand energetically. "Uncle Sam," he said. "It's good to see you again. It's been too long."

"I'll say," Sam agreed. "I wouldn't have recognized you, you've changed so much." Well, at least part of that was no lie!

"It's all the work I'm doing," Selah answered. "It either makes you grow or kills you."

"The way you work sometimes," his father said affectionately, "I swear you believe the latter's the likeliest." He laughed to show he didn't mean it. "Well, let's go see if Mary's warmed up your pie, eh, Sam? I'll wager that you're ready for it."

Sam's stomach obligingly complained. "I'd say you're right," he agreed.

The afternoon passed pleasantly enough. Sam ate the pie—which was every bit as tasty as Havens had promised—and nursed a couple of beers. He chatted with Selah and with Mary, who had a lively sense of humor. It was starting to get dark when Havens reappeared.

"I've cleared the small dining room," he told Sam quietly. "As soon as the coach arrives, you and your contact can have dinner there in private. I'll make certain no eager ears attend."

Sam thanked him and returned to nursing his drink. Al hadn't reappeared, and he wondered what had kept his friend. It couldn't simply be his desire to spy on Hannah; no matter how lecherous Al could get, he wouldn't let that interfere with his work. Something had to be happening, and Sam wished he knew what. Al was behaving rather oddly on this Leap. For some reason, he seemed to be awfully keen on Sam making love to Hannah. Maybe there was something going on here that he didn't know about. He felt so helpless, driven in different directions on this Leap by forces he couldn't control and didn't understand. So much was happening, and so little of it seemed to augur well.

Maybe Hannah was *supposed* to get pregnant about now. That might explain why Al was pushing the bedroom so strongly. But wouldn't he just come out and tell Sam this? Why would he hide it? It didn't make any sense. A lot about this Leap wasn't making much sense.

Then the coach arrived, with a clatter of horses and creaking of wood. Sam stayed where he was, listening to the bustle and fussing of the unloading. After a few minutes, Selah threw open the main door and escorted three travelers inside. Sam carefully studied them over the rim of his mug, wondering if he should pretend not to know any of them.

The decision was taken from him as a tall man strode over to him, grinning, and extended his hand. "Samuel! Good to see you again!"

Sam recognized the voice, if not the face. "Nathan Durham!" he replied, shaking the hand. "You've changed since we last met."

Indeed he had. Gone was the disguise he'd worn earlier. He'd shed several decades, the eye patch, and the limp, to become a moderately handsome thirtyish man. He *had* been a good disguise artist, without question. Durham grinned again. "Aye, that's true, thank the Lord. Well, man, Benjamin tells me that dinner will soon be ready for us—and I am more than ready for it." He glanced around, then beckoned one of the other passengers forward. This was a tall man, dressed in very fine clothing, clearly not homemade. His shirt was delicate, his trousers and jacket well fitted. His hat was new and very expensive in appearance. He wore a powdered wig and a cheery expression.

"Samuel," Durham said, "I'd like you to meet my good friend William Bradford. He'll be supping with us tonight."

Bradford . . . Bradford. . . . The name rang a bell somewhere. Sam shook his hand, then recalled where he had heard the name before.

William Bradford was the most notorious Tory sympathizer on Nassau Island, and a reputed British spy! Kirk and Townsend had expressed their desires to hang the man from any convenient tree.

Why was he meeting with Samuel Beckett? What *had* Sam gotten himself into?

CHAPTER
TWELVE

Alone with the baby, Hannah felt no better at all. As annoyed as she was with her husband, she missed his presence. Still, perhaps it was all for the best at the moment. Every time she looked at Samuel, she couldn't help feeling overwhelmingly angry at him. She had felt so comfortable and secure with him before that trip to Smithtown. Now she felt so lost and furious.

She busied herself with household chores, working with grim determination to use the jobs to take her mind off Samuel. The problem was that everything around her reminded her of him. The table he had made, the apples he had picked, the baby he had fathered. . . . The whole house positively reeked of him.

When she had married Samuel, she'd known him only a very short while. Their fathers had been friends, and both sets of parents had pushed them together. Hannah had resisted at first, but Samuel's cheery nature and his rugged good looks had won her over. She had grown to love him more since their wedding, and she had felt that she knew him so well.

128

And now this!

She broke one of the plates as she washed it, and then burst into tears as she threw it out. Why had Samuel betrayed her like this? Why had he ruined all of her happiness?

A small voice within her pointed out that if she'd let him talk, she might have some answers. Samuel had never lied to her, and she doubted that he would begin now. On the other hand, he'd never done anything that she was ashamed of before, and now she felt bitterly ashamed of his actions. Who knew what else about him might have changed? It was almost as if she didn't know him any more.

In the late afternoon she heard the sound of a horse approaching. Samuel was back! She felt the normal surge of anticipation, and then she forced it back, beating it down. Her anger and her disappointment in him wouldn't allow her to appear pleased to see him. She was annoyed with herself that she still wanted him. She glanced out of the window, then realized that the rider wasn't Samuel.

She went to the door cautiously. She wasn't afraid, but with the current state of things, it was better to be a little wary. As the rider reined in and dismounted, she recognized him and went outside quickly. "Isaiah! It's good to see you again."

"Hello, Hannah," Isaiah Watts replied, smiling. "You're looking just as radiant as always. No wonder Samuel's always talking about you." He glanced at the fields. "Is Samuel working?"

"No." Hannah's face lost her smile of greeting. "He's had to go away for a while. He didn't say where to, or when he'd be back."

"Oh." Isaiah stood beside his horse, shifting his feet

uncomfortably. "I just came to tell him that I'd followed his example and joined the militia." He patted the musket attached to his saddle. "I'm on my way to join Colonel Smith's men now."

"Be careful, Isaiah," Hannah said with concern. "This is no game. You might get injured. What would happen to Anne and the children then?"

"What will happen to them if we don't fight for what we believe in?" asked Isaiah. "Samuel made me realize that. He's made me really think about things lately."

"It's a shame he didn't think about some things more clearly," Hannah snapped. She was unable to keep the bitterness from her voice.

Concerned, Isaiah squinted at her. "Is something wrong? You sound unhappy."

"I *am* unhappy, Isaiah," she admitted, unable to keep it in any longer. "It's Samuel—he seems to have changed, somehow. He doesn't seem like the man I married any longer."

Isaiah took her arm gently and led her to one of the seats beside the house. "I'm not the wisest person in the world, Hannah," he said simply. "But I do care for you and Samuel. It pains me to see you in this distress. Perhaps you'd feel better if you talked about it. I'd be happy to listen, and offer what comfort I can."

"Thank you, Isaiah," she said gratefully. She *did* want to talk about it, and Isaiah was a good friend. Perhaps he could offer her some solace, even advice. He wasn't smart like Samuel, but he had a good heart, and often a fine, simple sensibility. She considered what to say to him. No matter how good a friend he was, she had no intention of mentioning Samuel's strange reluctance to perform his husbandly duties in bed. That was absolutely nobody's concern but hers and Samuel's.

130

"We were in Smithtown yesterday," she said, fighting back the urge to cry as she thought about it. "And I was given some very shocking news. Samuel has joined some Committee of Safety, whose purpose it is to go around intimidating people who disagree with them, and then throwing them from their homes. They employ violence to achieve their ends, and Samuel is a part of it."

Isaiah flushed, his pale skin becoming bright red. Even his straggly blond hair seemed to take on a darker hue. "That was my fault, Hannah," he said, bowing his head in shame. "I was the one who led him to the group."

"You?" Hannah echoed, shocked.

"Yes." In a quiet voice, he explained. "I was asked to join. George Townsend made it sound like the duty of a good patriot, to root out and remove all corrupting influences from our midst and to purify our society, ready for the day when we would be free of British rule. It sounded so good when he told me, and I happily joined up. When I told Samuel about it, he was very annoyed—a little with me, I suspect, but mostly with Townsend and the others. He insisted on accompanying me to the meeting and having his say. When he tried, however, John Kirk threatened to kill him if he wasn't on their side. Samuel then declared that he was. He told me afterward that he aimed to ensure that they were kept in check."

"In check!" Hannah was incredulous. "Isaiah, people were beaten and thrown out of their homes. How could Samuel be a part of that?"

"He wasn't," Isaiah answered. "He stopped Kirk when he tried to do such things. And he inspired me to do the same. I quit the Committee when I saw what their

131

real aims were. Thanks to Samuel, I'm out of their influence, and doing the right thing: fighting for my country, not fighting against my neighbors.''

Hannah was wavering. Isaiah's words were so sincere, and she *wanted* to believe the best about her husband. But she was terribly afraid that she might be making a dreadful mistake if she believed simply because she wanted to. "Samuel came home with a man's blood all over his shirt,'' she said. "He must have beaten a man near to death to get so stained, Isaiah.''

"*Beat* him?'' Isaiah shook his head. "No, Hannah, Samuel *saved* that man's life. He'd been whipped by Kirk's henchman, and was bleeding profusely. If Samuel hadn't seen to the wound and stitched it closed, the man would surely have died. Samuel saved his life. That blood was a badge of courage, not shame.''

Hannah stared at Isaiah, hope and embarrassment flooding over her. "You mean that I was wrong?'' she asked in a strangled voice. "That Samuel *didn't* behave wickedly?''

"Quite the reverse,'' Isaiah insisted. "He never faltered in his beliefs, and he showed me and several others that what we had become involved in was wrong. He shamed us into quitting the Committee. And he convinced me that joining the militia was the right way to work for our freedom.''

Hannah hung her head in shame. "I feel so terrible,'' she whispered. "I yelled at him and accused him of so much that he didn't do. . . .''

"Didn't he defend himself?'' asked Isaiah, puzzled. He seemed to be uncertain whether he should comfort her, and how to do it if he should.

"I would not listen,'' Hannah confessed miserably. "I refused to let him speak, so certain that he was guilty.

Oh, Isaiah, I feel so terrible! I can't believe I thought my beloved husband capable of such evil."

"I'm sure he'll understand and forgive you," Isaiah replied. "Samuel is a very understanding and forgiving man."

"That he is," said Hannah firmly. "Not that I deserve him, but he is." She straightened up. "And when he returns tonight, I shall confess my foolishness and ask him to forgive me." She patted Isaiah's hand. "Thank you, old friend. You have done a great deal to ease my mind. All that is left is for me to admit my errors and beg Samuel's indulgence again."

"Which I am certain he will give," Isaiah answered, blushing at the touch. "Well, I'm doubly glad that I stopped by today. It gives me pleasure to know that I've been able to heal a foolish rift between you. Don't be too hard on yourself, Hannah. Your mistake was made from righteous indignation against the actions that some are indeed undertaking. But be certain that Samuel is not one such man."

"I am," Hannah agreed. "And I should have known that all along. It was wrong of me to doubt him, and worse of me not to allow him to explain. But I shall make it up to him, I swear." She smiled happily at Isaiah. "Thank you, again. I shall be sure to give Samuel your message—*after* I have given him mine."

Nodding, Isaiah returned to his horse. "Be well," he called.

"God go with you, and keep you safe," Hannah replied. "I suspect that Samuel will follow you shortly and be with you again."

She watched Isaiah ride off. Then she danced a few steps back to the house, her heart singing again. She berated herself for her stubbornness and her foolish be-

133

lief in Samuel's guilt. But that could be atoned for, and she would be certain to apologize to him just as soon as he arrived home. She would make this night the best he had ever known. She still had some of that apple pie he loved, and plenty of chicken and corn chowder. Then again, perhaps she could be a trifle unfrugal this night and make him something special for dinner. Didn't he deserve it?

As she started to busy herself, she hummed happily. All was right with the world again. And this evening, she would accept no excuses from Samuel. Whatever was bothering him about their bed-riding, she was going to be sure he rode long and well this night.

Durham bustled Sam and Bradford into the small dining room, then called to Mary, "We're all here, now, lass—and so are our healthy appetites! Bustle us up food and some of your fine wine!" Without waiting for a reply, he closed the door. "Now, Samuel, William—we'll be eating well in a few minutes, I'll warrant. Our discussion can wait for the bowl after the meal. I'm sure that the two of you have appetites that almost rival my own." He rubbed his stomach. "And if we had taken an hour longer to get here, they'd have had to see if the coach could have run with one less horse!"

Bradford laughed. "Well, truth be told, I'll hold my own with you over the plates. It seems like yesterday since I last ate." He eyed Sam and chuckled. "Though if you've been here long, I imagine you've already had a fair sampling of Master Havens' kitchen."

"True enough," agreed Sam. "But that was a while ago. I may not be able to match you both, but I promise to try." Though he smiled, he was still very disturbed by this meeting. What was going on here? It looked as though he'd have to wait until after their meal to find out.

The door opened, and Mary came in with three pewter goblets. Sam accepted one, and sipped from it. It was a red wine, a trifle sweeter than he preferred, but pleasant enough otherwise. Both Bradford and Durham emptied half of theirs almost instantly.

"By the Lord," Durham said, "the dust of the road gives me a hearty thirst."

"Ah, so that's it, is it?" asked Mary, her eyes twinkling. "Well, I can see I'd better be ready to refill your glasses a few times this night."

"Love," growled Durham, "there's plenty of things you could fill for me this night. My bed, for example."

"I'm sure you can fill it amply enough alone," Mary shot back. "Especially after a good meal here. Your stomach wouldn't leave room for me."

Durham laughed. "God, you're a saucy one." He smacked her rear as she left the room.

"If you expect good service," Mary called back over her shoulder, "you'll use that hand for eating with, and nothing else."

Undeterred, Durham laughed. "Ah, that one has a sharp tongue in her head. I can't resist baiting her to see how she'll reply." He rubbed his hands together. "Well, gentlemen," he said, "I propose we take our seats and await our meals with anticipation."

Sam followed their lead, and the meal progressed well. It was a fine roast ham, with plenty of trimmings— and with the wine flowing as freely as Mary had promised. Most of the chatter over the food was idle, changing to ribald whenever Mary entered the room. She seemed to enjoy the attention she was getting from Durham, and, as he had claimed, managed to deflect his coarse humor with a joke and a smile. Sam paid the conversations little heed, wondering what he was going to discover when the talk turned serious.

Partway through the meal, Al popped in. He looked worried, then groaned when he saw the small gathering. "Jeez," he muttered, "just when I wanted a word or two in private." He scowled. "Can't you need to use the bathroom, or something?"

That wasn't a bad idea. "Excuse me," Sam said, getting to his feet. "Nature calls."

"I've heard it calling for a while," Durham answered, laughing, "but Mary won't let me answer it. You'll get no further with her, I suspect."

"Not *that* call," Sam answered. "Don't forget, I'm happily married."

"Aye," agreed Durham. "But Mary needn't know."

"Perhaps not," Sam agreed. "But I do." He left the room and looked around for the toilet.

"Out back," Al informed him. "The johns are all outdoors, remember?"

"Oh, yeah." Sam wandered into the yard. Al walked through the wall behind him. "So, what's up?"

"Plenty," Al answered. "Things are getting real complicated for you."

"I don't need you to tell me that," Sam answered, keeping his voice low. "Do you know who that guy in there with Durham is? William Bradford—the biggest British sympathizer on the island! What is Samuel up to? Is he secretly working for the British, as Kirk suspects?"

"You've got me there," Al replied. "I'll make it a top priority for Verbeena to ask Samuel, but don't expect quick results. Anyway, there's been a few new developments."

Sam sighed. "Let me guess—none of them are good, right?"

"Depends on your point of view," Al admitted. "The bad news is that your pal Isaiah has up and joined the militia. He's shouldered his rifle and marched off to the wars."

"Musket," Sam corrected him automatically. Then he winced. "He's left already?"

"Oh, yeah." Al frowned. "And, boy, is he eager. He's walking right into a bullet with his name on it."

"Please tell me that's just your usual pessimism showing, and not one of Ziggy's predictions," Sam begged.

"Well, so far it is," Al agreed. "But Ziggy projects a forty percent chance that Isaiah will be killed in the upcoming battle. And she still thinks that you're here to stop that from happening. So you'd better get ready to blow this joint, shoulder your own musket, and head after him."

"I can't do that just yet. I have to hear whatever Durham and Bradford want me—*Samuel*—to hear. Then I can go after Isaiah." He sighed. "I wish that kid would stop trying to sign up for all these good causes and simply stay home."

"You're beginning to sound like a father," Al groused.

"I'm beginning to *feel* like one," Sam admitted. "Anyway, I'm in the place of a father right now, so maybe it's natural. What else do you have to tell me that'll make this Leap even more wonderful?"

"Well, the good news is that Isaiah's cleared up that fight you were having with Hannah."

"He has?" That brightened Sam up. "She talked it over with him?"

"Yep." Al gave a tight smile. "And she now feels horribly embarrassed that she ever doubted you, and aims to apologize profusely when you get back home."

"I wish it could be tonight," Sam said. "But I'm stuck here at this meeting. I hate being at odds with her."

"Sam, Sam," Al said. "You're not *really* married to her, remember? You're just standing in for her hubby right now. As you keep telling me."

"I know," Sam admitted, sighing. "But there are times when I feel like she is my wife. It just feels natural and right somehow." He shook his head. "Even if it is just bleed-through from Samuel, it's real strong, Al."

Frustrated and knowing he wasn't going to get anywhere with Al, Sam glanced at the inn. "Look, I'd better get back inside, or they'll wonder what's keeping me."

"They'll probably suspect the serving maid," Al replied. "Speaking of which, she does seem to have the hots for you. And since you're technically not married. . . ."

"No," Sam said firmly. "Everyone here sees me as Hannah's husband, and I'll not have his reputation sullied."

Al sighed, "Sam Beckett. Boy scout. What a waste." Tapping the handset, he stepped back out the door.

Sam used the outside privy, then returned to the dining room. The plates had been cleared away, and Mary was refilling their wine goblets. She looked up with a smile as Sam entered.

"Will you be wanting anything else?" she asked him.

"I shall be," Durham answered, laughing and making a grab for her.

"That's enough of your sauciness," she snapped. "I

138

can see I'd best be leaving the three of you alone.'' She flounced out of the room.

''Well,'' said Bradford, settling back in his chair and taking out a clay pipe, ''if all the ribaldry is over, perhaps we can at last get down to business.''

''An admirable notion,'' agreed Durham. There were several clay pipes on the table, around a humidor. He took one, opened the canister, and started to pack his pipe. ''Samuel, will you at least indulge in a pipe?''

Sam didn't smoke, and he didn't really feel like trying the somewhat coarse weed in the humidor. ''Not this evening, thanks,'' he answered. ''I've had enough wine, and one indulgence an evening is sufficient for me.''

''More for us, then,'' Durham said. He used a taper to get a light for himself and Bradford from one of the candles on the table. When both pipes were lit, he shook out the taper, then puffed on his pipe to get the tobacco going.

Bradford leaned forward, a small cloud of smoke rising as he did so. ''You've kept admirably quiet all through the meal, Samuel,'' he said. ''But I've no doubt you've been wondering just what you've landed yourself in, meeting with such a notorious British agent.''

''The thought had crossed my mind,'' answered Sam honestly. ''Your reputation does precede you somewhat.''

''And I'm glad that it does,'' Bradford said, smiling. ''I'd be falling down in my duty if it didn't. I've worked long and hard to achieve that reputation, and I'm very proud of it. Thankfully, the British believe it implicitly.'' He took another draw on his pipe. ''It should come as no surprise to you, then, to hear that I'm one of the British army's most trusted spies.''

Sam's heart fell at this confession. He'd been hoping

against all hope that this whole thing was some kind of a scam or a mixup, but Bradford had just confessed to being a British spy quite openly.

It was looking worse and worse for Samuel Beckett every moment.

Morgan had seen more than enough. He hesitated only briefly, wondering if he should try to overhear what was being said in the meeting. He decided against it when a young, pretty serving girl stared at him suspiciously. Morgan knocked out his pipe against the inn wall and returned to his horse. What Beckett might be saying really wasn't that relevant. The fact was that he had met with William Bradford. That was enough.

You could always tell a man by the company he kept. And Beckett was consorting with a known British sympathizer in an out-of-the-way inn at night.

What other interpretation of this was possible except that Beckett was selling out the Committee of Safety to the British?

Kirk would know what to make of this news, and it was important that he hear it as soon as possible. Despite the arrival of night, Morgan knew it was his duty to head back as fast as he could and to alert the members of the Committee that one of their members was a traitor.

And then Beckett would get what was coming to him. . . .

CHAPTER

THIRTEEN

Sam was at a loss for words, but Bradford was clearly waiting for some response. Finally, Sam said, "You're taking a risk telling me such things." That was reasonably noncommittal. He still wasn't sure which side Samuel was supporting.

Bradford laughed. "Wisely chosen words," he approved. "But don't look so worried, Samuel. The British *know* I'm one of their most valuable spies. That makes me doubly effective for the Rebel cause. I slip the British snippets of information that will hardly do our cause harm, and in return I gain access to large amounts of information to pass along to the right people."

Almost gasping with relief, Sam sighed. "A double agent," he breathed.

"Precisely," Bradford agreed. He shrugged. "The British are certain of my loyalties, and the cold-shouldering I get from my neighbors is a small price to pay for the authenticity they lend to my guise. And when I'm with the British, I keep my ears and eyes open and soak up whatever I hear and see like a sponge."

Sam glanced at Durham. "It all sounds very plausible," he said. "But is there any proof for what he says?"

Durham smiled slightly. "Ah, I can't blame you for your suspicions, Samuel. His claims of working for us could be as fake as anything he claims, eh? Well, there's no real proof, of course. He'd be a fool to carry any documents on his person, since he's constantly being searched either by the British soldiers or by Patriots who'd rather hang him. But, for what it's worth, I can vouch for his trustworthiness. I have been his regular contact for a while now, and his information has proved to be most helpful."

Sam considered the point. The problem was that he didn't really know Durham the way that Samuel obviously did. Still, if Samuel trusted the man, could Sam do any less?

But—did Samuel *really* trust Durham? Or was that simply another layer in this complex game that his ancestor had been playing? He would have to have Al ask Samuel. . . . But would Samuel give an honest reply? That was the big problem involved when you started to doubt people's trustworthiness: there was no way of knowing when you could stop. Sam would have to work on the assumption that Samuel did indeed trust Durham. If that should prove to be untrue, he'd worry about the consequences later.

"Then that is a good enough recommendation for me," Sam replied. He saw the relief in both men's eyes. "Now, what would a clever double agent want with the likes of me?"

"A reasonable question," Bradford admitted. He puffed on his pipe for a moment. "You know that Colonel Smith is gathering a militia and preparing to engage the British in battle?''

"Yes," Sam replied. "In fact, I'm due to join that militia myself in the next day or so, as soon as my affairs are tidied up.''

"I thought as much," Bradford replied. "You are, after all, his nephew by marriage. That is one of the reasons I specifically requested to meet with you. I have urgent news that must be passed along to General Woodhull. Because of the buildup in forces in the Brooklyn area, there is no way for me to get through the American lines to deliver this news myself.''

"You'd most likely be hung on sight," Durham grunted.

Sam frowned. "Couldn't you get the British to let you through the area they control? If they thought you were spying up fresh information for them, surely they'd let you pass.''

"Possibly," Bradford agreed. "But then I'd have to return with something very valuable to justify that risk, and I'm not about to betray anything too useful to them. Plus, how would I, a known British sympathizer, be able to explain to any American forces I met on the way that I was to be taken to General Woodhull? They'd suspect treachery, and quite reasonably, too. No, I need an outside agent to deliver the message, one who will be accepted and trusted. You, to be precise.''

That made good sense. "I imagine I could get through Colonel Smith to General Woodhull," Sam agreed. "But only if I could slip past the battle lines. That isn't too likely—and my musket might be needed in the fight.''

"This information I have is of much more importance than one musket in a battle, Samuel," Bradford replied

143

earnestly. "It could affect the whole future of this area. Now, do I have your word that you will do your best to deliver this message for me?"

Sam considered the matter carefully. Aside from the fact that he had promised to fight with the militia, there was the problem that Isaiah had joined up. If he *was* here on this Leap to save Isaiah's life, then abandoning him in the battle could really screw things up. But, on the other hand, what if he was *really* here to ensure that Bradford's message got through? If Samuel had been killed by the Committee, as Ziggy had predicted, then presumably the message had remained undelivered. It might be Sam's task here to make certain that the message *did* get through.

Or would that change history? Without knowing what Bradford had uncovered, he had no way of knowing which way history would be affected by the delivery or nondelivery of the message. That was one of the great perils of Leaping: there were so many ways to screw up, and sometimes Sam had no idea whether his actions would have positive or adverse effects until afterward.

Still, given the situation as it now stood, what real options did Sam have? He had little choice but to agree, and that way discover what the message was. Then he could confer with Al and decide what was to be done about it. "I give you my word," he said carefully. "I will do my best to ensure that your message reaches General Woodhull."

Bradford sighed with relief. "Excellent. Samuel, you're a good man. I know that this will be very risky for you. Now, this is too sensitive to be written down. If the British or any Tory sympathizer should discover such a message on your person, you'd be shot as a spy. So pay careful attention and memorize what I'm about

144

to tell you." He leaned forward in his seat, lowering his voice to lessen even further any chance that they would be overheard.

"The British are committing themselves to winning the upcoming battle. They understand the strategic sense and morale involved in possessing the most important city in the Colonies. They are determined that New York and Nassau Island will remain in their hands. General Tryon is even now gathering his forces. They will number in excess of a thousand men, almost all trained and well armed. We all know that Colonel Smith's militia is a volunteer group, patchily armed and untrained. Without reinforcements from some regular army, they will not stand a chance in the upcoming fight."

None of this was news to Sam, and wouldn't really have been that surprising to Samuel. "I know we're badly outnumbered and outgunned," he agreed. "But that is not all that counts in a battle. There's the will to win and level of commitment, in both of which I think we beat the British."

"If that were all, I might be inclined to agree with you," Bradford replied. "But there is more. General Clinton is on his way to Southampton even as we talk, and is bringing two and a half thousand men. The idea is to form a pincer movement. In charge of the fight for the Colonies is Brigadier General Nathaniel Greene. If Greene somehow wins the first battle, his troops will then face Clinton's men advancing behind them. Clinton's troops will be fresh and will undoubtedly have the advantage. Smith and Greene must not be caught between the two forces, or we will have a massacre on our hands."

"That makes matters a lot worse," agreed Sam thoughtfully.

"There's more. I have seen copies of orders that say twenty-five British warships are under sail at this moment. They are expected to make Sag Harbor any day now. When they arrive, that will sway the balance of power so strongly in the British favor that we will be doomed."

Sam recalled that Sag Harbor was one of the larger ports. Twenty-five ships would carry a large number of troops, and if they were to combine with Clinton's men, it would create an impressive army at the Rebels' rear. "Then what can be done?" he asked.

"General Woodhull must commit his troops to this battle," Bradford answered. "The forces of General Tryon must be stopped, and then Sag Harbor must be reinforced, to prevent the British from landing. If those warships make harbor, Nassau Island is doomed to fall into their hands. That has to be prevented at all costs."

Sam nodded. "That makes sense. I'll do my very best to ensure that this message gets through to him. You can rely on me."

"Good man." Bradford smiled, and puffed on his pipe. "I'll be off in the morning to Southampton, to see if I can gather any further insight into what the British are planning. Nathan here will be about, ready to bring any further messages to you. As soon as you can, you should return to your farm. Nathan will contact you there with any further news."

"But what about my militia service?"

"Let that go, man," Bradford insisted. "This information-gathering is far more important to our cause."

To the cause, perhaps. But what about to Isaiah Watts? If Sam wasn't there to protect him, who knew what changes that might eventually make in the war? Or beyond? The problem was that Bradford could see only the present, and not the possible consequences to the future. "I'll do what I can," Sam promised.

"We can ask no more," Durham agreed. "Thank you, Samuel. Your work will be greatly appreciated. This is vital to the defense of our country."

"It's too late for me to start home tonight," Sam said. "I'll rest here, and set off at daybreak. Then, as soon as I've finished up at home, I'll head out to join the militia. That should be tomorrow afternoon." He frowned. "What is the date now?"

"The twenty-fifth," Durham replied.

Talk about cutting it close! The Battle of Brooklyn began on the twenty-seventh, Sam knew. If he were to deliver his message, it would have to be done very fast indeed. Where had the time gone? Farm chores, mostly. The days flew too quickly. "I'll hurry," he vowed. Standing, he nodded to the two men. "Good night, and good luck."

"Good night," replied Bradford, shaking his hand. "And Godspeed."

Sam entered the room that Mary had prepared for him. Talk about a complicated Leap! This one was putting him through an emotional wringer. He was a wreck already, and the pressure was hardly likely to let up. He pulled off his boots, then lay back on the bed. He felt bone weary. He wasn't used to riding a horse, and had done so much of it in the past week. His backside ached from it all. His muscles ached from the farm labor, and his heart ached over Hannah.

Still, according to Al, she had finally decided that Sam had been right, and was ready to forgive him and make it up to him when he got home. In one way, that was wonderful. He was happy that the breach had been mended. On the other hand, if Al was right, she aimed to make his homecoming tomorrow a very special one. And that could get very difficult indeed. It was all very well for Al to advocate bedding Hannah and forgetting the moral implications, but Sam couldn't do that.

No matter how much he wanted to.

Well, he'd have to deal with that problem when he ran into it. Meanwhile, he'd gained several new ones. First of all, the fact that he'd agreed to deliver Bradford's message. The spy was right, and the information he'd gained might well mark the difference between winning and losing Nassau Island for the Colonies.

The trouble was that Sam *knew* from his history that the British *did* take the island in the upcoming battle. If Sam kept his word and delivered the message, and if General Woodhull believed him, then Sam might be instrumental in changing the course of history.

And then what would happen? Would the British, determined to regain the island, commit even more troops to the battle? Would they bring over so many mercenaries and soldiers that they might actually win the war? Or would taking New York City so inspire the Revolutionaries that they might win the War of Independence even faster?

Could Sam chance either event happening?

He was almost certain that his Leaps were meant to affect only the lives of individual people, and not to rewrite history. And yet. . . . Hadn't he saved the life of Jackie Kennedy, when in his original history line she'd been murdered by Lee Harvey Oswald? That wasn't exactly a minor change in history. Who could possibly know what the result of that action had been? Sam had no real idea, since he hadn't had a chance to go back to his own time and see the effects, but he doubted that it was unaltered by the life of such an important person.

148

Perhaps he *was* here to change the history of the Revolutionary War after all.

Or was he simply getting delusions of grandeur now?

His head was starting to hurt from all of this speculation. The problem was that he had no real information either way. It was nothing but a huge pile of "what ifs." And there was yet another one. What if Isaiah Watts was killed in the Battle of Brooklyn because Samuel Beckett wasn't around to save his life? How would that alter his mission? How would it alter history?

How would Sam feel, knowing he could have saved a man's life but had failed to do so?

No matter how he thought about the quandary he was in, it refused to get any clearer. It seemed that no matter what he did, he'd be letting somebody down and maybe fouling up this Leap. This was one of the murkiest tangles he'd been involved in yet.

There was a flash of light, and Al appeared. He flicked the ash from his cigar. It vanished before hitting the floor. "So, how did the meeting go?"

"Wonderfully," Sam said bitterly. "It's given me even more to worry about." He sketched out what he had heard from Bradford. As he did so, Al's frown deepened.

"Jeez," he muttered when Sam finished. "This isn't good."

"That's what I told you. The question is, what can I do about this information?"

"Nothing," Al said emphatically. "We know that Woodhull never got it, so you daren't deliver it."

"That's the whole point. We don't know that he didn't get it. We just know he didn't act on it. Maybe Samuel was supposed to deliver the message and it was destined to be ignored."

"We don't know that," Al objected.

"The trouble is that we don't know *anything*," Sam complained. "I don't have the slightest clue as to what I should do here. I need information. Why don't you give the message to Samuel in the Waiting Room, and see what he'd do with it?"

"No way," Al replied firmly. "Suppose you Leap out of here in five minutes, and Samuel returns? Then he knows there's this message he's supposed to deliver. What's he going to do? Deliver it, that's what. And he could change history by doing that."

"How do you know we're not here to do just that?"

"To change history?" Al shook his head. "That's not our job."

"Al," Sam said, "we don't *know* what our job is. We're just doing what we *think* we should be doing. What Ziggy predicts we should be doing. So why don't you ask Ziggy what *she* thinks I should do?"

"That's simple enough," agreed Al. He tapped in some information on the handlink. He winced as he read the reply. "Ziggy basically agrees with me—forget any notion of changing history. I kind of rephrased that a bit. You don't want to know what her original words were."

"How can she be so sure?" asked Sam.

"She can't be *sure*. She works on probabilities, after all. But she still says that saving Isaiah should be your priority here. You can't deliver this message, Sam."

Disturbed, Sam chewed at his lower lip. "Al, I gave my word I'd do my best to deliver it. I can't just turn my back on that."

"You can't do anything else, Sam. If you do, you could alter every event in history. Something this big would have incredible repercussions. There are so many variables that even Ziggy can't estimate them all. You might rewrite history so that the British stomp out the Minutemen, and hang George Washington. What would that do to our world? What would it do to the Project? If the Brits kept control of America, *everything* would alter. You can't chance it, Sam. You've got to forget about ever hearing that message.''

Sam sighed. ''I know that. But can I simply turn my back on things at this stage in the game? I wish I knew.''

Al nodded. ''You're confused. I know that. Look, I'll go back and have a real serious talk with Gooshie and Ziggy about this. We'll run every projection we can think of overnight. Just don't make any decisions about this till I get back, okay?''

''Okay,'' Sam agreed. ''But unless you can come up with something real strong, I can't just walk away from this mission. It's too important. It might save thousands of lives. Or it might change the whole course of human events. I just wish I knew what would happen.''

''So do I,'' agreed Al, very soberly. ''So do I.''

CHAPTER

FOURTEEN

By morning, Sam still had made no decision. He'd spent a restless night struggling with the problems that faced him, but could see no real solutions to any of them. It appeared that no matter what he did, someone would suffer. And there was no way of telling which problem he was here to fix—except to guess. But in matters of this importance, how could he afford to guess?

He took his leave of Havens early in the morning. Then he rode hard, heading home. At this time of the morning, with the dew still fresh and a slight ground mist playing about, everything seemed so crisp and fresh. It was very hard to realize that some sixty miles away, two forces were even now drawing into position for a battle that would begin in just over twenty-four hours. A battle that Sam didn't know whether to join.

Old Flighty, for once, seemed to sense urgency in Sam's mood, and responded admirably. There were virtually no other travelers abroad this early in the day, and Sam had the roads mostly to himself. Ignoring distractions, he managed quite a respectable speed.

Al popped in beside him for a few minutes. "In a hurry?" he asked.

"There's so much to be done," said Sam, concentrating on the road. "Did you get anything useful for me yet?"

"No," Al admitted reluctantly. "Ziggy's hoping for some predictions in an hour or so. She's complaining about the huge number of variables she's got to juggle here, but I think that she's secretly kinda pleased to be asked to predict another outcome for the Revolutionary War. But you know how she is about making mistakes."

"What about Samuel?" asked Sam. "Get anywhere with him?"

"Dr. Beeks is still working on him." Al grimaced. "He's still thinking the whole thing might be a British trick to get him to talk. But Verbeena is doing a great job, I gotta say. Even if she still won't let me in the Waiting Room."

Al shook his head. "Can't you slow down? Whipping past the trees like this is giving me a headache."

"Sorry," Sam answered, insincerely. "I've got to get back to Hannah, and then on to Brooklyn. I can't afford to slow down."

"In which case, I'll go on ahead and meet you at the house," Al decided. "At least that stays in one spot. Be seeing you."

Alone again, Sam concentrated on the ride. He was no Paul Revere, but he was making respectable time on these shoddy roads. He had to stop to rest his horse for a while somewhere near Patchogue. Then he turned away from the shore and north toward the farm. Most of the way was through woodlands, but he did skirt Lake Ronkonkoma, the largest body of freshwater on the island, as he approached the Beckett farm.

153

And then he was back, reining in outside the house. He led Old Flighty into the barn and removed his saddle. The poor horse had worked up a sweat, so Sam began to rub him down.

There was a flicker in the light from the doorway, and then Hannah rushed in. "Samuel!" she exclaimed happily. "I was so worried when you didn't come home last night!" She threw herself onto him from behind, hugging him tightly and kissing the back of his neck.

It felt wonderful, but Sam tried to steel himself to resist the feelings. "I couldn't get back. I've been charged with a very important mission." Then he smiled. "You seem to have had a change of heart."

"That I have," she agreed, releasing him. She stared at the ground. "Samuel, I'm a wicked, uncaring, unfair woman. I don't know why you put up with me at all. I'm sorry for everything I've said to you these past few days, and I can only beg you to forgive me." She sounded very miserable and contrite.

Sam couldn't bear it. "There's no need to apologize," he told her, clasping her chin and forcing her to look up again. "I know why you were angry, and you would have been right to be so if I'd done what you believed I had."

"But you *didn't*!" she exclaimed. "And I refused to listen to your explanation. Samuel, I'm so sorry."

"Then let's just forget about it," Sam suggested. "It's all past, and we'll not speak of it again."

Hannah smiled widely and threw her arms around him again. "Ah, it's no wonder that I love you so much, Samuel. I deserve to be beaten, not forgiven."

"Don't be silly." Sam struggled free. "Now, let me see to Old Flighty before he collapses from hunger. He deserves better treatment than that."

Hannah stared at him. "Did you have any breakfast?"

"No," admitted Sam. "I was in too much of a hurry to get home."

"Hah!" she snapped, her eyes blazing. "Then I shall see to it that you have the best possible breakfast. You deserve it—and need it." She grinned wickedly. "You'll be needing all of your strength today."

Uh-oh. It sounded as if Al had been right in his reading of her reactions. Tempting as the offer was, Sam couldn't get caught up in that. "We'll see," he said, in a noncommittal fashion. "The breakfast as a starter sounds great."

She kissed the tip of his nose. "I'll get right to work," she promised, and hurried off.

As Sam bent back to seeing to the horse, Al's voice called, "What did I tell you?" He stepped through the stable wall, making Old Flighty buck and neigh until Sam calmed him down.

"Don't forget that animals can see you," Sam complained. As he measured out oats for the horse, he added, "And, yes, you were right. It looks like Hannah is all set for a grand reunion."

Al grinned wickedly. "Well, you know what they say: lay back and think of England. Or is that appropriate under the circumstances?" He shrugged. "This is one of those days when I envy you."

"Don't," Sam replied. "I've no intention of taking advantage of Hannah."

"She may not give you a choice. She's one tough-minded woman, if you ask me."

"I have to get to Brooklyn, remember? The battle starts tomorrow, and once it's begun, I won't be able to get through the lines with my message. I *have* to leave today, and the sooner the better."

"If you've got time for breakfast, you've got time for dessert," Al commented. "And, boy—what a dish!"

"Stop that! I'm not going to do it, and that's that."

"Well, I hope Hannah believes you." Al studied his cigar thoughtfully. "I'll just stick around to see how it turns out."

Sam frowned, but he could tell that Al wasn't going to vanish, no matter what. Having finished tending to Old Flighty, he set off for the house. His stomach was insisting that it was definitely his turn for food.

As she'd promised, Hannah had made a large meal for him—pancakes, eggs, and thick, salted bacon, with more of the rough bread and butter. Sam ate happily, washing it down with a glass of cider. Hannah pecked a little at her own, smaller plate, but Sam could see that she had other things than food on her mind.

Unfortunately, so did he, and his purposes were not in sync with hers. "I'm afraid I have to leave you again," he told her as he polished up the last of the food with a hunk of bread. "I have an important message to deliver to your uncle today."

"I understand, Samuel," she replied, removing the dishes. "It's to do with the upcoming battle?"

"Yes." He sighed. "I wish I could tell you more, but I can't. All I can say is that the message I carry could alter the whole future of our country."

"Then you'd best deliver it," she answered, returning to his side. "As soon as Old Flighty is ready to be ridden again." Her lips twitched. "Which should be within the hour, I'd say. And that means you have some time to waste. . . ." She grabbed him before he could move, and backed him against the nearest wall.

"Atta boy. Go for it!" Al added from somewhere in the room.

156

Sam didn't know what to do as Hannah pressed against him. "Uh, this may not be the best time . . . ," he protested, fighting off her hands.

"It may be the *only* time," she contradicted him. "Who knows when it will be safe for you to return to me, Samuel?" She glared at him with mock severity. "Stop all this fussing, Samuel. I'm a very determined woman, and I'll have my way this day, whatever has gotten into you."

Sam believed it, too. His body was quite certain that he didn't want to fight her off, and his mind was starting to lose the battle. The one thing right now that he *wanted* to do was exactly what Hannah had in mind, and be damned with the consequences.

Except . . . he simply couldn't. It would be wrong.

"Hannah," he gasped, squirming to extricate himself, "Hannah! There's something I've got to tell you."

"It can wait," she murmured, pressing against him.

"No, it can't," Sam insisted, on the verge of panic. "I *really* have to tell you this."

"Tell me in bed," she replied. "Afterward."

"No. It can't wait."

Hannah gave an exasperated sigh, and let him push her away. "Whatever ails you, Samuel Beckett? You've been acting so strangely these past few days. I swear, I don't know what has gotten into you." But she giggled, and started to unlace her dress.

"Don't *do* that," Sam begged, batting at her hands. "Please, Hannah, just listen to me. It really is very important."

She scowled. "You're a very frustrating man some days, Samuel."

"I'm worse than that," Sam replied. "Look, Hannah,

I know you're going to find this difficult to believe, but I'm not the person you think I am.''

"Sam!'' Al exclaimed. "No! You shouldn't tell her that!''

Hannah looked puzzled. "You have some dark, hidden secret? Something that you have to reveal to me at this very moment, Samuel? Can't it wait?''

"No,'' Sam answered. "You see . . .''

There was a sudden sound from outside, and Sam broke off. He had heard a horse. Could it be that in his haste he'd not closed the stable properly? Or did they have visitors? "Damn,'' he muttered. Either way, he had to check before he continued to explain to Hannah who he really was. Sam hated having to try and explain Project Quantum Leap to anyone, because it sounded so farfetched. But to Hannah—who didn't have the vaguest notions about physics or the concept of time travel? Still, what choice did he have? If he couldn't make her believe him, then she was determined to bed him. . . .

"I'd better see what the noise was,'' he told her. "I'll only be a minute.''

"Good,'' she said, firmly. "We have some unfinished business you'd best pay attention to.''

Sam sighed and headed for the door. He wasn't getting through to her. He strode outside, and then stopped, scowling at the sight that greeted him.

Townsend, Kirk, Morgan, and several other members of the Committee of Safety were there, all astride horses. Their eyes narrowed as they saw him.

"What is this?'' Sam demanded. "I thought I'd told you I was done with your Committee.''

"Maybe you are, Samuel Beckett,'' replied Townsend grimly. "But this Committee is not done with you. You stand accused of treason and conspiracy, and you shall face your judgment.''

''What are you talking about?'' Sam demanded. There was a sinking feeling in his stomach; the Committee had the air of a lynch mob about them.

''James?'' prompted Townsend.

Morgan sat forward in his saddle, a smug expression on his twisted features. ''Yesterday, I followed you as you rode from here, Samuel Beckett,'' he said. ''And I saw you yester evening consorting with a known traitor and British spy, William Bradford. There were several others who witnessed this, so there is no point in your denying it.''

''And so, Samuel Beckett,'' Townsend intoned, ''it is the opinion of this Committee of Safety that you also are a spy and a traitor, in the pay of the British, and a danger to all right-thinking men of this country.''

''You don't know what you're talking about,'' Sam said angrily. ''That accusation is ridiculous.''

''Careful, Sam,'' said Al, who'd walked through the wall to stand beside him. ''These nozzles look like they're ready to hang you, not start a debating club.''

Sam didn't need Al's warning on that score. He was already tense and prepared for action. It was quite clear that Kirk, Morgan, and Townsend had discovered their way to get the rest of the Committee onto Sam's case. The problem was that Sam couldn't explain to anyone—least of all this pack of vultures—the truth behind his meeting. ''This is my land,'' he said, coldly. ''Get off it now.''

''We'll not listen to you.'' Kirk spat, prodding his horse several paces closer. ''You have to answer for your crimes, Samuel Beckett.''

''What crimes?'' Sam snapped. ''I've done nothing

wrong, and I won't be intimidated by the likes of you.''

There was a sound from the house, and Hannah emerged. Her dress was fully laced again, and she frowned. "What is it, Samuel?" she asked. "What is going on?''

''Go back inside, Hannah,'' Sam said, turning to her. ''This isn't your concern.''

That was a mistake, and Sam realized it almost as soon as he'd turned. Morgan seized his chance, and his whip was in the air instantly. It cracked, and whirled toward Sam.

He couldn't move out of its path with Hannah standing directly behind him. If it missed him, it would flay her instead. With only a second to think about it, Sam did the only thing he could—he threw himself into the path of the whip.

By doing so, he moved inside the deadly weighted tip, avoiding its slicing into his skin. The bulk of the whip, however, slammed across his shoulders. He barely avoided a scream of agony as fire jumped from shoulder to shoulder. Wincing, he fastened his hand about the whip and jerked forward.

Morgan was prepared for this, and didn't let go of the handle. Instead, he crowded his horse forward, intending to ram it against Sam. Sam released the whip and ducked under Morgan's outstretched arm, flinching at the pain that burned across his back as he did so. He brought his right arm up, striking at Morgan above him, punching hard. Morgan howled with pain as the blow caught him in the small of his back.

And then a rope settled over Sam's upraised arm, and it was jerked. Sam, his arm a pillar of pain, was hauled backward and to the ground. He slammed down hard, knocking the wind from his lungs. Dazedly, he saw that

Kirk held the other end of the rope that had tightened about his wrist.

Sam struggled to regain his feet, but Kirk backed his horse up, dragging Sam away from the house. Shaking his head to clear it, Sam heard Hannah scream. He tried to focus in on the sound, and saw her dive back into the house. Good, she'd be safer there. Let the men concentrate on him instead.

He managed to scramble to his feet. His entire back was a mass of pain now, and the circulation was being cut off in his wrist. He tried to free his hand, but Townsend slammed his horse against Sam. The blow sent Sam to the ground again, and he hit the baked earth hard. His head shook, and he couldn't focus.

"Sam!" he heard Al yell at him. "You gotta get up! They'll kill you if you don't fight back!"

Like he wasn't already aware of this? What did he think Sam was doing? Angry, confused, and hurting, Sam tried to get back to his feet as another horse slammed into him, sending him rolling in agony again.

"Leave him alone, you animals!" screamed Hannah. Sam's vision was very blurred, but he could see that she'd emerged again from the house, this time carrying Samuel's musket. He wasn't surprised that she would know how to shoot—she was a very capable lady, after all. But the gun had only one bullet, and against a gang like this it would do little good.

"No!" he cried. "Hannah, don't!"

But it was too late. As he struggled to get back to his feet, he saw, dimly, Morgan's arm draw back as he prepared another strike with his whip.

There was a loud report as the musket went off.

Morgan screamed, and the whip went flying in a spray of his blood.

There was a second shot—a *second* shot? For an instant, Sam couldn't understand it, but then he heard Hannah scream and saw her spin around, redness on her shoulder.

"Hannah!" he cried in panic. He regained his feet, blind rage wiping away much of the pain he felt. But it was no good. Another horse slammed into him, and then something hard came down on his back. All the paths of pain flared up again as he lay on the ground.

"Sam!" Al cried urgently. "Get up! You've got to get up! Hannah's been shot! You've got to help her!"

Save her? Much as he wanted to, there was no way Sam could go to her aid. He could barely twitch a muscle. Struggling inside, he attempted to overcome all the agony he was suffering, but it was no good.

Something heavy crashed into the back of his head, and everything went very, very black.

CHAPTER
FIFTEEN

Everything had happened so fast that Al wasn't the only one who froze. The moment after Sam fell, nobody moved a muscle. Then Al bent over him, frantically waving a hand through his face.

"Sam," he begged, "Sam, don't be out cold. Not now!" But he knew it was a vain hope. The musket butt that had slammed into the back of Sam's head had been all too solid. Sam was out of action for several hours, at the very least. Which left the situation in a very difficult state. Al straightened up and stared across at where Hannah lay by the door, blood flowing from her shoulder. "Ziggy!" Al snapped. "Zero in on Hannah. How's she doing?"

"Not well," came Ziggy's pleasant tones. Even though she was a computer, there was no missing the concern in her voice. "She is likely to die if no action is taken."

"Damn," muttered Al, striding across the yard toward her. There was absolutely nothing he could do to help her. He was unable to interact with her in any way, and Sam was the only one who could even see him.

Then the assembled men broke out of whatever spell had held them. "Get him on a horse," Townsend commanded, gesturing toward Sam's limp body. "We'd best be out of here."

"But what about his wife?" objected one of the other riders. "She needs medical attention."

"She's not our concern," Kirk snarled. "She shouldn't have interfered. She got what she deserved."

The objector shook his head. "I never agreed to ride with you to make war on women," he replied. "If Sam'l Beckett is a traitor, then I say he should stand trial. But no one has accused his wife of any ill dealings. I'll not see her die."

Townsend whirled his horse about, seeing that one of his other riders had slung Sam across the front of his saddle. "Do as you will, George Burke. But we'll have none of you if you help the wife of a traitor."

"Better that than her death on my conscience," Burke answered, climbing down from his horse. "You . . . *patriots* . . . had better leave, if helping a woman to live is too hard on your stomachs."

"Fool!" Townsend glared at the rest of the riders. "If anyone else feels that way about a traitor's whore, he'd better stay, too. The rest of you, ride with me." Setting his knees to his horse, he headed away from the house.

Al glanced at the Committee members. Several looked back at Burke with anguish on their faces, but only one other man stayed when the rest rode away. He called down to Burke, "I'll fetch a medic as fast as possible, George. I'm with you on this."

"Good man, Isaac." Burke then ignored him, hurrying over to where Hannah lay. Al followed Burke, determined to see what would be done. There was, after

164

all, nothing he could do to help Sam right now.

Al could see that the wound was a serious one. The blood was bright against Hannah's skin, and there was blood pooling under her. The shot must have cut clean through her shoulder. It hadn't touched anything vital, but it wouldn't have to, from the amount of blood she was losing. Burke was not exactly skilled, but he'd obviously had some experience in the past in treating cuts—probably his farm animals. Cursing to himself, he worked on cleaning the wound and then stanching the flow of blood. He dressed the wound as well as he could, using cloth he found in the house. Unwilling to risk opening the wound again by moving her, he put a pillow under her head and draped a blanket over her to keep her warm.

Al had watched the whole thing without a word. With a groan, he straightened up. "What do you think?" he asked Ziggy.

"She appears to be stabilized for now," the computer answered. "It would have been preferable for Dr. Beckett to have dressed her wound, but this man performed adequately. If medical help arrives shortly—and if it is of at least minimal skill—then she should live. I estimate the odds in favor of her as being approximately sixty-eight percent."

"Well, that's something," Al muttered. He then realized he was hearing a sound that had been going on for a while, but he hadn't focused on it. "Jeez, the baby's crying."

"That is hardly surprising," Ziggy commented, "considering the level of distracting sound for the past fifteen minutes."

Fifteen minutes? Was that all it had been? It had seemed like hours to Al. He strode through the walls of the house and into the bedroom. Little Daniel was bawling his young lungs out. "Sorry, kid," Al apologized. "There's nothing much I can do to help you." He winced. "I *hate* noisy kids. I gotta get outta here."

"An admirable, if somewhat cowardly, decision," Ziggy approved. "I will continue to monitor the situation here, Admiral Calavicci, and if anything changes, I will alert you."

"Okay." Al considered his options. "Sam's been abducted, Hannah's been shot, and Watts is off fighting for his country. And I can't do a damned thing about it. I think it's time I had a little chat with Samuel."

"Dr. Beeks might not agree," Ziggy pointed out, as Al returned to the Imaging Chamber door and left the room.

"Dr. Beeks can kiss my . . . anywhere she pleases," Al muttered. He strode down the corridor that linked the Imaging Chamber to the Waiting Room, ignoring the technicians he passed. He was determined to listen to none of her theories this time around.

He had reached the Waiting Room now, and saw Verbeena standing there, her face tense. "Sam's been abducted, and Hannah's been shot," he said brusquely. "And right now I'm not worried about possibly altering the past by talking with Samuel. He's the only one who might be able to add something constructive to this lousy situation, and I'm gonna talk to him. I mean it Verbeena."

"I know, Al," the psychologist replied. "I'm as concerned with Dr. Beckett's welfare as you are. I concur with your decision to speak with Samuel. It may be the only way."

"Oh." Al hadn't been expecting this easy compliance, and it left his mounting anger and apprehension without a solid target. "Right." He tapped his access code on the door panel. Striding in, he checked to see that Samuel Beckett was away from the door and that Dr. Beeks had followed him through before closing it firmly behind him. Now would not be a good time to lose the transfer subject. "Keep quiet," he said softly, before Verbeena could speak.

"You again!" yelled Beckett, hurrying over to him. "Are you in charge here? What are you doing to me? I demand that you release me at once, so that I may return home to my wife!"

"It's not that simple," Al protested, stepping back. It was astonishing how much the man looked like Sam. His hair was darker, and his face a little chubbier, but the resemblance was uncanny. For this Leap, Sam wouldn't have really needed the masking effect of the aura to help convince people he was Samuel Beckett. The problem was that this worked in reverse, and it would be easy to forget that he wasn't really dealing with Sam himself. This man was two hundred years antique in his thinking, and he had zero grasp on the realities of what was involved. "It's not up to me when you go home."

"Then contact your superiors," Samuel snapped. "Get them to agree to release me. I must be with my wife and country at this time."

"Look, you've got my honest sympathy. And if I could, I'd gladly send you back." Al glanced upward, wishing that God or Fate or whatever was behind this would suddenly switch Sam and Samuel. "But even if I could, It wouldn't help. You wouldn't go home, you'd just trade places with Sam again. And he's in no position to help anyone right now."

"What are you talking about?"

Al winced. Naturally, Verbeena had explained virtually nothing about Leaping to Samuel. Al did his best to give the poor slob a rundown on what had happened so far. Dr. Beeks stood behind him, clucking in irritation as he did so, but at least she didn't stop him. "The man who's taken your place has been captured," Al finished. "If you were to switch back right now, you'd be a captive."

"You're lying!" Beckett replied, but Al could see that his confidence had been shaken.

"Why the heck would I lie about this?" asked Al, exasperated. "Listen, bozo, I'd *love* to be rid of you. All you've done is to complicate everything for me. If you'd just *helped* a little more, a lot of this could have been avoided. But now, Sam's been whacked over the head and your wife has been shot. Both of them are in serious trouble, and all you can do is kvetch at me. Now, shape up and start talking if you really want to help Hannah."

Samuel stared at him, anger and pain on his features. He hesitated, obviously caught in a dilemma. Clearly, he was still not about to trust Al or anyone at the Project, but he did at least understand that making demands loudly wasn't going to get him anywhere. Finally, a little more quietly, he said, "I will not betray my trust to help a man who cannot convince me he is not my enemy."

"Boy," muttered Al. "How can I possibly convince you that you're not being fooled by the Brits? Okay, tell me—what would make you believe that everything I've said is true?"

"Send me back."

"Listen, I've just told you that's impossible!" Al yelled. "It's not up to me. You don't get to go home until Sam's done whatever it is he's supposed to do in your place."

Samuel swallowed and appeared to be composing himself with great difficulty. "Please," he said, "bear with me. I will try and make *my* position clear to you. Let me see if I understand the situation correctly. You say that I am in the future, and that my place has been taken in my own time by a man who is my own descendant, correct?"

"Right."

Samuel nodded. "A man who looks so much like me that even my own wife cannot tell us apart." He frowned. "Surely you can understand the anguish that this causes me, especially when I think of her cozying up to this man in my stead?"

"Yeah, I can see that this might be a bummer," agreed Al.

"Now, suppose for a moment that I accept that your preposterous tale of the two of us somehow being switched is true," Samuel continued. "You then tell me that this Sam Beckett is in my guise to perform some action that I would or could not, and that it is for my own good that he will do this."

"Or the good of others," Al added.

"As you say," agreed Samuel. "But you do not know what this action is, and you do not know why I would or could not do it, and you cannot say when it will happen. You do not know what will cause Sam Beckett and myself to switch back to our rightful places again, or when it might occur. You have some . . . thinking machine . . . that is making gambler's odds for or against certain causes of action, but even it cannot fathom what must be done. Then you tell me that I alone can help by providing you with information—information that I would rather die than provide to my foes. Can you not see how difficult it is for me to accept that your story is true?''

Al paced the Waiting Room in frustration. "Look, I know it's hard to believe," he agreed. "But try some very definite facts. One, your wife's been shot, and she needs help. The best possible help is Sam, because he's a doctor in *this* time period, which means he's two hundred years up on whatever quacks and leeches you guys are used to. Two, if anything happens to Sam—like those jackasses kill him or something—then you're *never* going back. You can go back only if Sam Leaps, and he won't be Leaping if he's dead. *Cappish?* Three, if anything happens to both Hannah and Sam, then your kid doesn't have much chance of a life. Four, Sam's been given a message that he's supposed to deliver to General Woodhull, one that might change the course of the war for you. He can't do that if he's Townsend's prisoner. So, even if my story's a bit hard to swallow, *try*, for God's sake. And for Hannah's sake. And Sam's sake. And Daniel's sake. And the whole bloody war's sake. Try!''

He could see the confusion and suspicion on Samuel's face as the man struggled with all of the facts and worries that filled him. Dr. Beeks tapped Al on the shoulder.

"It might be best to allow him to think about this for a while," she suggested. "It has to be very hard for him." She turned and left the Waiting Room.

Al hated the thought of more delay, but her suggestion made sense. "Okay," he said, in as kindly a fashion as he could manage. "We'll talk again in a while." He started to turn to leave, punching in his code to open the door.

"All right," agreed Samuel, his voice choking. "And—I'm sorry."

Hearing the catch in Samuel's tone, Al started to turn back. As he did, Samuel's fist caught him across the chin. Pain lanced through him as he staggered back, dropping the handlink and flailing to regain his balance. The fact that there was regret in the look that Samuel shot at him as he fled didn't help at all.

Then a wall hit him in the back, and Al groaned, sliding to the floor. "Ziggy!" he yelled, and then wished he'd spoken a little softer. His jaw was on fire. "Samuel's out. Sound the intruder alarm and get him back—in one piece." He rubbed at his jaw, wincing with pain. "Then get me a medic. I'm getting too old for this kind of thing."

"Understood," agreed Ziggy, and Al heard the blare of the general alarm sounding throughout the warren that was Project Quantum Leap.

In a second, Verbeena was back in the Waiting Room. She knelt beside Al and cautiously examined him. "Admiral" she said, "what will happen if Samuel sees—" Al cut her off.

"There is nothing we can do except get him back. Pronto." Al lay back, groaning. So far, just about everything that could get screwed up with this Leap had happened. The only thing that hadn't happened was Ziggy crashing.

Some days weren't worth getting out of bed. Especially a bed shared with Tina. Al wished he'd called in sick this morning. He certainly felt pretty sick right now.

Tina was on her way to a meeting with Donna when the alarms began to blare. She winced; the noise always went through her like nails scraping on a chalkboard. "What's wrong, Ziggy?" she asked.

"Samuel Beckett has escaped from the Waiting

171

Room," the computer replied. "He punched Admiral Calavicci."

"Al? Is he okay?"

"I suspect he is malingering. And feeling sorry for himself." If the computer had shoulders, she'd have been shrugging them about now. "It's a human trait."

"One you share often enough," muttered Tina. She glanced down the empty corridor. "Where is Samuel now?"

"Heading in your general direction," the computer replied. "If you continue along your present path, you will intercept his flight." There was the slightest of pauses. "As will one of the security guards, so there is no need to hurry."

No need to hurry? Tina set off like a rocket. Samuel might be making a break for it, thinking in his confusion that he was a prisoner of the British, but he would not be prepared for what he'd encounter. Major culture shock was incipient if she didn't get him back to the Waiting Room fast. He might already have seen too much.

Imagine the consequences if Samuel Beckett returned to the eighteenth century with knowledge of the twenty-first. . . . He *had* to be contained!

Tina skidded around the bend in the corridor, in time to see Samuel dashing toward her—and an armed security guard between them.

"Stay where you are!" the guard yelled, his revolver out and pointing, his feet braced for trouble. "You've got three seconds."

"No!" Tina yelled. Samuel might realize that the guard in front of him was holding a weapon, but she wasn't willing to bet on it. The modern revolver didn't

172

look much like the pistols of Samuel's day. "Don't shoot!"

Distracted by her order, the guard half-turned. Samuel closed the gap between them, and shouldered the startled guard aside. Tina moved to block his path, and he slowed his pace.

"Out of my way, if you please," Samuel gasped. "I must be free, but I do not wish to strike a lady." He made a move to dash past her, but he was human. He couldn't help staring. Tina was dressed, as usual, in a bright, short, tight, lowcut dress. And Samuel was from a period when showing an ankle was considered daring. . . .

Tina struck out with the side of her hand, short and sharp to Samuel's stomach. Gasping, he doubled over, and she brought her hand down again on his neck. With a groan, Samuel collapsed. Tina raised an eyebrow as she stood over him. "I ain't no lady," she said. "And that's for punching Al." She glanced up at the guard, who was walking over to her.

"I'll take over now, Ms. Martinez-O'Farrell," the man said apologetically. "I'll see he's returned to the Waiting Room safely."

An idea slid into Tina's head. She bent over the dazed Samuel. "Do you still think you're a prisoner of the British?" she demanded.

"Who else?" asked Samuel, wincing in pain.

Tina held her hand out to the guard. "Give me your gun," she ordered.

"Huh?"

"Your gun—hand it over." A moment later the puzzled guard laid the weapon in her hand. Then she bent back to Samuel. "All right," she said. "Let's suppose we're the British, and you're correct. Why would we want to hold you here and question you?''

"To learn what I know of the Patriots' plans, to help you win the war,'' he answered. "You know that as well as I do.''

"Really?'' She held the revolver close to his face. "Take a look at this, fella.'' Samuel reluctantly dragged his eyes away from her ample cleavage to the proferred weapon. "I'll lay odds you've never seen a gun this sophisticated in your life. If we have guns like this, why would we need any information from you? We could walk over any army you could field with a few of these.''

Samuel stared at the weapon with concern, then disbelief. "That is no pistol,'' he finally said. "It could not be—so small and with no room for powder or shot.''

"It's all internal,'' Tina assured him. She glanced down the corridor. On the wall at the far end was a particularly ugly painting. She suspected that Al had hung it there. "See that picture? Watch.'' She raised the revolver and squeezed off a single shot. The sound of the gun in the narrow corridor was almost deafening, but Tina saw with satisfaction that she'd hit the painting dead center. "Now what do you say?''

Samuel's face was expressing a number of emotions, from shock to disbelief to shock again, and finally to something close to awe. "That *is* a weapon,'' he breathed.

"Yes,'' agreed Tina. She handed it back to the guard, who holstered it. "It can fire a number of times before it needs reloading. And it's a lot more accurate than any pistol you've ever fired. With that gun and a few clips of bullets, I could wipe out your whole army before it got within firing range of me. So—I repeat: Why would we need you to tell us anything?'' She smiled at him.

"Think about that while they take you back to the Waiting Room. Then, maybe, you'll be a bit more cooperative." She nodded to the guard. "He's all yours. I've got to go check on Admiral Calavicci." She headed down the corridor.

"I already told you that he's malingering," Ziggy commented.

"Maybe," agreed Tina. "But I've got a great bedside manner."

"So I've heard," the computer answered. She was obviously learning sarcasm.

CHAPTER
SIXTEEN

By the following morning, Al was almost boiling over with frustration and concern. Samuel had finally started talking—and it was proving almost impossible to get him to stop. Tina had spent the entire evening with him, much to Al's disgust, asking questions and gathering data. He suspected that more than a half of Samuel's newfound belief was based more on how much of Tina's charms he could see than on the logic of the pistol. The problem was that very little of what he was now saying was of any use. With Sam's capture, a lot of their options had been curtailed.

The fact that Sam still hadn't recovered from being knocked out bothered Al more than he wanted to admit. The blow had been pretty severe. Ziggy, constantly monitoring, insisted that Sam was not in grave danger—but why wouldn't he wake up?

He was on his third cigar of the early morning when Ziggy interrupted his brooding.

"I have finished calculating the changes that Dr. Beckett might create by revealing the information he gathered from his clandestine rendezvous," the computer announced.

"About time," Al said grouchily. "Anyone would think we were paying you by the hour."

"You are not paying me at all," Ziggy replied somewhat huffily. "And there were a considerable number of variables to include in my calculations."

"Okay, okay." Al waved aside her protests with his cigar. "So—what did you finally figure out?"

There was a slight pause. "Dr. Beckett isn't going to like this," Ziggy warned him.

"Then maybe I won't tell him," Al answered. "Quit stalling, and tell me what you've got." He swilled down the dregs of his now-cold breakfast coffee and made a face.

"The information will have absolutely no effect on the outcome of the war whatsoever."

Al scowled up at the ceiling. "It took you all this time to figure out that nothing will be changed?" he groused. "How do you figure that?"

"Dr. Beckett's capture has delayed all possible delivery of the message," Ziggy answered primly. "If he were somehow to escape immediately and contact General Woodhull, the Revolutionary forces are already committed to the Battle of Brooklyn—which has already begun. There are no troops left to even contemplate intercepting further British landings. Nothing that Dr. Beckett can do now will alter the outcome of the battle in any significant way."

"That's one load off my mind, at least," Al admitted grudgingly. "The thought of him screwing up our country's history was starting to give me the willies. So, where does that leave us?"

"Where we were before Dr. Beckett was given the

message. I still calculate the odds as being sixty percent that Dr. Beckett is there to save Isaac Watts; thirty percent that he is there to save Hannah Beckett; and ten percent that he is there to save Daniel Beckett.''

"Well, he's not doing anything at the moment," Al complained. He thought hard. "Okay, let's start doing the rounds, I guess." He strode to the door to the Imaging Chamber. "You'd better center me on Hannah to start with. That way, I can at least check on two of the three.''

"Of course," agreed Ziggy, opening the door for him. "It is a wise course of action."

"It's the only thing I can do," Al snapped. He clicked on the handlink and stood in the chamber. "Okay, do it.''

The room about him darkened and blurred, then came up again, bright and different. He seemed to be standing inside the Becketts' bedroom. In actuality, of course, he was still in the Imaging Chamber, and everything about him was no more than a hologram that he couldn't interact with in any way.

Al strode to the bed, where Hannah lay. He saw that she'd been undressed and that her shoulder had a bandage over it. Blood stained the cloth slightly, but Hannah seemed to be reasonably well. Al wished he knew more about medicine, but she looked to be out of danger. She was taking shallow, regular breaths, and she seemed to be a healthy enough color.

He crossed to the baby's crib and peered inside.

Empty.

"Uh-oh," he muttered. "Where's the brat?" He glanced around the bedroom, but it was obvious that he wasn't there. Shrugging, Al walked through the wall and into the house's main room.

There was a strange woman there, stirring broth over the fire with one hand, and holding Daniel to her hip with the other. The baby was making the soft cooing noises that always seemed to set women sighing happily and set Al's teeth on edge. This woman was no exception. She grinned down at Daniel.

"You're a bonny child, and no mistake," she said, rubbing her nose against his and making him produce further burbles of happiness. "Don't worry about your mother; she'll be fine in a few days, I promise you that." A cloud passed over her eyes. "If any of us are, that is," she added. "These are terrible times we live in, child. But you're too young to know about much other than your mother's milk and warmth, aren't you?"

"Well, it seems as though everything's under control here," Al commented. "What do you think, Ziggy?"

"The baby is certainly in good health," agreed the computer. "I am forced to revise my estimate down to five percent that Dr. Beckett is here to help him. And Hannah Beckett, though injured, seems to be sturdy and on the road to recovery. The medicine of this age may well be primitive, but it would appear to have been sufficient in this case. This means that it is most likely now that Dr. Beckett is here to save Isaac Watts."

"Yeah," agreed Al. "There aren't many more options. Any signs of Sam waking up yet?"

"Not at this time," Ziggy answered. "His breathing is regular, and he would appear to have made the transition into regular sleep. I will alert you when he recovers."

"Good." Al sighed. "Okay, Ziggy—orient me on Isaac Watts now. I may not be able to do anything, but at least I can see what's going on."

The scenery flickered about him, then changed completely.

Al had been to Brooklyn a number of times in his life, but he had never seen it like this. Instead of the built-up, run-down streets filled with cars and people, he was in open fields. All around were people, but they were not shoppers, petty crooks, or workmen. Many of them were no longer alive.

The sporadic sound of gunshots was mixed with the groans, moans, and curses of the injured and dying. What might have been pleasant fields to walk in of an evening were littered with wounded men. Al's experiences in Vietnam had steeled him to the sight of death during warfare, but he couldn't help feeling sorry for the victims all about him.

They were all obviously locals—many of them farmers, and almost all of them young. The dead had been abandoned where they had fallen, limbs sprawled in the mud, mouths gaping and buzzing with flies. Blood and water mingled beneath the battered corpses. Not all were dead, however. Without moving from the spot where he had materialized, Al could see three badly wounded men, none of whom had much chance of survival. One had lost the lower part of his right arm, presumably to a bayonet slash. A rough tourniquet had been applied, but judging from the redness of the dressing over the stump and the man's pasty skin, it had been too little too late. There was a rattling sound issuing from his lungs. Al, hurting inside, turned his head.

A second man had been shot in the stomach. He was propped against a tree, his hand over his belly, blood bubbling around his fingers. He was moaning softly, the sound getting fainter all the time. The third wounded man was simply kneeling in the mud, screaming wordlessly, his hand clasping a blood-soaked rag to his head. He was shaking with either cold or shock.

Knowing there was nothing he could do for these men, or for any of the others here, Al forced himself to turn his back on them. He was facing north now, and could see that the American troops were retreating in a disorganized way through the fields and across the hills. Many were injured, and some were throwing away their weapons to lighten their burdens.

"Ziggy," Al called, "where's Isaiah? I can't see him. Is he okay?"

"He is close to you," came the computer's voice. "About twelve yards north of where you now stand. He is still alive at the moment."

Al moved toward the indicated spot. There was a slight hollow in the ground, and he finally could see the man. With relief, he realized that Isaiah was uninjured, even though he was not on his feet. As he drew closer, he saw that the lanky farmer was bent over the body of one of his comrades. Al peered over Isaiah's shoulder. The man had died from a stab wound to the chest.

"It's no good," he said with sympathy, even though Isaiah couldn't hear him. "Your friend's dead. And so will you be if you don't get moving soon. Haven't you heard? The British are coming!"

Isaiah, naturally, paid him no attention. Tears were rolling down his dirty cheeks, and he stood looking down at the dead man. "I must go, Thomas," he muttered. "I must go. I'm sorry I have to leave you."

"Yeah, but you *don't* go," Al complained. "Jeez, get some smarts, kid, and shift into high gear, will you?" He glanced nervously over his shoulder. How much time did Isaiah have? "Ziggy, can you take me up a couple of hundred feet, so I can get a look at what's happening?"

"No problem, Admiral," the computer replied.

Al, abruptly shooting up like a rocket, almost lost his breakfast. "A bit slower!" he begged. His headlong rush slowed to a smooth crawl, and he felt better. Finally, he was apparently standing in midair above the hill, and he had a terrific view of the disaster.

To the south, he could make out Coney Island and Gravesend Bay. The land there had sizable towns. In the bay, several ships were anchored. Each flew the British flag. "Landed from the sea?" he asked Ziggy.

"Last night," Ziggy replied. "The troops came ashore at midnight, and made their way through the town to attack the Revolutionary forces early this morning."

Al nodded. He could see thousands of red-coated men ahead of him, advancing northward. They were hunting survivors as they went, and shouting in guttural tones. "They don't sound very British," he complained.

"Most of them aren't," Ziggy explained. "General Howe has about fifteen thousand men thrown into this battle. Most of them are Germans—Hessian mercenaries. Really, Admiral, I thought you knew your history better. The British didn't want to use British troops against people who were most likely their own relatives."

"Yeah, I just forgot for a moment." Al could make out a number of darker faces to one side of the British forces. "They got slaves, too?"

"No," Ziggy answered with a sigh. "Those are troops from the British West Indies, fighting for the British—two regiments of them."

"Oh." Al peered around, trying to get an idea of what

was happening. "It looks like they've whomped the Rebels badly."

"That's one way to put it," Ziggy concurred. "The American forces numbered about twelve thousand, most of them from New England or Maryland. They are under the command of General Israel Putnam. The problem is that he did not know the lay of the land, and didn't take advice from Colonel Smith or any of the local militiamen. There are currently four passes through this region of Brooklyn, and he neglected to defend one of them. The British forces made an attack there, and managed to overrun the defenders. What you are now seeing is the start of the rout."

Al swallowed, watching the British forces advancing relentlessly. "Isn't this battle supposed to last a couple of days?" he asked. "At this rate, it's all going to be over within an hour."

"This stage of the battle lasted barely the morning," Ziggy answered. "The troops toward the north are digging into trenches already. Those will hold the British for a short while, prolonging the fighting. The British have already effectively won, however."

"So what happens next?"

"The British will press northward, trying to reach the East River to attack Manhattan. A storm will spring up this evening, preventing the fleet that you see moored there in the bay from joining the fight. Two regiments from Massachusetts will be able to rescue nine thousand of the American troops and take them across to Manhattan. There, General Washington and General Woodhull will be able to rally the men and then retreat to White Plains for the next phase of the war."

"And what about Isaiah?"

There was a slight pause. "I cannot be certain, of

course," Ziggy replied reluctantly. "He is in a very dangerous situation. Many of the American troops will escape, and we may indeed hope that he will. But there is a strong chance that without outside help, he will perish. He is young, inexperienced, and somewhat foolish. The prognosis is not favorable."

"Unless we can get Sam back on the case, eh?" asked Al, chewing at his cigar in frustration.

"Exactly. Dr. Beckett is more than capable of looking after Isaiah—when he is capable of looking after himself."

This was depressing Al. "Okay," he ordered, gesturing with his cigar, "take me down. *Slowly*." He didn't want to get nauseated again.

The landscape rose to meet him, and a moment later, he was apparently standing on solid ground again. Glancing around, he saw that Isaiah had moved from the hollow and was retreating with the other militia members, though he constantly looked back to where his dead friend lay. "War's always hell," muttered Al. "Only the weaponry changes." In the background was the dull *thoom* of a British cannon. No shots came near, so it was presumably firing at other refugees from the battle.

The retreat might better be described as a rout. The Revolutionaries had lost the battle fairly quickly, and few of them had the stomach to stand and fight against the Hessian mercenaries. The latter were grim, efficient, and eager to kill anyone who stood against them. The Americans were now demoralized and confused, their chains of command broken. Most of the militia had been buoyed up by their enthusiasm for the cause, and were stunned by their all-too-easy defeat. Discouraged, they were retreating to their homes, or attempting to stay with the body of the troops pressing back toward the East

River and Manhattan. The troops from Maryland had been decimated, having taken the brunt of the British attack, and the survivors had lost their enthusiasm to defend other people's land. Tired, wounded, and spiritually battered, the Americans retreated.

From time to time, Al went aloft to get a better view of what was happening. Almost all he could see was wave upon wave of the Redcoats advancing through small towns and along the country lanes. The Americans were burning some of the homesteads and farms as they retreated, leaving more misery in their wake. They were obviously hoping to slow the mercenaries' advance, and also cutting off the possibility that their enemies might be able to live off the land. In doing so, however, they were alienating many of their neighbors and potential allies, who saw the Patriots as depriving them of their homes and livelihood.

It reminded Al all too much of his days in Vietnam.

Isaiah stumbled along with four other militiamen. All looked like zombies, their faces pale, their tired feet plodding along the road; they were not thinking about what they were doing, just placing one foot after the other, knowing that the British weren't far behind them. They had no food, and they did no more than sip from the water skins slung at their waists. Al wondered how long they could keep this up.

"I am sorry to disturb you," Ziggy said, breaking into Al's thoughts. "But I believe you wished to know when Dr. Beckett recovered."

For the first time in hours, Al felt a surge of hope. "Okay!" he exclaimed. "Right, Ziggy, home me in on his location, right now."

There was a shimmering of light about him, and the scene shifted again. He was now standing indoors, in the dimmest of light. The room was cramped, obviously some sort of cellar, without a window. Light seeped into the room from cracks overhead. Al was glad the hologram program didn't incorporate smells, because he doubted he'd like what the result would be.

The room had one door, which he didn't need to check to know it would be locked. There were a couple of pallets on the floor, and some half-filled sacks. The only other item in the room was Sam. He'd been slung onto one of the pallets and left. Now, groaning, he rolled over and stared at the ceiling. He fingered the back of his neck and groaned even louder. Al couldn't make out any details in the gloom, but he expected that Sam had a bruise and maybe even a lump.

"Sam!" he called out. "How are you feeling? Come on, you've got to get back on your feet."

Sam didn't reply. Instead, wincing with pain, he managed to scrabble his way into a sitting position, his head bowed and his hand on the back of his neck.

"Attaboy," Al said encouragingly. "You can do it, Sam. Let's go—on your feet. We've got to get you out of here."

Sam still didn't reply, but he staggered erect. He stood there, swaying, for a moment, then he threw out his left hand to support himself against the closest wall.

Al stared at Sam's hand, which appeared to have gone right through his chest. "Hey, cut that out," he complained. "I hate it when you do that." He stepped to one side, then scowled. Sam wasn't even looking at him. "Come on, will you?" he grumbled. "Get with it, Sam." There was still no reply. "Sam?" Worried, he waved his hand in front of Sam's eyes. "Sam, tell me you can hear me!"

No response. Sam simply stood there, swaying, his head bowed.

"Ziggy," Al called. "What's wrong?"

"It would appear," Ziggy said gently, "that Dr. Beckett cannot see or hear you."

"What?" Al made a fist and punched the air in front of Sam. There was no flicker of anything in his friend. "How could that be possible?"

"I can think of only one possibility," Ziggy answered. "You are attuned to Dr. Beckett's brain waves, so he should be able to see you. Since he cannot, his brain waves must have changed. It would appear that the blow to his head caused a concussion, scrambling his mind."

Al scowled. "You're saying that his brain's scrambled even more than normal? Well, change the settings for me, and get me in line with whatever he's thinking now."

"That is not possible," Ziggy said. "I do not know what his brain waves have changed to. I cannot monitor him this way. Unless or until he recovers, there is nothing that either of us can do. Dr. Beckett is on his own."

CHAPTER

SEVENTEEN

"And I had to wonder how this Leap could possibly get any worse," Al muttered. "Okay, Ziggy, what's your best guess on him recovering?"

The computer hesitated for a moment or two. "As far as I can ascertain, Dr. Beckett is in reasonable condition. There is evidence of some trauma, but I believe that he is strong enough to recover, if he is allowed to rest. Once he sleeps again, he may return to normal."

"May?" echoed Al.

"The human mind is difficult to predict, even for me. It may be that Dr. Beckett's neural net has been sufficiently damaged that he will never recover. However, I do not think that this is likely. I estimate a sixty-four percent chance that he will recover after his next sleep period."

"I wish I knew how you worked out these odds of yours," Al complained. "I'm beginning to suspect you just pull random numbers from the air."

"There is no need to get insulting, Admiral," Ziggy answered huffily. "I could no more explain my mental processes to you than you could explain your own to a kitten."

"Okay, okay." Al waved his hand dismissively. "Now, pipe down and let's see what Sam's up to. He might not be able to see me, but he's still got a sharp mind. He's got to be up to something."

Sam had straightened, and moved to the door. He breathed deeply, then hammered on the wood. "Whoever's out there!" he yelled. "Come on!" He banged and yelled for a few minutes before there was any kind of reply.

"Shut up, Beckett!" roared Morgan. "I've no patience with traitors and scum."

"Let me out of here!" Sam answered. "You've no right to keep me here. Let me go back to my wife."

Morgan laughed at him. "The only way you're getting out of here is in a pine box. As soon as we hear that the Patriots have defeated the Tories' army, you're going to be taken out and hung for the traitor that you are."

"You'll have a long wait," Al muttered.

"You can't do that!" Sam replied. "I'm no traitor. I'm a Patriot, too."

Morgan laughed, a nasty, harsh sound. "Forget it, Beckett. You're dead, just as soon as I get the word."

Sam shook his head in frustration. "What about my wife?" he asked. "Hannah. What happened to her?"

Another nasty laugh. "I hope the harlot is dead," Morgan answered. "We left her in her own stinking blood. Now, shut up. I'm listening to no more of your whining." There was the sound of heavy feet on stairs outside.

Sam flung himself away from the door and back onto the sacking. "Hannah!" he groaned, tears trickling

189

down his face. "Is that true? Are you dead? Oh, my dear, dear wife. . . ." He fell into a heap on the make-shift bed.

Staring down at him in shock, Al shook his head. "He's delirious. He's gotta be."

"It would appear that the blow to his head has caused further mental problems," agreed Ziggy. "Dr. Beckett has seemingly taken on the personality of Samuel Beckett. He really believes that Hannah is his wife, and that he is of this period."

"Oh, great!" Al felt like punching something, but nothing here was real. "This Leap keeps getting worse all the time. What more can possibly go wrong?"

There was a pause, which didn't surprise him, since his question was meant to be purely rhetorical. Then Ziggy answered it.

"I hate to be the bearer of bad tidings, Admiral," she apologized. "But I really think we should return to Hannah Beckett at this moment. There has been a fresh development."

"Terrific!" He was definitely going to have to give up wondering what else could go wrong—so far, each and every time, he'd discovered the answer. "Okay," he sighed. "Get me back to her."

Once more, there was that momentary disorientation, and then Al was back in Hannah's bedroom. She was out of bed, finishing lacing up her dress one-handed. "Great timing," muttered Al. "How come I always miss the good bits?" Ziggy ignored the question, as he'd expected her to do. "What does she think she's doing?"

"She is getting dressed," Ziggy responded. "Evidently she is planning a trip. In her condition, this is not wise."

That was an understatement. No matter how strong a

woman she normally was, Hannah had taken a wound to the shoulder and lost a fair amount of blood. Once more, Al was frustrated at not being able to interact. "What she needs is a good smack on the fanny," he growled. "She should be in bed recuperating, not playing around." He prowled about the room like a caged tiger, watching her struggle into her shoes. Then she pulled a basket from under the bed, and crossed to the baby's crib.

Daniel was still sleeping. Carefully, crooning softly to the child, she managed with some difficulty to transfer him to the carrier and slipped it onto her good shoulder. Al saw her wince with pain as she straightened up. Then, crossing to the clothing chest, she burrowed inside it for a moment.

Her hand emerged with a small pistol and a pouch. Slowly, glancing over her shoulder at the bedroom door, she loaded the pistol. She slipped the pouch in with Daniel, then took the weapon in her good hand. It was obviously an effort for her to move, but she crossed to the door.

"What does she think she's doing?" Al asked incredulously. He walked through the wall into the main room. The woman he'd seen before was still there, and now she'd been joined by Burke, the man who had saved Hannah's life. Both of them looked around when the bedroom door opened. Their eyes widened with shock as they saw the pistol covering them.

"Stay where you are," Hannah warned them. She walked slowly across the room. "I don't want to hurt you, since you've been so kind to me, but I will if I must." She crossed to the outside door. "Where are they keeping my husband?"

Burke started to rise, but the pistol gently pointed him

191

back to his seat. Sweating, he allowed himself to fall back. "Hannah," he said gently, "you're sick. You must rest."

"And allow them to kill my husband?" she snapped. "George Burke, either you tell me where he is, or I promise before God that you'll depart this world before Samuel does."

Burke swallowed and licked his lips nervously. "They will kill me if I speak."

"And I will kill you if you don't," Hannah informed him coldly. "If Samuel dies, I shall lose all reason to live. So—choose, now."

Burke clearly didn't know what to do. He was obviously afraid of what the Committee of Safety would do, but he was equally certain that Hannah wasn't bluffing. Al was just as sure as Burke was that she'd pull the trigger if she felt it necessary. Burke tried again. "There's nothing you could do if you went there," he protested.

"I don't care. I will do what I can."

"They'll kill you, too!"

"They may try," she agreed. "They may even succeed. But I will not abandon my husband to such vermin. Now—tell me where he is, or you'll die before either of us Becketts."

Burke hesitated again, sweating profusely. The woman—obviously his wife—then blurted out: "He's being held at James Morgan's house!"

Burke glared at his wife. "You should not have told her! She will only be killed."

"Better her than you," Mrs. Burke answered crossly. She glared at Hannah. "Go and die if you must—but leave the baby here with us. We'll look after him, I promise."

Hannah shook her head. "I believe you, Molly, and I thank you. But he is a Beckett, too. If his father and mother must die, then he'll have to take his chances with us. If we live, we'll need Daniel with us. I doubt we could stay here on the Island any longer, even if we wished it." She hesitated, her hand on the door. "Don't follow me, and don't try to warn this hell-bent Committee that I'm coming."

Burke nodded. "We'll not interfere with you," he promised. "You're going to the grave, but you're a brave woman, Hannah Beckett. God go with you."

Then Hannah slipped out of the door, closing it behind her. Al stayed, to listen to what the Burkes would say to one another. They seemed to be decent people, but they might be capable of trying to stop Hannah.

Actually, he rather wished they *would* try and stop her. They were right—what she was contemplating was suicide.

The woman clasped her husband's hand, squeezing it. "I'm sorry, George," she apologized. "She would have shot you if I hadn't spoken."

He nodded again. "I do believe you're right. She is a strong woman, that one. But I do not believe she's strong enough to rescue Samuel." He bit at his lip nervously. "Perhaps I should go with her."

"And die beside her? She has no chance. You know that. Stay with me, and out of this. It is not your fight. You've harmed yourself enough already by saving her life. Kirk and Morgan have no love for you after that. If the Patriots win through, then you're likely enough in trouble as it is. Don't add more blame to your account."

"Blame?" Burke sighed. "For doing what is right? Molly, what times are these when a person is punished or killed for doing good?"

"Troubled times, husband," she answered. "Times of war. Times we must live through."

Al had heard enough. Burke meant well, but he was a weak man. He'd not hinder Hannah, but neither would he help her. He'd already performed to the limits of his courage. Now he'd sit and wait to see who would win, and which way the winds of change would blow him next. With a sigh, Al walked through the wall and into the yard.

There he saw Hannah leading Old Flighty from the barn. She had saddled the steed, and as he watched, she stood on a log to mount the horse. It wasn't easy for her, weak as she was and encumbered with the baby, but she made it. Al shook his head. She was a stubborn, determined woman, and she aimed to rescue Sam or die with him. He was proud of her and cursing her at the same time. This was really complicating their problems. There was still nothing that he could do.

"Ziggy!" he called. "How's Sam doing?"

"He has fallen back asleep," the computer answered.

"And Isaiah?"

"Still fleeing the battlefield."

Al chewed his cigar thoughtfully. "Okay, close down the Imaging Chamber. I'd better talk to Samuel while there's a lull in all these screwups." The hologram about him dissolved, and the door of the chamber hissed open. Fastening the handlink to his belt, Al marched from the room and down the corridor to the Waiting Room. He hesitated a second before punching in his access code, then glanced warily around the opening door.

Samuel Beckett was in the middle of the room, pacing up and down, swearing. Al entered and closed the door behind him.

"You've been told what Hannah's up to?" he asked.

"Aye." Samuel turned to him, his expression concerned. "George Burke is correct: she's off to her death."

"She thinks she's going to rescue you," Al informed him. "She's some woman."

"She's brave enough, I'll grant you," agreed Samuel, his face twisted with pain. "But she's just as much stubborn and foolish. Morgan, Kirk, and Townsend are not as timid or vacillating as George Burke. And they are at least three to her one. All she will do is get herself and the child killed, along with this descendant of mine."

"You may be right."

Samuel scowled as a thought struck him. "You say that I can return to my own place and time only if this Sam Beckett . . . Leaps again?"

"That's right."

"Then what will happen if he is executed before he can perform this Leaping?"

Al sighed. "I wish I knew. My best guess is that he'll be dead and you'll be stuck here for the rest of your natural life. So we'd both better pray that doesn't happen."

Samuel nodded. "There are some . . . attractions to this time and place of yours," he said. "But my place is with my wife and child. I must go back to care for them."

"And we'll do everything we can to make sure that's what happens," Al promised, knowing there was no way he could fulfill that vow at the moment. "So, time to help us again. How far from your farm is Morgan's house? How long is it likely to take Hannah to get there?"

Thinking hard, Samuel shook his head. "Morgan lives on the farther side of Smithtown from us. I could be there in an hour or less. But Hannah is not much of a rider, and she is injured and encumbered. It is difficult to be certain, but I would say the better part of two hours.''

"Two hours?'' Al echoed. "Jeez, that doesn't give us much time, does it?'' He considered his options for a moment, but they were pitifully few. "Okay, stay here and I'll have Dr. Beeks keep you informed of what happens. If anything—anything at all—useful occurs to you, just tell her. She'll have Ziggy relay the information to me.''

Samuel nodded. "I do not like the idea of standing and waiting while my wife rides into danger. But there is, it would seem, nothing more that I can do. Very well, I will obey your instructions and do that. Meanwhile, what do you plan? You *do* have a plan, I trust?''

"Not so much a plan as a prayer,'' Al was forced to confess. "I'm gonna go back and try to wake Sam up. With any luck, the rest he's had will have reset his brain patterns, and he'll be back to normal. In that case, we can work together to get him out before Hannah gets there and rides into trouble.''

"And what if he has not healed?'' asked Samuel in concern. "He has not had much rest.''

"In that case,'' Al admitted, "I'm likely to lose my best friend, and you're gonna be a bachelor once again.''

CHAPTER
EIGHTEEN

Darkness retreated slowly from Sam's mind, ebbing and flowing like a violent ocean tide. Wave upon wave of nausea, buzzing, and giddiness almost swamped him. He struggled to retain the slender grip he had on consciousness, dimly aware that someone was yelling at him from an immense distance. It was so very hard to fight the blackness, but Sam knew that it was important, and he refused to surrender. Eventually he started to become aware of his surroundings, and the crashing in his mind faded to a numbing noise, then drifted into background pain.

With a groan, he finally managed to open his eyes. Blurrily, he could make out a face, and then sounds within the noises.

"Wake up, Sam. You gotta wake up. Sam!"

"I *am* awake," Sam complained. He closed his eyes again to reduce some of the pain, then opened them to see Al staring happily at him.

"You can hear me!" he exclaimed.

"Yeah," agreed Sam. "You're way too loud." He

197

moaned again as he moved his head. "Ow!" He felt the back of his neck, which was tender and swollen. "Is it night?"

"No, it's afternoon," Al replied. "Sam, I'm so glad you're back to normal."

"This is normal?" Sam asked wearily. "I feel like I've been chewed up and spat out by a saber-toothed tiger." He managed to struggle into a sitting position. He hoped the world would stop break dancing and settle back to normal fairly quickly. "What's going on?"

"Trouble, of course," Al answered. "Lots of it."

Sam groaned. "Why don't you just let me die, so I can get some peace?" he begged. His head was still swimming.

"That may yet happen," Al informed him grimly. "If Kirk and his pals have anything to say about it. They've got the rope and the tree branch all ready for your own private hanging."

"Oh." Sam focused his mind, and started to remember what had happened. "Right. Kirk and Morgan captured me at the house and. . . ." He broke off as his memory flooded back to him. "Hannah! Is she . . . ?"

"She's alive for the moment," Al replied. "And she's on her way here, playing Rambo, to try and rescue you. Sam, she's going to be killed if she goes through with it."

Sam moaned again. "Tell me that's all the bad news," he begged. "*Please* tell me there isn't more."

"Sorry," Al apologized. "It gets worse. You slept through the Battle of Brooklyn. The Brits have won it, and are swarming all over the island. You can forget about the secret message stuff now—you wouldn't be able to get through to General Woodhull, and there wouldn't be anything he could do about it anyway. The

Patriots are retreating from New York, and the British are going to take over.''

"Marvelous!" Sam managed to stumble to his feet. "Well, that solves one of my dilemmas, at any rate. What about Isaiah?"

"Ziggy's keeping an eye on him. He survived the battle, but he may not survive the retreat. The kid's got a good heart, but his sense of direction needs some work. He's circling around, and seems to be too depressed to care that the British are getting closer to him. He really needs a nursemaid right now, Sam.''

"And I guess I've been elected," said Sam, sighing. "Okay, let me make sure I can stay on my feet without keeling over, and then we'll see about getting out of here." He took an exploratory step forward. Though he felt giddy and unsteady on his feet, he didn't fall down. "Okay, I feel well enough to make it to the door sometime this week." He took a deep breath and let it out. "I guess it would be too much to hope that the door's unlocked."

"Way too much," agreed Al. "But it's the only way out of here."

Sam nodded, then wished he hadn't. He waited until his head returned to the vicinity of his shoulders. "Then it's time for another daring jailbreak, I assume. You wouldn't have any ideas that might help me, would you? My brains are still kind of scrambled."

Al rubbed his chin. "Maybe you could call for help and then pretend to be sick and jump Morgan when he comes."

"I don't think that would work. I can remember waking up before. I was kind of fuzzy, but I know he didn't come in." He licked his lips. "And they don't seem to be in any hurry to feed me or give me water. I guess they figure it's a waste of time, since they aim to kill me."

Al shrugged. "Then how do we get you out? It's got to be through that door, and they've got to open it for you."

Sam managed a thin smile. "I guess I'll just have to make them mad enough at me to come in here to teach me a lesson." He was feeling a little stronger now. The buzz in his head had dropped down to the loudness of a circular saw, and the room was only shaking instead of reeling. He chanced his luck and bent down to examine the pallet he'd been left to sleep on. He was thankful when he didn't pitch forward to the ground again.

Throwing aside the sacking, he saw that the pallet consisted of three long planks over three crosspieces. Gripping the middle long plank at one end, he stood on the other. Pulling hard, he heard the plank splintering, and then it broke free. He grinned as he hefted the wood in his hands. It was about four feet long and six inches thick. "This should do it," he said. He glanced upward, and then brought the plank up with as much strength as he could muster, slamming it into the ceiling with a loud thud. Taking a breath and praying that he'd stay conscious long enough, he repeated the action.

"What the devil are you doing?" Al demanded.

"Worrying them," Sam answered, making a third swing. "They're bound to think I'm trying to break out somehow. They're going to come running down those stairs any second." *Slam*. "You'd better pop outside and let me know the second they open that door." He grinned slightly. *Slam*. "It opens outward."

Al caught the grin and returned it. "Gotcha." He

strode through the wall. "Keep it up!" he yelled encouragingly.

"Easy for you to say," Sam grunted, slamming the plank upward again. He felt weak enough to begin with, and his strength was ebbing each time he swung the plank. He wasn't going to be able to keep it up for very long. His body had taken quite a beating.

Slam. How long would it take his captors to get worried about him? *Slam.* Was there, in fact, anyone here? *Slam.* Surely there had to be. They'd definitely post a guard, at least, just in case. *Slam.*

Wouldn't they?

"That's it!" yelled Al. Over the sound of the plank slamming into the ceiling again, Sam could hear an angry yell outside, and then feet hurrying down the stairs. "Get ready!"

Sam heaved the plank upward one more time, then let it fall with a clatter onto the pallet. Pulling together every tattered remnant of his strength, he crouched slightly as he heard a sound at the door.

"Now!" Al howled.

Sam sprang, and kicked the door with all of his strength.

Kirk had started to open it when Sam hit it. The blow knocked him backward into a hard wall. He yelped from the pain of both blows, and then Sam was upon him. There was no time for finesse, so Sam punched the man as hard as he could on the jaw. Kirk's head snapped back, cracking against the stone wall behind him. He crumpled to the ground without another sound.

His chest heaving and his head spinning, Sam sucked in the air of freedom. He stood there for several seconds, trying to reorient himself. "Is there anyone else here?" he finally gasped.

"I'll check," Al answered, and vanished. Sam bent over Kirk's unconscious form, feeling for a pulse in his neck. It was fast but regular, and Sam was relieved that he'd done no more than render the man unconscious. Kirk might want Samuel dead, but Sam hated to kill anyone—even pond scum like this—unless it was really necessary. Then he frisked the man. He found a knife, which he tucked into his belt, and a small purse. The struggle with his conscience was very short: Kirk owed the Becketts for what he'd done, and this could be useful. Sam slipped it into his pocket. Then he hit the jackpot, discovering a pistol in one of Kirk's coat pockets, and powder and shot in the other. While he was waiting for Al to return, Sam carefully loaded and primed the pistol. This might very well even the odds.

Then Al was back, walking out of the stone wall in front of him. "There's just Morgan left here," he reported. "And he's getting awfully suspicious of the lack of noise down here."

"Then let's give him some," Sam suggested. Throwing back his head, he let out a loud scream, and then called, "No . . . no more, please!"

Al laughed. "Nice performance. That should please his sick little heart."

"While he thinks Kirk is beating me up," Sam said softly, "let's head on up." Holding the pistol at the ready, he quietly climbed the wooden steps. At the top of the stairs was a trapdoor, which had been left open when Kirk had rushed down. Sam nodded upward to Al, who nodded in return, then rose until the top half of his body was poking through the floorboards.

"It's okay," he called out. "He's staring out of the window, not this way and. . . . Uh-oh." There was a slight pause. "Sam, I think it's Hannah coming. Morgan's got a blunderbuss, or whatever you call those guns. . . .''

He didn't need to say any more. Sam drew on his remaining strength and dashed up the remaining steps. As he emerged into the house's one main room, he yelled, "Morgan!"

The thug whirled around, startled, his musket wavering. Sam saw the shock change to fury as the big man started to aim the musket. With a savage howl of anger, Sam fired first.

The pistol was primitive by twentieth-century standards, but it was still more than effective, especially at such short range. Morgan grew a large, red hole in his chest, just above the musket. His eyes bulged, and his fingers clenched convulsively on the trigger. The shot went into the floor as he pitched forward. The life had gone from his eyes as he gurgled up blood, crashing to the floor and not moving.

"About time he got it," said Al with satisfaction. He aimed a kick at the dead man's body, but his foot went through it. "No-good sadist."

Sam staggered forward, struggling to keep hold of the pistol. He might yet have need of it. This was no more than the first rung on the ladder to freedom. His head was swimming again as he made his unsteady way to the door. He could hear the sound of a horse approaching now. Gripping the door firmly, he pulled it open and stumbled into the warm afternoon light.

Morgan's house was on the edge of woods, which meant that with luck, the short fight hadn't been heard by anyone else. As Sam clutched the door frame for support, he saw the horse and rider rein in.

"Samuel!"

"Hannah," he gasped, with a grin. "Stay where you are! I'll come to you."

"But you're injured," she protested.

"So are you." He shook his head and wiped the hair from his eyes. She still looked absolutely delectable, but he could see that she was pale and shaking. There was blood on the shoulder of her dress. "You shouldn't have ridden here."

"I couldn't leave you to the slender mercies of these rogues," she replied. "I was too afraid for you, Samuel."

"I know." God, he wished she were his woman! She was brave, resourceful, and determined, all fueled by her love for his ancestor. Samuel was a very lucky man indeed. "We can't stay here and talk. Kirk is unconscious and Morgan is dead. Others will be coming soon. We've got to be on our way. And it can't be back to the house. The Committee is bound to check our farm when they find me gone."

"I had suspected as much," Hannah said simply. She patted a bulky bundle across the saddle behind her. "I have Daniel here, husband."

Sam smiled again as he walked slowly to join her. "Smart girl," he said approvingly. "Now we can get out of here." He patted her hand as he drew level with Old Flighty. "Morgan's got to have a horse or two around here. I think Old Flighty has enough weight to carry. Stay here, and watch the road. Warn me if you see or hear anything." He started for the back of the house. "You keep an eye on her," he muttered under his breath to Al.

"Don't forget about Isaiah," Al cautioned him, then moved back to stay with Hannah.

Sam walked carefully. He was feeling exhausted, and

his neck and head still ached from the blow he'd received. Despite this, his spirits had raised considerably. Though this Leap was proving to be extremely troublesome, at least a few of the difficult choices he had been facing had been simplified. Since delivering his secret message was no longer possible, he didn't have to worry about changing history. And now that the Committee had attacked him and the Battle of Brooklyn had been fought and lost, his next course of action was obvious. He had to get Hannah and Daniel off the island and to safety in Connecticut. When it became clear that the British had won, the Loyalists would begin to exact their revenge on the Rebels. It was all falling into place, as he knew from his family history that it must.

The only remaining complication was Isaiah. It appeared that the lanky farmer had survived the battle, but not necessarily the war. Sam couldn't simply abandon him to fate. He hadn't Leaped out of here yet, so he obviously had something left to do—and with Hannah and Daniel reasonably safe, that left Isaiah.

As he had suspected, there were two horses in a small fenced field behind the house. Sam quickly caught one of them, then saddled up. It hurt his neck when he used his arms, but he forced himself to endure the pain. He had to have a horse. Finally he mounted the animal, and rode back to join Hannah.

"I am so very glad to see you again," she told him. "I was desperately afraid that I would not be in time, and all I would have left of you would be your corpse hanging from a tree."

"You don't get rid of me that easily," Sam joked, giving her a kiss on the cheek as he reached her. "You can't know how glad I am to see that you're all right," he added. "When I saw you shot...." He scowled at her. "How does your shoulder feel?"

"As though someone has lit a fire inside it. But it's slow-burning, and I can endure it while I must." She sighed. "If we cannot go back to our home, Samuel, what are we to do now?"

"We have to leave the island. I'm sure we can get a boat to New England from the north shore. We have friends there who will help us." At least he hoped that was true! "We'll have to start over again, I'm afraid, but we have little choice."

Hannah laid a hand on his arm. "As long as I have you, Samuel, and Daniel, then I am content. Everything else is just frivolity."

"Hardly that," Sam answered with a laugh. "But it does me good to hear you say it." He chewed on his lip. "Hannah, I'll ride with you as far as the main road to Oyster Bay. After that, you'll have to go on alone. I'll rejoin you as soon as I am able."

She stared at him in concern. "Why? What are you planning to do?"

"I have to go after Isaiah. He's survived the battle, but he needs my help. Otherwise, he'll be captured or killed by the British."

Frowning, she asked, "But how can you possibly know that?"

How indeed? "I can't explain right now," Sam answered. "You must trust me on this."

"Of course I trust you, Samuel. But will you at least allow me to worry about you?"

"Certainly." Sam agreed. "That'll save me one chore, at least." He urged his horse to motion. "Come on. We don't know when any of the other Committee members might arrive here. We'd best get moving." He heard Old Flighty start moving behind him. "Al," he breathed, so that Hannah wouldn't hear him apparently talking to himself, "you'd better provide me with directions."

Al slid into place beside him, keeping up with the horse. "Do I look like a road map?"

Sam couldn't resist a grin. "Actually," he said, studying Al's green and blue suit, brown shirt, and dark tie, "you do bear a certain resemblance to one."

"Thanks a lot." Al sniffed, then drew on his cigar. "Okay, just follow this road north for a couple of miles. It joins the main road into Oyster Bay then. Hannah can take it pretty safely the rest of the way, while you turn west from there. I'll just scout on ahead and make sure that Townsend and the rest of his finks aren't heading toward you." He tapped in a command on the handlink, and shot down the trail at about thirty miles an hour. Sam watched him go, then turned back to Hannah.

"Are you sure you're up to this?"

She managed a thin smile. "I have to be, don't I? What other option do we have?" She touched her shoulder and winced. "But I shall bolster my spirits by thinking of a nice long rest in a nice warm bed." She smiled wider. "With you beside me."

Sam felt the familiar stirring of desire. He wished he could fight it off better, but she seemed to kindle a spark within him that refused to die. "There's nowhere else I'd rather be," he said honestly.

"Then perhaps when we have a chance to rest, we can start on planning our second child," Hannah murmured. "A new child, for a new life."

"Perhaps we can," agreed Sam. With any luck, he'd have Leaped by then, and she could have her real husband back.

Much as he wished that wouldn't be the case!

To keep his mind off thoughts of enjoying the pleasures of Hannah's body, Sam tried to concentrate on his task. He hadn't had much chance to examine Hannah's wound, but if she was talking about getting frisky in bed, she probably wasn't too badly hurt. And Daniel, sleeping in his makeshift bed on the saddle, seemed to be healthy enough. That meant Ziggy had to be right—he was here to save Isaiah.

Unless, of course, there was something unseen still to occur. And, given how this Leap had gone so far, he couldn't rule it out. Expect the unexpected. . . .

And nothing unexpected happened for the next half-hour. He and Hannah kept up a stream of inconsequential chatter until they reached the crossroads. Al was waiting for them, sitting cross-legged in thin air like some technological pixie, smoking happily.

"Took your time," he observed. "Been having some fun on the way, eh?" He grinned lasciviously, knowing Sam couldn't deny it. Then he gestured to the smaller road. "That's the way to Oyster Bay. Say good-bye to the little lady, and get ready to do the Lone Ranger gallop thataway." He gestured to the wider road. "There's plenty of traffic, but no sign of real trouble."

Sam reined in at the junction, and leaned across to Hannah. "Take care," he told her tenderly. "I'll be back as soon as I can." He glanced at the sky. The sun was falling toward the horizon. He handed her the purse he'd taken from Kirk. "Get yourself a bed for the night, and something to eat," he ordered. "I won't be able to join you until tomorrow afternoon at the earliest, but it won't be a second longer than it has to be. I promise."

Hannah nodded, clutching at his hand instead of the purse. "Be careful," she whispered anxiously. Then she leaned forward and kissed him on the lips.

It felt wonderful, and he wished it didn't have to stop. But he had little choice in the matter. Disengaging his lips, he smiled. "I promise. Save some more of that for when I return. It's just the tonic I need to speed my recovery."

"That and much more," Hannah vowed. "It will be good for me, too." She couldn't hide all of her concern, however. "I love you, Samuel."

"And I love you, Hannah." Sam knew that he wasn't simply saying the right thing between a husband and his wife. On many different levels of his being, he meant precisely what he had just said. Reluctantly, he tore himself away from her, and wheeled his stolen horse around. Before he could regret the action, he dug his knees in. The horse started down the road that Al had indicated. Sam risked one glance back, and saw Hannah watching and waving. He waved back, then concentrated on the ride.

It would be hard being separated from her again. He was becoming quite addicted to her. She was so perfect, it seemed—exactly right for him. She had somehow nestled into his mind and emotions, and the thought of Leaping made his heart sink. He didn't want to leave her, never to see her again. Not that he had any option— when his task was done, he would Leap whether he wanted to or not.

But here and now, living with Hannah, was starting to feel more real and more desirable than the future he had come from, and about which he recalled so infuriatingly little. Only pieces of his own life were left to him, and he could recall too few details about his personal history. Most of that had been supplied to him by Al. He knew the names of Ziggy, Gooshie, and Tina, for example, but he couldn't put faces to any of them. Most of what he knew about his life and friends back in the future was based on what Al had told him.

He had even lost details about many of the Leaps he had made. Some he could recall with perfect clarity, while others were no more than a vague, lingering thought. As a result, he suspected, this current Leap seemed that much more real to him. Maybe he felt this way on all Leaps, and then forgot about it. Maybe all of his surrogate lives felt as though they were perfectly real.

But . . . there was something else, something *more* about Hannah, and he simply couldn't put a mental finger on it. It was as though he had known her for years, not simply days. He could imagine her moods, her laughter, her passions.

He didn't want to give her up, ever. He found himself wishing that this Leap would never end. Maybe even that he could *deliberately* screw it up in order to stay here. . . .

But that wasn't merely selfish, it was disastrous. He was here for a purpose, an important one, and to forget that even for an instant was reprehensible. Besides, he had no way of knowing whether failing on a Leap would leave him here. Suppose it didn't? What if he failed, then Leaped anyway? He'd have the burden of guilt carried over into his next mission. How much worse would be feel if he lost Hannah and also deliberately failed his task? No, he had to go through with whatever he was supposed to do. Even if it meant that he was bound to lose Hannah. The very thought of never seeing her again sent as sharp a pain through him as any from the blow to the neck.

Whatever he did, he was going to regret it.

Still he would do his duty, even if it meant losing Hannah. Even if he'd go on to the next Leap with a burden of loss. What else could he do, and still remain true to himself?

The sun was sinking slowly, but he knew it would be night before he reached the Brooklyn area. That would complicate matters a bit, but the cover of darkness might be a help in avoiding the patrols that the British were bound to have out. Sam wasn't too happy with having only a knife and a single-shot pistol as weapons. If he ran into a British patrol, that could prove fatal. Still, in this time period he was unlikely to find an AK-47 just lying around. . . . He'd have to make do with what he could.

As the last rays of the sun faded, Sam passed through New Lots. This was on the southern outskirts of Brooklyn, and consisted of little more than large, widely spread farms. He was forced to slow his exhausted mount to a walking pace. Anxiously, Sam looked all around; he could see very little.

"Al," he called, "you're going to have to guide me in now. Are we far away?"

Al shook his head. "About fifteen minutes on foot," he replied. "But there's complications."

"Why am I not surprised?" Sam sighed as he dismounted from the horse, then tied the reins to a nearby tree. "Stay put," he ordered it. Then to Al, "So— what's the surprise?"

"Isaiah's gone to ground. He seems to be snapping out of his depression a little, and had that much sense, anyway. The problem is that the British patrols have passed him by. They're only about five minutes ahead of you now. You're gonna have to sneak past them to get to Isaiah."

"Well, nothing about this Leap has been simple so far. It's a bit late to expect it to improve right now. Okay, can you locate the patrols for me, and help me avoid them?"

"It's a cinch," Al answered breezily. "Ziggy, increase the resolution of the Imaging Chamber, then increase my refractive index."

A moment later, Al was glowing with an inner light. Sam grinned. "Just like a Christmas tree."

"And, thanks to Ziggy's enhancing of the hologram, everything's as clear as day out there to me." Al waved his cigar forward. "Let's go, Kemo Sabe. Stick close to me, and you'll be fine. And try not to make any noise. The Brits might not be able to see you, but there's nothing wrong with their ears. Except Prince Charles's, of course. You ever seen the size of his ears?"

"Al, try and keep the conversation to a minimum," Sam begged. "It will help my concentration."

Al shrugged. "Just trying to help with the morale." He started walking.

Keeping to the trees, Sam followed him down the dark road. For the past half-hour, he'd seen nobody on the road. Before that, he'd passed a steady stream of refugees. Some had been militiamen, but most had been farmers and other settlers displaced and scared by the fighting. Many of the houses he'd passed, though, were still occupied. For the majority of the locals, life would go on as usual. The British weren't interested in reprisals—after all, the majority of the settlers were still at least vaguely loyal to the Crown. Letting the mercenaries wreak havoc would only alienate the colonists, and the British had no desire to do that. They aimed to finish this war swiftly and then get back to business as usual.

They couldn't even begin to imagine that they were destined to lose.

Walking carefully, Sam kept Al in sight. Al was sauntering down the center of the road, hands in his pockets, whistling. Well, he could afford to take this casually. He couldn't be seen or injured. Sam wasn't so fortunate.

"Patrol coming up," Al called back. "Three of them, kind of sloppy. They're even smoking on duty."

Ducking into the woods, Sam peered out at the road. A moment later, he made out three dark outlines, each preceded by the small glow from a clay pipe. There was a low murmur of conversation as they passed. They clearly were not taking this too seriously. They still thought this was more a matter of beating a few country bumpkins, then collecting their pay and going home. They had no idea of what was in store for them.

As soon as it was safe, Sam slipped back to the road and continued on his way. Even with Al playing scout for him, he took care where he stepped. It was always possible that Al might miss one or two troopers. A twig snapped under Sam's shoes could cause trouble.

For another ten minutes, Sam continued to advance. There were occasional sounds of firing in the distance, and at one point Sam saw the faint glow of a fire on the horizon. Other than that, there was little to indicate that a major battle had been fought a few miles from this spot. Just ahead, Al was leaning into a tree and waiting for Sam to catch up.

"In here," he said, gesturing with his cigar. "Isaiah's about thirty feet into the woods. There's a little hollow in the ground, and he's gone to earth there. Watch how you go, though. There's brambles all about."

Isaiah was obviously smarter than he sometimes appeared to be. If any patrol blundered toward him, they'd

213

give him plenty of warning by stumbling through the brambles. "Any more British?" Sam asked in a low voice.

"There's another patrol on the way. They'll be here in about ten minutes, so now's a good time to slip in and get Isaiah."

Sam nodded, then followed the faint trail that Al had indicated. It was very dark, but with care Sam could make his way through the growth. Isaiah had picked a good hiding place, that was for certain. Gingerly, Sam plunged deeper into the woods.

Walking through another tree, Al stopped about ten feet ahead. He gestured downward. "He's here, and still awake," he called out. "Poor kid is shivering from either cold or fear."

Since it was a warm summer night, Sam had a good idea which it was. "Isaiah," he called softly. "It's Samuel Beckett. Can you hear me, Isaiah?"

There was a slight pause, and Sam continued forward. Then he heard a hesitant voice. "Samuel? Is it really you?"

"Yes, it's really me, Isaiah. I've come to get you out of here and to safety."

A dark shape rose from the ground ahead of him, brushing off leaves and twigs. "Samuel! I never expected to see you here! How did you ever manage to find me?" Isaiah's voice was filled with astonishment.

"I had a little help from a friend with great eyesight. Anyway, that's not important right now. How are you? Are you hurt?"

"No. Tired and more than a little frightened, I'll tell you. It was dreadful, Samuel. The British just kept coming and coming, and there was nothing we could do to stop them. It was like the fields had been seeded, and they'd all sprung up with red coats. They just walked right through us, as if we weren't even there, Samuel." He shook his head. "We don't stand a chance against them, do we?"

"Sure we do," Sam replied encouragingly. "General Washington will show them how we Patriots can fight soon enough, believe me. Let them have this one little victory for now. But, for the moment, let's forget about the war. The battle's been lost, and there's going to be lots of trouble in store. The best thing we can do is to get off the island and to New England for safety."

Isaiah nodded. "I've been thinking about that all day, Samuel. I've got to get Anne and the children out of here. It's not going to be pleasant under British rule, and plenty of people know we're Whigs. There's bound to be reprisals against them as soon as things settle down."

"There will indeed," agreed Sam. "Kirk, Townsend, and the Committee of Safety showed the way while they thought they had the upper hand. Now the British have got control of the whole New York area, the Tories are going to take a leaf from Townsend's book and start striking back at the Patriots. I've already had Hannah and Daniel go on to Oyster Bay. They'll wait for us there. We have to get Anne and your children, and join her there tomorrow. I'm certain we can get a boat over to Connecticut and safety. There we can rejoin the militia, and I know we'll win the next fight."

Isaiah managed a smile. "You can always make me feel better, Samuel. You're a good friend. I'm ready. Do you think we can make our way through the night? There are plenty of British patrols about."

"Yes. If we can't see them, they can't see us, either. Besides, I've a horse waiting for us up ahead." *And an ace up my sleeve*, he added to himself. He couldn't even begin to explain Al to Isaiah, so he had no intention of raising the subject.

All they had to do was get through the British lines, get Isaiah's family, and then rejoin Hannah. Compared to what he'd been through, this had to be a piece of cake.

Then he heard the sound of a branch snapping under someone's foot. He whirled around, and saw several shadowy shapes in the darkness.

A heavily accented voice called, "Hands up! *Schnell!*"

This was followed by Al's "Sorry, Sam. I guess I was looking in the wrong direction at the wrong time."

Which, Sam reflected, was not a lot of help, considering they had just been caught by the Hessian mercenaries.

CHAPTER
NINETEEN

"What should we do?" Isaiah asked in low tones. He still gripped his musket. Sam could only pray he'd kept it loaded.

It was too gloomy to make out more than vague shapes—which meant that the troopers were at the same disadvantage. They *might* not be able to get off a good shot. . . .

"Follow my lead," Sam breathed. "Go left when I move."

"*Schnell!*" the mercenary repeated loudly.

Sam could make out three shapes in the darkness. It had to be the other patrol that Al had mentioned; they must have heard him talking to Isaiah, then investigated. Surely they had only the vaguest idea where their "captives" stood. He had to rely on that hope. He eased the pistol from his pocket. "Al, point them out to me," he muttered.

Al slipped back in the darkness, then stood still. "He's the head bozo," he called, gesturing with his cigar. "My butt's right over his heart."

Sam moved swiftly to his right, then fired. There was a scream, followed by a crash. A musket fired wildly.

"Nice shot," Al approved. Then the other two Hessians fired.

Both shots went wide as Sam dived for cover. He thrust the pistol back into his pocket and removed the knife from his belt. As he did, he heard Isaiah dive to the left, as he'd been ordered, then fire off a single shot. One of the Hessians howled in pain and fell to the forest floor.

"Al!" Sam whispered. "How are we doing?"

There was a slight pause. "One dead, one out of the fight for now. Number three's over here." Sam saw him gesture toward the ground. "He's trying to reload, and botching it in the dark. He should save his effort."

Sam rose to his feet and sprinted toward the spot Al had indicated. He hated to do this, but he had very little choice. Taking a life wasn't easy for him, even if this was war. But if he didn't, he and his mission were doomed. Someone had probably heard the shots, and there were a lot of British troops in this area. Crashing through the undergrowth, he leaped at the spot where Al was stabbing at the ground with his cigar. He connected with a squirming, grunting bundle of fighting man. His first thrust was deflected by the stock of the mercenary's musket. His second went home in his opponent's shoulder. Sam twisted the knife, heard the man scream with pain, and felt him go limp beneath him.

"He's a goner," Al reported. Sam could feel the man's lifeblood pumping onto his hands. He pulled back in horror and disgust. "You got all three of them. You're safe for now, but there's bound to be reinforcements."

"I know that," Sam snapped. He felt polluted and sickened by what he'd been forced to do. "Just keep your eyes open, and help us get out of here." As the man he'd attacked shivered and died, Sam wiped his hands and knife clean on the man's tunic. Shaking, he regained his feet. "It's over," he called out.

Isaiah clambered to his feet. "That was amazing," he gasped, a quiver in his voice. "How did you know where to go in this poor light?"

"I have excellent night vision," Sam lied. "I eat a lot of carrots." He felt sick, but knew he didn't have the option of being weak right now. "I wouldn't want to gamble our lives on the hope that nobody heard this fight," he said. "We'd better get moving. Follow me—closely." He stumbled out to the road, Isaiah behind him. He wanted to be sick, but instead, he turned to follow the road back to where he had hidden the horse. Al drifted out of the woods to walk beside him. "Go on ahead," Sam muttered to him. "And this time make sure you see anyone heading in our direction."

"Boy, what a grouch," Al muttered. He moved ahead swiftly, doing as he'd been asked.

Isaiah came abreast of Sam. "You sound as if you're talking to someone," he commented.

"Just talking to myself. I can't believe I let that patrol sneak up on us like that."

"I'm amazed that you could handle it at all. I hit the one man only because I saw his gun flash when he fired. It was a lucky shot."

"It helped us a lot," Sam told him.

Isaiah swallowed. "I feel sick. That's the first man I've ever killed, and even though he was the enemy. . . ."

"You hate how you feel," Sam finished for him. He placed a hand on his friend's shoulder. "Don't be ashamed of that feeling. He was a human being. You

219

should never take another life without question. I hope you always feel that way, Isaiah. It's not a light thing we've both done this night, but it's one that we may both be forced to do again before this war is over.''

Isaiah nodded. ''I know that. But it makes me feel better to hear you say it, Samuel. Thank you.''

''Enough talk,'' Sam replied. ''We don't want to alert anyone heading after us.'' He was growing rather fond of this simple farmer. Some of Isaiah's decisions reflected questionable judgment, but his heart and passions were in the right place. All they lacked was a good cause. But he might have discovered one now, in this fight for independence.

Al blinked back into gaudy existence ahead of them. ''I've checked the road back to that nag you stole,'' he reported. ''The first patrol is still going on. They didn't hear the shooting. You're only about five minutes from the horse, and I'll be back before you reach it. I'm going to check the back path now.''

Sam nodded, and Al vanished again. Well, at least something was going right at last. Even if they were being pursued, with Al's help they should be able to make their escape. With Isaiah trailing him, Sam made his way down the road. A moment later, Al reappeared.

''Everything's clear for now,'' he said. ''The closest patrol's still way back, and they'll never catch you before morning. Okay, your horse is off to the right here.''

Following Al's directions, Sam soon reclaimed the steed he'd stolen. Clambering into the saddle, he helped Isaiah up behind him.

''You seem to be able to see remarkably well in this darkness,'' Isaiah commented. ''But, unless this horse is blessed with similar powers, I doubt we'll be able to travel far tonight.''

"We don't have to go too far," Sam replied, "just as long as we outdistance the British patrols tonight. We can make the bulk of our journey when the sun comes up."

"He's got a point, Sam," Al commented. "Maybe you'd better travel for just an hour, then get some rest."

Sam nodded. "We'll just go a short distance," he promised Isaiah. "Hang on." He prodded the reluctant mount forward, and made his way carefully back to the road. It would be dangerous to press the horse for speed, so he allowed it to walk.

The rhythm of the ride almost lulled him to sleep. His body needed a lot of rest. He was still recovering from the blow he'd suffered. But there was too much at stake right now to take a vacation. . . . Then he was aware that Isaiah was pressing against his back, a dead weight.

"Al," he muttered, "I think he's dozed off."

"You can't blame him," Al replied, floating beside the horse. "It's been a long, rough day for him. And it hasn't exactly been easy for you, either. Look, I think you've gone far enough for one night. Why don't you pull off the road and find somewhere to lay your head? I'll keep watch and let you know if anyone comes close."

"That's what you said right before you let those mercenaries stumble over us."

"Everyone's allowed to make a mistake now and then," grumbled Al. "I'll be more careful this time. You're gonna need your strength come tomorrow."

Sam considered this. He was bone weary, no doubt about it. And tomorrow was going to be a real strain, that was certain. "Okay," he finally agreed. "But make certain you *do* stay awake."

"Scout's honor."

"You were never a scout," Sam snorted.

"Was too," Al protested. "I earned lots of badges. I was real good with knots. You should see my sheep-shank some day." He grinned. "I liked the crossover meetings with the Guides best."

"I'm sure you did." Sam carefully shook Isaiah. "Come on," he said softly. "Time to get down before you fall down. We'll stay here tonight, and move on when it's light."

Isaiah obediently scrambled off the horse, then fell asleep again on the ground. He really had to be exhausted! Sam hobbled the horse, and lay down to sleep.

It seemed as if he'd barely closed his eyes when he heard Al's urgent voice. Shaking his head, he opened his eyes and groaned at the light flooding in.

"Come on, Sleeping Beauty," Al grumbled. "The morning's wasting, and you're just sleeping your life away."

Rubbing his eyes, Sam clambered to his feet. He felt tired, but it was obvious that he'd slept for hours. His neck still hurt, but not as badly. He glanced around and saw Isaiah curled up in a fetal position on the grass. "Okay," he told Al, yawning and stretching. "I'm up and raring to go."

"Great." Al yawned in his turn. "Now I can get some shut-eye. It's not easy keeping watch by night. I'm bushed." He pointed down the road. "This will take you back toward Smithtown. I'm sure Isaiah can guide you to his home once you're close. I'll be back when I'm rested. There's no patrols close by, so you should be fine without me to watch over you."

Sam nodded. "Thanks, Al. See you later."

Waving, Al stepped back through the door that Ziggy opened for him, then vanished.

Hungry, thirsty, and still tired, Sam tried to ignore all the complaints his anatomy was sending his brain. He shook Isaiah until he woke up. "Time to go."

Isaiah sat up, yawning and scratching. "I feel better this morning," he said, glancing around. "It seems so peaceful, doesn't it? Hard to realize the British are out hunting us."

"Well, they're looking in all the wrong places, then," Sam informed him. He crossed to where the horse was grazing. "Now what I'd like to hunt for is a good, hot breakfast."

"I'm sure Anne will insist on feeding us when we arrive," Isaiah said with a grin. "She won't want to start out for a new life on an empty stomach."

"That sounds marvelous," Sam admitted, swinging into the saddle. He helped Isaiah on behind him. "Let's get started right away."

In the fresh morning light, the road ahead was clear and free. They hurried along, passing few others on the road and skirting the main towns in case the British had already occupied them. Sam's stomach rumbled, and his throat ached, but he didn't dare stop. He'd settle his needs when they reached Isaiah's farm.

They made it there shortly before noon. As soon as the horse drew close to the house, the door flew open and a young woman rushed out. "Isaiah!" she shouted happily, "I was so afraid for you!"

Slipping from the saddle, Isaiah rushed to collide with her in a tangle of arms and kisses. Sam smiled, watching them greet one another. After a moment, Isaiah broke free.

"We have to leave here, Anne. It's not going to be safe any longer. The British won the battle. If it wasn't for Samuel here, I'd be dead or a captive."

"Thank you, Samuel," Anne said gratefully. "I owe you more than I can ever repay."

"Well," Sam answered, "a hot bite to eat and a gallon of water would go a long way to pay off the debt."

"What am I thinking of?" Anne asked, aghast. "Of course, you poor dears. Come in, come in. We'll talk about fleeing after lunch." She shoved them both into the house.

It was very much like Samuel's, only with two small rooms on the side instead of one. The second was obviously for their two children, who greeted their father happily. One was a girl of about two, and the other a boy who couldn't be more than one. From the look of Anne's slightly rotund frame, there was to be another addition to the family in about six months.

Anne was almost as good a cook as Hannah, and she whipped up two large plates of eggs and salt pork, along with glasses of strong cider to drink. Sam cleaned his plate, and mopped up the remnants with cornmeal bread. While they ate, Isaiah related most of their adventures and thoughts to his wife.

"So you see," Sam added, "we have to get out of here. It's not going to be safe for any of us now that the British have control over the island."

"I can see that," Anne agreed. She glanced around the house and sighed. "I hate leaving all of this behind, but what must be, must be." She clapped her hands together. "Rachel! Thomas! Come along. We have to get ready for a journey." She turned to her husband. "Can you and Sam gather what we'll need while I get them dressed?"

"Of course."

There was very little that they could take. Sam helped Isaiah to get the family's cart ready, and tied his own horse to the back. They loaded on just a bundle of clothing, some food wrapped for travel, the family Bible—which Anne refused to leave behind—and a few other small items. Sam knew how painful it had to be for them to leave behind everything they'd built up, but there was no choice. Finally, Isaiah took a small bag of coins from a chest.

"This should help pay our way," he said. "I wish it were more, but it'll have to suffice." He clapped Sam on the shoulder. "Thank you for all of your help."

"No problem," Sam answered with a smile. "Now, we'd best head for Oyster Bay. Hannah's going to be getting worried." It was early afternoon, and it might well be evening before they arrived. Every hour Hannah waited would worry her more, and he wanted to save her all the stress he could.

And, of course, he wanted to see her and hold her again, no matter how wrong it was to desire that.

Anne fussed and scurried to get the children onto the wagon beside her husband. Sam settled in the rear of the cart, giving his horse a chance to rest for a while. Isaiah slapped the reins and started them on their way.

As Anne looked back, there were tears in her eyes. "It's such a shame to be leaving our home," she said, sighing. "To be forced out of it like this!"

"At least we're still alive," Isaiah reminded her gently. "There are plenty of men who died yesterday and who will die while this war goes on. What will their families do?"

"I know I should be grateful," Anne agreed. "And I am. But we put so much work into this farm, Isaiah."

"And I've no doubt we'll put as much or more into the next," he replied, chuckling slightly. "Let's look forward and not back, wife."

Anne managed a resolute nod, and turned to watch the way ahead.

Sam felt sorry for them all. To have to give up everything like this was very hard. He knew that Samuel would be just as affected when he returned to his own life. Sam could be stoical about it, since this wasn't really his home, but he could imagine how they felt. If his father had lost their farm, it would have devastated him.

And there were many more like the Becketts and the Wattses. The war would force many Patriots to relocate away from Long Island. This was the start of a large exodus while the British moved in. Anyone who stayed would have to discover either an old love of the Crown or a fresh love for it.

The two children were not affected by the somber mood. All they knew was that they were going on a trip, and that generally meant time in town and maybe even candies at the store. Both were excited and bouncing, and that raised the spirits of their parents somewhat. Nevertheless, it was a long, slow trip. Sam transferred to his borrowed horse after a while, riding slightly ahead of the cart to allow the family some privacy. He was eager to speed ahead and rejoin Hannah, but he didn't dare. They might be away from the area of British occupation at the moment, but things could still go wrong. He had to stay with Isaiah and the others and look after them, much as he wanted to be with Hannah.

The sun was starting to wane when they rode down the dusty road that led into Oyster Bay again. It seemed like an eternity since he'd last been here, but it was barely more than a week. And, once again, he was here under less than cheerful circumstances.

Hannah, who had obviously been waiting anxiously for them, waved and called out to them as they approached. Since they were safe enough for now, Sam rode ahead to greet her. She almost jerked him from the saddle to embrace him happily.

"It is so good to see you again, Samuel," she cried, crushing him to her chest.

"If you don't do it a little more gently, I may not survive," Sam replied, gasping. As she eased up a little, he hugged her. "It's good to see you again, Hannah."

"Daniel is resting," she told him. "I've got us a room at the inn here, and I've found a boatman who'll take all of us across to Connecticut. He's a friend of my father's, and I've paid him already."

"You've been busy," Sam said approvingly. "I don't know what you need me for."

"I can think of at least one thing," Hannah answered, smiling.

Oh, wonderful! Sam was torn again. One half of him wanted to panic; the other half wanted to take her inside this very moment. His conscience survived the ordeal as the four Wattses reached them. Anne and Hannah embraced, and started talking about how much they already missed their homes.

"Hannah's arranged the boat," Sam told Isaiah. "As soon as she can untangle herself, I think she'll let us know the details."

"Mind that tongue of yours," Hannah said, mock-frowning. "The boat will be set to sail this evening. There's talk that the British will be bringing their fleet around to blockade any boats heading across to New England, so Dermott wished to go as soon as possible. Since I was sure you'd be here tonight, I agreed to that."

"Good idea," said Sam. "The sooner we're off the island, the safer we'll be." He glanced at the sea, which seemed calm enough. It wasn't a long crossing, he knew, but it would take a couple of hours, at the very least. "Maybe we should go straight down."

"Not until dark," Hannah told him. "There are already murmurings going about the town that there are Patriots who'll be fleeing. Some of the Tories are talking about capturing them and holding them for trial. I don't think they'll cause us any real problems, but it's best not to tempt fate and their good natures."

"Makes sense," agreed Sam. "A habit you indulge in frequently." His stomach rumbled again, reminding him that it had been hours since he'd eaten. "Maybe we'd best get some food inside us to fortify us for the crossing."

"A sound idea," said Isaiah. "I was starting to eye that horse of yours and wonder how well he'd go with gravy."

Laughing, mostly from relief, they went into the small inn. Sam felt good, knowing that the end of the journey was at hand. In a couple of hours, they'd be setting off for their new lives. Everything seemed to be safe and in order again.

So—why hadn't he Leaped yet? Not that he was complaining, since he was still with Hannah, but it did seem to indicate that there was trouble ahead. The others appeared to be happy, buoyed by their relief that they had survived their troubles so far. Sam couldn't ignore the nagging feeling that there would be further problems to face.

But he'd face them better on a full stomach.

After a simple but filling meal, he did feel a little better. Night was starting to fall, so they could make their way down to the docks now and be on their way. Hannah collected Daniel from her room, along with her few possessions, and Isaiah fussed his small family along. They went outside into the warm evening air.

Sam froze in place. Gathered about them in a semi-circle were several men whom he and Isaiah instantly recognized.

"So," growled George Townsend, his face dark with anger, "the rats are fleeing, eh? It's a shame you didn't hide your tracks better. Well, I think we'll have something to say about that, won't we, men?"

The rest of the Committee of Safety nodded grimly. Kirk stepped forward, his musket primed and ready.

"It's time that justice be served," he said. "For the betrayal of our country, and for the murder of the patriot James Morgan, you are sentenced to die, Samuel Beckett!"

CHAPTER
TWENTY

Sam stared helplessly. There were eight members of the Committee here, all of them Kirk's staunchest supporters, and each had a musket pointing at him, Isaiah, or one of the women. Knowing that if he made a move, he would be cut down and probably precipitate a massacre of his companions, Sam had no choice but to remain still.

"We'll do this properly, John," Townsend said gently. "You can shoot him after he's been tried and found guilty."

"Shoot him?" echoed one of the others. "He should hang like the common criminal he is."

"Shot, hung, who cares?" growled Kirk. "Just as long as he pays for his crimes."

"Crimes?" Hannah repeated, furiously. "What right do any of you have to accuse my husband of anything? He's a decent, God-fearing man who does his best by everyone. You pack of hypocrites and Satan's spawn!"

"Easy," Sam urged her, trying to remain calm. "It's best not to bait them while they hold all the weapons."

"I'll not allow them to kill you while I stand back and do nothing," Hannah snapped. "They will have to kill me before they kill you."

"Aye," growled Kirk, scowling at her. "One bullet was not enough to silence your wicked tongue, I see."

"Leave her alone," Sam said. "Your quarrel is with me, not with her—or with Isaiah or Anne, either. Let them go."

Isaiah moved to his side. "No, Samuel," he said firmly. "If it's murder they have in mind, they'd best be ready to make it two killings."

"Three," said Hannah. "For if they don't kill me, I will surely kill each and every one of them."

"Six," Anne added, moving forward with her children. "I hope it's a massacre you've the stomach for, John Kirk, because that's what it will have to be, pure and simple."

Townsend growled. "Stop all this foolish prattle, women," he commanded. "We are here to mete out justice, not to commit murder. Samuel Beckett, you have been previously accused by James Morgan of consorting with known British sympathizers and traitors. Brother Morgan cannot be with us because he is now dead—and John Kirk accuses you of being the man who felled him. How do you respond to this charge?"

Sam bunched his fists, wishing he could wipe the floor with the fatuous man. "This is no proper court of law," he pointed out. "I don't have to answer to any of you for anything."

Kirk raised his musket. "You had better answer us, anyway," he said softly. "Or you'll have to try arguing your case with the Devil himself."

"In that case," Sam answered slowly, "I admit to shooting Morgan—in self-defense. He was trying to kill me at the time. And he shot and wounded my wife.''

"In his self-defense!" Kirk roared. "She had a gun aimed at him at the time! And he was merely trying to ensure that you stayed in the jail and rotted, where you belonged when you shot him down.''.

"He had no right at all to imprison me," Sam shot back.

"It is the duty of all loyal Patriots to fight for justice," Townsend announced pompously. "Brother Morgan was merely doing his duty by holding you for trial." He sat forward on his horse. "You've all heard him admit to killing James Morgan. What is your verdict?"

"Guilty!" the men thundered.

"As if you hadn't made up your minds before you came here," Sam snapped back. "This isn't justice! It's murder."

Townsend shook his head. "You have been found guilty by this Committee, Samuel Beckett," he announced. "And now you must pay the penalty."

"Sorry I'm late," Al said suddenly, stepping through the wall of the inn. At another time, Sam would have laughed at how Al was dressed, but the situation was too serious for that. Scratching himself under his bright pink pajamas, Al walked to join Sam. "Verbeena had Ziggy wake me up, and I came in on the tail end of this kangaroo court.''

"Do something," Sam hissed, looking at the leveled muskets.

Hannah heard him and obviously thought Sam was referring to her. She stepped forward, attempting to get between him and the weapons. "They will have to shoot me down before they reach you," she said. She was obviously scared, but grimly determined.

"No," Sam said, even more firmly. "Get back." He

pushed her, hard, and there were snickers from the men of the Committee as she stumbled back.

"Get ready!" Al yelled, then leaped forward, directly at Townsend's horse. "Ya!" he screamed loudly. "Booga-wooga!" And he punched the animal's nose.

Like all animals, the horse could see Al. It didn't know that he was simply an image that could do him no harm. At this apparent attack, it panicked and reared up, flailing out with its hooves, snorting and whinnying.

Townsend went flying backward from the saddle, his musket discharging harmlessly in the air. He howled as he fell.

The other Committee members whirled to see what was happening, and Sam seized his chance to leap at Kirk. He slapped the barrel of the musket aside, hearing it discharge, then followed through with a right hook to Kirk's jaw. Sam's neck still hurt when he did this, but the pain he felt was more than compensated for by the pleasure he got from sending Kirk sprawling once again.

The other six men realized that a fight had begun, and they started to turn to open fire. Isaiah hadn't waited. As soon as Sam had moved, so did he. The tall man plowed, head down, into one of their attackers, sending him reeling and gasping for breath. Sam whirled from the felled Kirk to kick out high and hard at another of their attackers. Hannah also had seized her chance, and headbutted the man closest to her.

Which left three armed men, all of whom zeroed in on Sam. As he swung about, he found himself facing three muskets, all leveled on him.

"Stand where you are, and lower those weapons!" a loud voice cried.

Sam blinked, and stared beyond the men facing him. There were eight men surrounding this fight, all with

233

muskets of their own, and all aimed at the remaining Committee members. At their head was Gentry, looking considerably better than when Sam had last seen him. The three men looked around and saw that they were outgunned. They lowered their weapons.

"Disarm them," Gentry ordered, pushing past the men. He stopped in front of Townsend, who lay on the ground, his face ashen and his arm hanging limply. "I hope that hurts a lot," he said coldly. "We've had more than enough of the likes of you, George Townsend." He spared a glance for the gasping Kirk. "And you, too, John Kirk. It wasn't that long ago that you and yours were terrorizing this town and beating up the innocent. Well, now the shoe's on the other foot, isn't it? Let's see how you feel about turnaround. It's your turn to be the victims." He nodded to his men, who had gathered up all the loose weapons. "Lock them up. I'm tempted to tell you to throw away the key, but we'll wait for true justice to be served on them all."

Then he turned back to Sam with a smile. "Samuel Beckett, if it weren't for you, I wouldn't be alive this day to help you in your hour of need."

"Well, I'm even more grateful now than I was then that I saved your life," Sam replied sincerely and with great relief. "I thought I was done for."

"Not while there are still honest and decent men in this town," Gentry informed him. "You helped us as best you were able, and we can do no less for you. Still, you do leave us in a bit of a quandary, don't you? After all, you are technically a traitor to the Crown."

Hannah stepped forward. "I wish to add my thanks to those of my husband," she said gratefully. "You've saved his life, and I won't forget that."

Gentry acknowledged her thanks with a nod. "Ah,"

he said slowly. "You're getting ready to leave for safer parts, I take it?" Sam nodded, and Gentry smiled. "Well, as a Loyalist, it's my duty to stop you from going, and to hold you for trial and possible punishment." He pretended to think about it, but Sam could see the smile in the man's eyes. "Well, we have to take this scum off and find some place to secure them till they can be transferred to a proper jail. I'm afraid it'll take all of us to do that. Once we're finished, though, we'll certainly have to come looking for you. That'll be after breakfast, of course. Can't do work like that while you're tired, or on an empty stomach." He winked. "Will that be long enough for you?"

"We'll be leaving tonight," Sam promised him.

"Good enough," Gentry answered. "Shame, but it looks like you might just get clean away from us. Ah, well, with eight Whigs here, I doubt the King will complain about two or four that managed to fool us and escape, eh?"

"Thank you again," Sam said simply.

"My pleasure—this time." Gentry nodded. "No offense, but I'll be happy if I never see any of you again. Good luck, and God go with you." He waved to his men. "All right, let's get these scoundrels out of here, and clean the air for decent folks to breathe."

Hannah hugged Sam ferociously, and together they watched Gentry and the other townsfolk march Kirk, Townsend, and the rest away under guard. "What will happen to them?" she asked Sam. "You know I'm not a vengeful woman, but I hope they pay for what they've done."

Recalling what Al had told him earlier, Sam said, "They will." Kirk would die in jail, and the rest would be imprisoned while the British held the island. It was

235

no less than they deserved, considering what they had done and meant to do. "Now we'd better get out of here, and not waste the chance that Gentry's given us."

Hannah nodded. "This way to the boat," she said. Sam took the basket with Daniel in it from her, then followed as she led the way. He heard Isaiah, Anne, and their children behind them. Hannah moved to snuggle against him. "Your own good deeds helped save you," she said. "I am content—and so very, very proud of you."

"And I of you. That poor guy you head-butted is still gasping for breath."

"Well, you told me I have a stubborn, hard head. I thought I'd best put it to some use." She kissed his cheek. "It's all over now."

Is it? Sam wondered. If that was the case, why hadn't he Leaped?

What was still to come?

CHAPTER
TWENTY-ONE

The boat that the man named Dermott owned was a shallop—about twenty feet long and six across at the center. It had a single mast, with a lantern swinging from it, and several benches for rowers or passengers. Dermott was a bulky man in his early thirties, blunt and friendly. Two of his brothers were to help him with the boat.

"If there's rowing to be done, you and your friend will have to pitch in, too," he warned Sam.

"Fair enough," Sam agreed. "Thank you for agreeing to take us over."

Dermott shrugged. "I've no love for the king, understand. My own folks came over from Ireland, and we've our own grudges with George for that. Besides, Hannah's family and mine have been friends for twenty years." He grinned. "A pretty lass like that asking for my help—how could I refuse her?"

"I have a hard enough time, myself, refusing her anything," Sam admitted.

"It's the women who rule this world, underneath it all," Dermott agreed. "Through ruling us. Still, that's one monarch I'll not be rebelling against. Not if I've any sense left, eh?'' He moved to prepare for sailing.

Chuckling, Sam stowed the few possessions he and Hannah had brought with them, then helped Isaiah. They all clambered into the shallop, which swayed under them.

''I hope I'll not disgrace you by being seasick,'' Hannah said uncertainly.

''You could never disgrace me,'' Sam said. ''I could hardly be more proud of you than I am.''

She blushed slightly. ''Honestly, what a tongue you have in your head. You'll turn my head with all that flattery.''

''And a prettier head I could hardly find.''

She kissed him quickly. ''I'll remind you of that later tonight, when we've reached land,'' she vowed. Sam fought to keep his desires down.

It was time to get his mind on other things. . . .

''How are you doing, Isaiah?'' he asked.

Isaiah smiled. ''Well, I'm eager for the start of this new life of ours. It's an adventure, isn't it?''

''Yes,'' Sam agreed. He paused to tickle little Rachel, making her giggle. ''And we've both got everything we need with us.''

''Aye.'' Isaiah contemplated his wife and children with pride. ''We're both of us very lucky men, Samuel.''

Dermott jumped down into the shallop, and made his way to the bow. ''Cast us off!'' he called to the brother still on the dock. ''Let's make sail!''

Sam settled down beside Hannah, and she nestled close to him, Daniel clutched securely in her lap. She seemed to be more than content, despite everything that had happened over the past several days. As Dermott and his brothers got the small craft under way, Sam sat back and tried to relax. There was nothing he could do during the crossing except wait and see if he was needed to row if the wind dropped. Otherwise, he'd simply get in the sailors' way. Exhaustion swept over him after all he'd been through, and he found himself dozing. Hannah smiled indulgently at him and stroked his temples gently.

When he awoke, it was to a sharp pitching motion. Bewildered, Sam sat up and almost lost his seating. The small craft was rolling like a drunk on a bender. And rain was falling.

"What's happening?" he asked Hannah, moving closer to her and the baby.

"We're on the edge of a storm. It seems to be getting worse."

"You should have woken me earlier."

"Why?" she asked, smiling slightly. "Can you still a storm, now, as well as everything else you've done? There was nothing you could do, and you needed your sleep, you poor thing."

The night was dark, and the circle of light cast by the lantern barely extended beyond the sides of the boat. But Sam could see that the waves were high, and he could definitely feel the pitching up and down of the vessel. He looked back to where Isaiah and his family were. They were huddled together under a tarpaulin, looking thoroughly miserable. Sam realized that he was partly under a similar sheet with Hannah and Daniel.

"How are they doing?" he asked Hannah. He had to raise his voice to be heard over the wind.

"Poor Rachel is suffering grievously," she replied. "Anne, too, is quite ill. But it is an illness that they can survive. Dermott tells me that this wind is our ally as well as our foe. It is giving us queasy stomachs, but it is also driving us faster toward the shore. We should arrive within the hour, he believes.''

''It won't be too soon for some of us,'' Sam muttered, looking at the unfortunates behind them. Even Daniel, normally the most placid of babies, was wailing softly and looking decidedly unhappy.

For the next fifteen minutes, Sam sat and watched. Al popped in, shrugged, then disappeared. There was nothing he could do right now, and it wouldn't be possible to carry on a conversation with him over the noise of the storm. The rain and wind were chilly, though it was the height of summer. And the constant roller-coaster motion of the ship was unsettling, even if he wasn't actually seasick.

It was quite clear that he was fortunate in that regard. Isaiah and his family were definitely suffering. Rachel, especially, was trembling and gagging constantly, when she wasn't crying with pain. She was only two, and she didn't know why she had to endure this.

''I'm going to see if I can help,'' he told Hannah. ''Will you be all right until I get back?''

''I'll miss you, but I am fairly certain I can survive that.'' She smiled fondly at him. ''I'm not at all sick, Samuel, so don't be concerned for me.''

He nodded at her and rose to his feet. He waited for the ship to plunge down another wave, then staggered across the seat and back to join the Watts family.

As he did so, the shallop hit the bottom of the trough and started to rise. Little Rachel went almost green, and she tore herself away from her mother to be violently sick. The boat rose through the wave, crested, then plunged almost instantly into the trough beyond.

Rachel's small scream was almost lost in the crashing of the waves and the howl of the wind. Isaiah leaped for his daughter, grabbing her just before she was swept overboard. He pushed her back toward her mother, and the shallop bottomed out again. As it rose, Isaiah lost his footing on the slippery planks, and a hard edge of water slapped into him over the side of the boat. With a faint yell, he toppled backward into the sea.

"Dear God!" Sam gasped. Striving to retain his balance, he reached the side of the boat. He could just see Isaiah's head in the dark waters, and one waving arm.

"He can't swim!" screamed Anne.

Sam stripped off his jacket and glanced around. The rope that had been used to tie the boat to the quay was curled in the bow. Dermott was fighting the tiller, and his brothers were struggling with the mast, trying to keep the boat on course.

"Neither can you, Samuel!" yelled Hannah.

Now he knew why he hadn't Leaped before this! Samuel, like many men of his time, had never learned to swim. *This* was when Isaiah died, swept overboard and lost at sea.

But *he* could swim. . . .

Ignoring Hannah's terrified scream, Sam gripped the rope, took a deep breath and threw himself into the raging sea.

It was icy cold, and he could feel it numbing his skin and shocking his muscles. Holding his breath as long as he could, Sam struck out toward where he had seen Isaiah. In the darkness, it was almost impossible to make anything out, especially as he drew away from the small light cast by the lantern. He was in a freezing sea, without anything to guide him, and in grave danger of dying of exposure.

"Here, Sam!"

Gulping in air and water as he rose again to the surface, Sam looked up. He saw Al, floating about a foot above the angry waves, gesturing downward. "Isaiah's here!" he yelled. "Come on, you can make it! I know you can!"

Holding onto the rope for dear life, Sam swam toward where Al was hovering. As he drew closer, shaking with cold, he could just make out a soaked bundle being battered by the waves. Grimly he pressed on, then grabbed hold of it.

It was Isaiah, battered and unconscious. *Be alive!* Sam thought feverishly, as he whipped the rope about the limp body. Then, holding Isaiah's head above the waves as best he could, Sam started to swim toward the boat.

It was no use. The waves were too strong, the wind too harsh. He simply didn't have the strength left for a hard swim. He was chilled to the core, and his neck was hurting like crazy again. It was impossible. He wasn't going to make it.

He wouldn't save Isaiah; instead, they would both drown.

Then he felt a gentle but insistent pull on the rope, and realized that they were being reeled in. His strength was renewed by this, and his resolve bolstered. Holding Isaiah's head up, he stroked for the shallop.

Moments later, strong hands and two very feminine ones hauled him across the side of the boat and onto solid planking. Coughing, he spat out seawater and struggled to regain his balance. He saw Dermott and Hannah drag Isaiah back into the boat.

"Smart move, taking the rope!" Dermott yelled. "It enabled us to save you, at least." He bent over Isaiah. "He's not breathing!"

Sam forced himself to overcome his chill, his weariness, and his pain. He slid over to where Isaiah lay on the bottom of the boat. "Leave him to me," he ordered. Ignoring everyone now, he gripped Isaiah's still form and started mouth-to-mouth resuscitation. He alternated this with CPR, trying to will life back into his unfortunate friend.

It seemed as though he was doing this forever, but it could have been only a minute or less. Then Isaiah gave a shudder and choked, spitting out water.

"Yes!" Sam exclaimed. "That's it! Live, damn you, live!"

Again Isaiah coughed, and more water dribbled from his mouth. Then he made a sharp intake of breath, and the worst was over. Sam grabbed a tarpaulin and wrapped it about the skinny body.

"We have to get him warm," Sam yelled over the howl of the wind. "But he should be fine now."

"You saved his life!" Hannah gasped happily. "How did you ever do that? What did you do?"

"I'll explain later," Sam lied. He couldn't, really. Let them think it was dumb luck, or some craziness that paid off.

"You're the most amazing man, Samuel Beckett," Hannah said, kissing him happily on the lips. He could feel her body through her clothing, and once again it aroused him.

"You can say that again, lady," Al added, stepping onto the boat. "I hate to break the bad news to you, Sam, but Ziggy says you've done it. You're going to. . . ."

Sam clutched desperately at Hannah, willing hard to stay where he was, where he wanted to be, where he wanted to stay. He didn't want to go home, or go save any more lives. All he desired was to stay here and love this woman.

Instead, he Leaped.

AFTERWORD

Al felt as if he'd been through a small war. He stepped out of the Imaging Chamber and sighed wearily. Then he started down the corridor to the computer room.

Donna met him halfway. "How is he?"

"As well as can be expected," Al replied, shrugging. "Considering what he'd been through these past few days, he's in remarkable health."

"Does he remember Hannah?" asked Donna.

"A little. He seems to have forgotten some of the passion he felt for her, at least. He just remembers her fondly right now. He's Leaped into a young kid in 1988 who's dying of AIDS, and he's using his own strength to keep the boy alive long enough for him to be reconciled with his estranged older brother. You know Sam—he's focusing all of his energies on that, and not worrying about his own problems."

"Yes," Donna agreed dully. "I know Sam. He's always been like that. That's why he's so perfect for his role, isn't it?"

"I guess." Al rubbed at his chin. He needed a shave. He'd forgotten all about it since Samuel Beckett had wakened him early this morning. "Did you see Samuel while he was here?"

"Only on the monitor," Donna replied. "He looked so much like Sam, didn't he?"

"Yeah." Al grimaced. "I guess it's a good thing Samuel didn't see you, isn't it?"

Donna nodded. "It might have ruined everything if he had. He'd have been even more certain then that you were lying to him." She wound a strand of her hair about her finger absent-mindedly. "Did . . . did Sam ever work out why he was so attracted to Hannah?"

"Nah," Al said with certainty. "I kept him off that line of thought by making him think it was all his gonads at work. He never had a clue." He stared at Donna, Donna who was the image of Hannah, only in twenty-first century garb. "He didn't know it was because she looked so much like you." He shrugged. "Maybe there's some kind of genetic thing to this love business. Isn't it ironic that both men married women who look almost identical?"

"Amazing," Donna answered drily. "But Sam still doesn't remember me at all? Not even with Hannah there?"

"No," Al answered gently. "He just knew that he was incredibly attracted to her; he didn't know why. And I never mention you when I talk with him." He paused. "I guess that even though he doesn't remember you, he still loves you."

"It's undoubtedly for the best." Donna replied softly. "After all, until he gets back here, we can't be together again. It's best this way. It really is." She nodded to him. "Good night, Al." She turned away and walked back down the corridor.

Al watched Donna Elesee Beckett leave. He tried to pretend he hadn't seen the tear on her cheek.

"Yeah," he said softly. "It's all for the best."

AUTHOR'S NOTE

A large number of the details in this story are historically based. I've taken a few liberties with the facts, of course, in order to tell the story. I'm indebted especially to Van and Mary Field of the Moriches Bay Historical Society for their aid; all mistakes are my own.

The Committee of Safety (as well as Kirk and Townsend) were, sadly, all too real. So, too, were the Battle of Brooklyn and its aftermath. Many of the people in this story actually existed, although I've sprinkled in quite a few of my own characters.

Of special interest is the Havens Inn. This existed back then, and it still stands as the Ketcham Inn in Center Moriches. It is being restored and is a registered charity, one that I'm very interested in. Many towns have their own historical societies, which can be both fun and educational to join.

SUMMER '96...LIVE THE 3-D VIRTUAL ADVENTURE!

T-2 TERMINATOR-2 3-D

UNIVERSAL STUDIOS FLORIDA®

For more information call (407) 363-8000 or visit our web site at http://www.usf.com

YOU'LL WISH IT WAS JUST A MOVIE.

COMING SUMMER '96

UNIVERSAL STUDIOS HOLLYWOOD

For more information on Universal Studios Hollywood Vacations call (800) 825-4974.

TM and © 1996 UCS and Amblin